# BREAKFAST UNDER A CORNISH SUN

Kate Golightly desperately needs to move forward with her life. And what better way to do so than with a trip to the Cornish coast, accompanied by Izzy, her boss and best friend? The sea breeze is just what Kate needs to finally relax and begin to let go of her past. Except for one little problem: she's agreed to attend the wedding of her old high school friend-turned-enemy, saying she's bringing a boyfriend who looks just like Ross Poldark — but he doesn't exist! So Kate now has just two weeks to find the smouldering scythe-wielder of her dreams . . .

SAMANTHA TONGE

# BREAKFAST UNDER A CORNISH SUN

*Complete and Unabridged*

# ULVERSCROFT
Leicester

First published in Great Britain in 2016 by
Carina
An imprint of
HarperCollins*Publishers*
London

First Large Print Edition
published 2017
by arrangement with
HarperCollins*Publishers*
London

A catalogue record for this book is available
from the British Library.

ISBN 978–1–4448–3518–2

Published by
F. A. Thorpe (Publishing)
Anstey, Leicestershire

Set by Words & Graphics Ltd.
Anstey, Leicestershire
Printed and bound in Great Britain by
T. J. International Ltd., Padstow, Cornwall

This book is printed on acid-free paper

Thanks for always believing in me, Mum.
I miss you more than words can say.

# 1

Taut bare chest boasting a natural-looking six-pack. Muscular arms wielding a scythe. Raven curls rippling in the breeze. Smouldering expression tense as the grass-cutting implement is raised in the air. The hint of manly, musky perspiration. All this set against rugged Cornish countryside . . .

Mmm. Thanks to scenes from my *Poldark* box set, any free window of time in my head is easily filled. For those of you unfamiliar with the hit Cornish mining television series, book yourself a doctor's appointment. You must be seriously loopy — as in out of the loop!

OK. Apologies. Perhaps that was a bit rude. Not everyone, like me, is a self-confessed geek when it comes to historical books and films — for example, did you know the original title for *Pride and Prejudice* was *First Impressions*? Talking of which, I probably didn't look my most appealing at the moment, having just bitten into a black cherry doughnut. I suspected a splodge of the filling had stuck to my nose. But mmm . . . the oozing maroon sauce tasted almost alcoholic and offered the same effect as a cheerful cocktail — that is a feel-good warmth flowing down my throat to the rest of my body.

Eyes closed, I made an appreciative noise as I savoured another bite, its piquant flavours heightened by a mouthful of rich hot espresso.

'Dreaming of unpaid overtime, are you? Honestly, Kate, stop being such a workaholic.'

'Ha, ha — aren't you funny?' I opened my eyes. 'Not that paying me more would be a problem, due to the profit this place makes. In fact, perhaps I was dreaming of a huge pay rise.'

I grinned across the table at my boss, Izzy. I say 'boss' — she's become more like my best friend, in the two years I've been waitressing at Donuts & Daiquiris. I know — strange name, people usually think of that sugary snack as accompanying caffeinated drinks. I never know whether to tell people I work in a café or bar as it's both. Come six o'clock, purple neon lights shoot across the room and tall glasses replace ceramic mugs.

Izzy loves neon. Adores bright colours and her appearance in the morning never fails to cheer me up. Imagine the shortest ash-blonde hair, accompanied by a slash of scarlet lipstick and clothes that look as if they've been dipped in a rainbow. Tie-dye is her favourite. What a contrast to brown-haired, less conspicuous me, who prefers muted, autumnal colours — ironic, considering I'm a very unmuted singer.

'I offered you a salary hike only last month,' she protested.

'Charity, I don't need,' I said and Izzy blushed. 'You can't pay me more than the other staff.'

'But you work the hardest,' she said. 'If only you weren't so stubborn, Kate. I know things are tight for you at the moment.'

'Nice jumpsuit,' I said, rapidly changing the subject. I admired how her eyeshadow exactly matched the material's shade of Dory blue. Yes, that was a *Finding Nemo* reference. Izzy also loved Disney movies and, between us, I didn't mind watching *Frozen* with her half as much as I declared. When it came to the staff's clothes, Izzy was pretty relaxed, as long as our outfits were clean, ironed and covered by one of her branded aprons — think white cloth edged with mini doughnuts and cocktails. Unlike the after-school club job I had before this one, where the way we looked after the kids was as regimented as their uniform. I couldn't carry on treating children like numbers instead of individuals.

It was two-thirty in the afternoon — the perfect opportunity for a quick break between the lunchtime and after-school rush. The . . . let's call it a café-bar — fulfilled the needs of an array of customers, with its colourful tables and gilt bar. At eight in the morning, we'd serve espressos and cinnamon ring doughnuts to the sleepy breakfast brigade. Mid-morning saw people out to treat themselves to a frothy latte and a chocolate-filled delight. At lunch we bring out the savoury options. Izzy is nothing but inventive and her most popular creations are herbed doughnuts filled with cream cheese. Then, at the end of their school day, children wanted glazed ones topped with colourful sprinkles, accompanied by a fizzy drink.

It's the evening I liked best though, when we dimmed the lights and put out the cocktail menus. Nothing accompanied a Cosmopolitan better than a prettily iced doughnut filled with orange crème. Or a cucumber gin and tonic slipped down nicely with a cheddar and jalapeno batter ring. And Izzy baked the prettiest mini caramel ones, the size of macaroons, to complement richer toffee Martinis. We had our regular drinkers, as well as the hen party crowds. Take Sheila and Frank. They always dressed up and ordered two Snowballs. At their wedding, in the fifties, the first dance song was 'My Funny Valentine' by Frank Sinatra. Sometimes I'd sing it for them. And I mustn't forget Mrs Sharp and her daughter. They swooned over Izzy's special tiramisu doughnuts, made from Marsala-infused batter and filled with mascarpone. Mmm.

Sorry. I'm rambling. Thanks to Izzy, I'm a bit of a doughnut geek as well. I yawned.

'How did the gig go last night?' said Izzy and wiped her mouth with a napkin.

'Not a bad crowd. Bit older than usual. In the end I veered away from the trendy stuff and stuck to seventies disco. Gloria Gaynor always goes down well.'

Yes, when I'm not serving cocktails during the evening shift, I race off to sing at some party or in a pub. Big dreams I've got. Would love to be a singer-songwriter — if I ever pluck up the courage to perform some of my own stuff. My style is kind of like . . . Adele's. But I am less operatic with just a touch of cockney Lily Allen. And some say my voice has the depths of Joss Stone . . . Hmm, OK, maybe I can't be tidily pigeon-holed. I like pop, rock and country and could never restrict my songwriting to one genre. Not that I have written anything for a while.

'Heard any more from Stanley Hotel?' she said. 'Is that regular singing slot definitely cancelled?'

My stomach scrunched and I pushed away the last mouthful of cherry gorgeousness, suddenly losing my appetite. I placed my elbows on the table and rested my chin on my hands. 'Yes. Can't believe it. My first regular gig for ages and within a week of agreeing the terms, it's all over.'

'Do you know why yet?'

'I rang up last night. The manager didn't know the hotel was about to go into liquidation. It's been bought out. This time next year it will be a nursing home. The poor guy was so apologetic — promised to book me for his fiftieth birthday party, later this year.'

Izzy leant forward as my phone rang and squeezed my hand. 'Something else will come up, lovely. Remember to bring in more business cards for the doughnut counter, the pile is running low. And we're hosting two hen nights next week ... I bet they'd appreciate some fun singing à la Katy Perry or old-school Madonna. I'll pay you the going rate.'

My chest glowed as I picked up my mobile. Izzy was the best. If I went around to hers because I was still missing Johnny ... A lump rose in my throat. Despite all my hopeful Facebook messages to him, over the last ten months, I still never got a response. At the beginning, I'd click obsessively, longing to spot the marker 'seen' pop up. And when it never did, my chest felt as if someone had placed me in a vice and turned the handle as tight as they could.

Many an evening, Izzy had invited me over to cheer me up and tolerated watching a few episodes of my favourite historical series on Netflix — as long as she had time for a few rounds of Bejeweled before bed or a catch-up episode of her latest favourite baking show. And she always had a box of tissues on her coffee table — along with, of course, a sample of her latest battered circular creation. A friendship with Izzy would be futile if you suffered from indigestion, but was perfect if your heart was breaking, over a boyfriend.

'Hello?' I said, not recognising the number that had dialled.

'Is that you? Katie?' said a voice as smooth as treacle.

I shuddered. No one called me that. Not since school. A shiver ran up and down my spine and my mouth felt as if I'd eaten a handful of dry cream crackers. That liquid sugar tone sounded so familiar yet I just couldn't identify the owner. It sounded like the meow of a cat that had just spied the mouse it wished to pounce upon.

'Katie Golightly?'

My stomach tightened further as I recalled

what an unfortunate surname that had been at school. You see with my love of vintage clothes and retro music, I stuck out from the crowd. A group of girls made up alternative surnames — Godrearily, Goseriously, Goboringly were just a few. I smiled. Thank goodness for Guvnah who taught me spiteful opinions weren't worth a moment's thought.

Ooh, quick explanation — my granddad always jokingly called my gran the Governor. When I learnt how to write, Guvnah seemed the obvious spelling and the nickname has kind of stuck.

'Katie, hi. It's Saffron!'

I dropped my teaspoon. Size eight, glossy-haired Miss Perfect, head of the spiteful crew.

'Oh,' I managed. 'How nice to hear from you' would be the polite response, but I just couldn't squeeze that sentence from my mouth.

'Surprised you, have I?' she said in bright tones. As she giggled, I could just imagine Saffron tossing her blonde mane. It was still blonde. I knew that from Facebook. You see, about six months ago, she'd sent me a friend request and one of my worst personality traits is my uncontrollable sense of curiosity. For example, if spam gets sent straight to my junk mail box, I have an overwhelming urge to open it. So I accepted Saffron's friend request with the lesson still to learn that curiosity might kill Kate, as much as the cat.

A small part of me was hoping that twelve years later she'd be frumpy and dumpy — but no. She was still the golden girl, with lots of friends and worked as an English teacher. Plus she had a fiancé — called Miles.

'Yes. You have surprised me. It's . . . been a while.'

Come on. We were adults. I could do this. The past was the past. Surely I could forget the way she'd dumped me suddenly at high school, after us being best friends for years? We had it all mapped out a junior school, you know — after the sixth form we'd share an apartment in London and own a dog. Saffron was going to be an actress, me a pop star. We'd cook together, go shopping . . . honestly, the hours we spent discussing the decor of our flat.

But then she ditched me. Found trendier friends. Became Miss Popular with girls and boys alike. No explanation. At first, I didn't realise what was happening. I recall it clearly, the very first time I realised she was laughing at me, not with. We bumped into each other at the swimming pool. I'd gone on my own. Saffron and her new friends all wore skimpy bikinis. I wore my black sports costume that hugged every generous curve and a swimming cap that gave me hamster cheeks but

9

Mum insisted I wear it, for the sake of my hair. Cue snide whispers about puppy fat, moon faces and unwaxed legs. Saffron giggled with her posse, yet couldn't quite give me eye contact. The broken trust broke my heart and it was a long time before I invested that much emotion in another person again. Dear Izzy renewed my belief that good people existed. As did my darling Johnny.

To my surprise, Saffron and I did have one thing in common now: an obsession with *Poldark*. She was always posting photos of the programme's lead, with his tousled black hair, brooding looks and hairy chest. Do you know, the BBC actually employ someone to trim that, during filming? Nice work if you can get it. In fact I'd pay the television company to let me do Poldark Pruning. Her Facebook banner featured that iconic image of him topless, cutting grass, and her profile photo was of her made up like his redheaded wife Demelza, for a fancy-dress party.

I cleared my throat. 'How did you . . . ?'

'Get your phone number?' Her laugh tinkled down the phone once more. 'A bit of detective work. You're in the entertainment business now, aren't you? You linked a website to your Facebook page once, where singers could advertise their services and your profile is on there.'

Ah. Of course.

'How are you?' she said. 'You look fab from your Facebook profile.'

My cheeks burned hot. Was she silent-laughing down her end of the phone? Did she really like the boho chocolate dress, with hanging beads and my shoulder-length hair, with a fifties short fringe? Izzy looked at me again as I pursed my lips. My eyes tingled. This was ridiculous. How could a simple phone call summon up demons I thought I'd well and truly exorcised? Images of sneering faces, on non-uniform days appeared in my mind. I was the third eldest of six children and was rarely bought new clothes or schoolbags. Keeping up with fashion? Even if I'd been interested, I'd never have had the cash.

'And how great to follow your dream and be a singer. What's the biggest gig you've played?'

My cheeks burned hotter. 'Riverside Stadium.'

'Wow. Sounds like a huge venue. How many thousands did you play to?'

I swallowed. 'Not many. That's actually the name of a bar. But it was for a fortieth birthday and brought me a couple of other bookings . . . ' I rambled, bracing myself for some sarcastic response — like the time I'd

11

come top in a French test. She'd laughed when one of her cronies muttered that Katie Gochastely may know the French language but had undoubtedly never once been French-kissed.

However, Saffron simply congratulated me. 'Must be hard, trying to find singing work — no doubt you support your dream with a solid job?'

'Yes. I work in catering,' I said and swallowed. I looked down as Izzy's brightly nail-varnished fingers curled over my free hand on the table. She squeezed tight and I forced a smile.

'Ooh, can you cook? I love watching Jamie Oliver.'

'No. I'm a waitress,' I said in a smaller voice and braced myself for a snigger.

'I imagine a flexible job like that fits in well around your sporadic singing commitments,' she said in a breezy voice.

What? No insult. My shoulders relaxed. Izzy smiled and I nodded. She took away her hand and started to clear our plates.

'Yes, it does actually. And you're a teacher?'

'I know! Never thought I'd end up going back to school. I met Miles on one of the careers' days. He's the uncle of one of my students and came in to give a talk on being an accountant.'

'Congratulations on your engagement,' I said. Why on earth had she rung? When would this torture end?

'Thanks. Yes. Miles is wonderful. I'm a very lucky lady. And . . . are you with someone, Katie?'

Shoulders tight again, I grimaced. Oh great. She'd already won in the intellectual professional stakes, what with her following a life of academia and having a solid direction and career. Child-minding and waitressing had seemed natural for me, after looking after younger siblings for years whilst Mum worked. And now Saffron wanted to ram home her victory by claiming the best personal life. If only this conversation had taken place earlier last year, when Johnny was still around. That would have shown her. Johnny, with his crinkly teasing eyes, and cheeks that crumpled adoringly when he enjoyed a joke; whose kisses sent prickles of heat from my head to my toes. I had a sudden urge to message him. *Johnny. Guess who's contacted me? Let's go to her wedding — show her how I've landed the dream boyfriend.*

I sighed. People said I should move on. Date someone new. Leave the memory of Johnny behind. But they wouldn't say that, would they, if I'd been married to him for years or had kids? No, but because I was

13

young and we weren't even engaged, I'm supposed to have a new boyfriend by now. But getting over Johnny? Social media made that even harder. All his photos on Instagram . . . I just hadn't been able to bring myself to unfollow.

I bit my lip. Who cared what Saffron thought? I was pursuing my dream. I loved my doughnut job and had wonderful friends.

'Yes, my boyfriend and I are very happy,' I said airily, before I could stop the false words. Clearly I cared about her opinion more than I should. Arrghh, why had I lied? Me, who was normally so honest? I'd go back to a supermarket if they'd accidentally under-charged.

I stood up to pace around and, for a moment, I forgot I was at work, with Izzy just a metre away. All I could picture was the other girls' superior faces as I sat down during the slow dance at the school prom, whilst they were all whisked to their feet by boys. 'I don't post about him on Facebook . . . he doesn't approve of social media.'

To my surprise, Saffron replied, 'Very sensible. A particular friend of mine always posts whilst drunk and another picked up a stalker. I'm very careful with my privacy settings. Facebook must be essential for you though, in terms of networking with bands.'

'Yes, it is,' I said flatly and thought how clever she'd become over the years at hiding her real feelings. I mean, why the sudden turnaround? Why treat me like an equal when all she'd ever done at high school was put me down?

'What does your boyfriend do?' she said.

'He ... he ... ' He's Ross Poldark, I wished I could say. There would be no way she could beat that.

My mind tripped back, again, to that famous grass-cutting scene from the show, in Saffron's Facebook banner. 'He's a gardener. Self-employed. A landscape designer,' I said, warming to my theme. 'He's called Ross.'

'Really? How wonderful. People always need work doing in their gardens. He must be terribly fit to cope.'

'Oh yes,' I said, knots in my stomach unfurling. 'In fact, he looks just like Poldark — dark curly hair, tanned from his job and gorgeous eyes. There is nothing quite like a six-pack that's acquired from good honest work and not some gym where everyone is obsessing over their body fat ratio or biceps size, wouldn't you agree?'

'The only six-pack Miles knows contains packets of cheese and onion crisps! Well, good for you,' she said.

Oh. Disappointing. She'd managed to hide

every trace of envy in that voice.

'In fact, that's great because the reason I'm ringing is . . . I'd like to invite you to my wedding next month,' she blurted out. 'Could you give me your address? I can't wait to meet Ross, your plus-one.'

*What?* I closed my eyes. Fair dos, universe, this is a swift punishment for my lie. Perhaps she'd guessed I wasn't telling the truth. I mean, why else would she want me there?

'That's . . . very kind of you,' I said, 'but . . . Saffron . . . I'm really busy during the coming months and . . . I'm sure there are closer friends you'd like to invite instead of me.'

Didn't the non-confrontational British just love an understatement?

Silence. Awkward. I awaited the shallow, meaningless retort.

'It would mean a lot to me. Really. And several friends from school are going to be there,' she said with a super-soft tone.

I squirmed. Then it truly would be the wedding from hell. But once again, curiosity piqued me and, despite some deep-set feelings of inadequacy that occasionally made a reappearance, for the most I wasn't that insecure teenager any more. Plus, I was trying to build myself as a singer, and weddings were the best opportunity to subtly leave out business cards.

'You'd be doing me a favour, Katie. I couldn't invite everyone I wanted but two family members have just dropped out, due to illness. That's why my invite is quite late notice. Please. Do consider it.'

Maybe things hadn't changed so much after all — I clearly wasn't her first choice of guest.

'OK,' I found myself saying. 'Ross and I would love to attend. I'll message you my address. Right. I'd better go — customers await.'

I pressed 'end call', put my mobile on the table and sank into my chair. How I would have preferred to say 'Yes, I have a boyfriend called *Johnny*.' My fingers flexed as if wanting to message him on Facebook, even though, deep down, I knew it was fruitless trying to exchange words with someone who was . . . dead. My eyes tingled and I gave myself a shake. I wasn't one of life's wallowers. Ever lost my job? I'd be the first in the queue at the employment office. Argue with a sibling or Mum? It was usually me to phone first and smooth things over. But losing someone isn't the same, is it? Deep-felt feelings can't be shaken away like salt out of a salt cellar. And messaging him was still possible, you see, because after . . . the accident, his family memorialised his Facebook profile. That meant friends could still visit his page to flick through photo albums. It meant, in my darkest hours, I could pretend that he was alive but simply ignoring my heartfelt words.

I gave a sigh and gradually my mind cleared of images of Johnny and uncomfortable school memories, until before me I saw . . . Ah. Izzy, mouth open, with one eyebrow disappearing into her hairline, clearly having heard me talk of a supposed new boyfriend called Ross . . .

# 2

With a sigh, I opened the lounge window, before collapsing onto my squat plum-coloured sofa. Well, the throw was plum. It hid threadbare blue cushions. I loved my flat, even though the kitchen was tiny and my clothes hung on a rail in this living room, due to the bedroom being so small that it could only house a bed *or* a wardrobe, not both. After years of sharing my personal space with siblings, however cramped, life here felt luxurious. I blinked rapidly and still couldn't believe my landlord's announcement, last week, that he wanted me out in two months. He'd decided to refurbish and sell because he needed the money to move back to Australia. Apparently ten years of grey English winters had taken their toll.

I bit the inside of my cheeks. No point moping but I'd miss old Mrs Bird from next door. She'd call on me whenever she needed a light bulb changing, as these days she was wobbly on her feet. Often I'd stay for a cup of tea and a biscuit and she'd play her old vinyl records, her favourites by Doris Day.

I inhaled and breathed out slowly. I'd

already started searching the rental ads in the local paper. Little point worrying over things that couldn't be changed, as Johnny always used to say.

I gazed up at the ceiling, in the corner of the lounge, at the shiny, red, heart-shaped wind spinner he had given me soon after we met. With every turn, the angled metal gave the impression that it pulsated. I hadn't dared hang it in the garden, in case the damp weather turned it rusty and brown.

'Whenever you look at it, remember,' he'd said, 'it pulsates with my love. I love you Kate Golightly and this is a constant reminder to follow your heart.'

'Oh, Johnny,' I murmured and flinched at that vice-like feeling across my chest. I sniffed, picked up my mobile and clicked on the Facebook icon. Very quickly, I found his profile and messaged: *Johnny . . . How are you? I'm missing you still, every time the wind spinner catches my eye. Oh what I'd give just to hear one more of your laughs — just to kiss those lips that had a hotline to my heart.* I swallowed, the typed words for a moment looking blurry. *What should I do? Soon I'll be homeless. Mum has relocated to Scotland with her new job. Shall I follow her there?*

I know. Pathetic, wasn't it — the irrational part of me still wanting a response? But I'd never been able to talk to anyone like I could to him, apart from Guvnah. As for moving to Scotland, my instincts already knew the answer. I'd been brought up by a woman determined not to sponge off relatives or claim benefits. Mum had held down three jobs at one point, to manage on her own. 'Independence is the key to happiness and self-respect,' she always said. True words. Nothing beat the feeling of paying your own bills or finally buying something you'd saved up for. But not even Guvnah lived nearby any more. After five years of widowhood, she'd met a lovely bloke and moved to Cornwall to marry him last year.

I couldn't help grinning at the memory of my sixty-seven-year-old grandma on her Big Day. Cupid had unexpectedly shot his arrow at her, during a bowling match, when her friend Bill had brought his friend, Geoff, visiting from the South-west. All of a sudden stubborn techno-phobe Guvnah learnt to text and Skype. She even bought a selfie stick. It gave me faith that it would never be too late to find my soulmate.

I gave the wind spinner one last glance, before prising open my laptop. If only Guvnah lived nearer or I had more paid days off work to go visit. Scrub that. I couldn't even afford the petrol to get there. Money was tight. That's why I'd offered to work a double shift today, because Suze, the afternoon waitress, had fallen ill. Mind you, Izzy's requests were hard to resist when she shook a plate of fresh Oreo-inspired dough-nuts under your nose.

Clothes feeling sticky and feet swollen, I yawned. Nothing beat waking up to summer blue skies but a warm café-bar wasn't the best place to work when temperatures tipped into the mid-twenties Celsius. Not that industrious wasps seemed to agree, having spent the afternoon mounting a well-thought-out campaign against customers and their sweet guilty pleasures. I kicked off my shoes and stared at the screen. Spiteful Saffron. Wedding. Plus-one. This was an emergency situation. I had four weeks to find a partner who looked exactly like a brooding mine owner. So that meant emergency chocolate, right? With an evening ahead of me, registering with as many dating sites as possible, cooking wouldn't feature on the agenda. Not that it often did, what with me living above the Egg and Whistle, a cheap and cheerful café. Izzy despaired and occasionally forced me to eat an apple during my tea break. I know. How paradoxical — her running a fast-food diner yet obsessing with fresh foods and vitamin C.

Having said that, she prided herself on baking with the freshest, best quality ingredients. And stewed fruit often bubbled away in the kitchen, to make fillings, plus her savoury doughnuts often required chopped veg. I slipped a hand under one of the faded blue cushions and pulled out a huge bar of fruit and nut chocolate. I stashed it there, kidding myself it was hidden and not offering temptation.

Mouth watering, I slipped my fingers along the wrapper. The rectangle looked misshapen, due to melting in the summer heat — not a problem us English chocolate-lovers often suffered from. I went to tug it open when the doorbell rang. At half past eight? Who could that be? Perhaps some local incarnation of Poldark, complete with eighteenth-century tricorn hat, frock coat and roguish smile, offering to escort me to Saffron's Big Day. I slipped the chocolate back under the cushion and headed to the window, stuck my head out into the muggy evening air and stared down at the pavement.

'Who's there?'

'The most considerate boss you'll ever have the honour of meeting,' called a voice.

'Izzy,' I said in a faux bored voice. 'What do you want? Isn't it enough that you listen to my erudite conversation all day, every day?'

She stepped backwards, into view, and we grinned at each other, although my chest squeezed. I'd avoided her after Saffron's phone call, not wanting to answer embarrassing questions about my fictional boyfriend, Ross. I headed over to the front door and pressed the button to let her in. Eventually, footsteps sounded in the hallway and I opened the door.

Izzy walked in, carrying a large plastic bag and humming, headed straight for the kitchen. With her yellow shorts and strawberry-red T-shirt, she reminded me of a garnished Pina Colada cocktail.

'Make yourself at home,' I said and she caught my eye. We chuckled and I shut the front door.

'Thanks for working that double shift,' she said. 'Figured I owed you a decent dinner as it was so busy. When I left, a group of eighteen-year-olds came in . . . or at least said they were. I prompted James to check their ID and, as a result, most had to order mocktails instead. So I think he's having a quiet night.'

'I'm surprised you didn't stay to help your newest employee,' I said, airily.

Izzy swung around.

'Goodness, how flushed your cheeks look, must be the heat.' I grinned. 'Or the thought of how his muscles show through a tight T-shirt. That man must live in the gym.'

'You know me, Kate — ever the professional. I would never have a relationship with someone I'd hired . . . ' She cleared her throat. 'So if I have to fire him for not thinking to check those girls' IDs on his own, well, so be it.'

'Izzy!'

Her shoulders moved up and down as she laughed. 'Only joking. Sure, he's cute, but a bit young for me.' With a flourish she pulled out a bottle of Prosecco.

'Ooh. What are we celebrating?'

She shrugged. 'There's no law against fizz on a week night, is there — especially if you've had a challenging day?'

My throat went tight.

'I saw your face after that phone call,' she said softly. 'No need to explain if you don't want to. I just thought your evening might benefit from a bit of sparkle. But Auntie Izzy is here if you need a chat.'

My mouth quirked up — 'Auntie' indeed. Izzy was only a couple of years older than me, although to be fair, she fussed over all her employees, apart from the ones she sacked for turning up late or helping themselves to too many doughnuts. Gooey as her heart was, like untried batter, kind Izzy was no pushover.

My throat tightened further as, for a few seconds, I relived the teenage feelings of inadequacy, embarrassment, self-hatred — feelings belonging to Katie Golightly, the round peg in a square hole girl.

'Oh, Izzy. What have I got myself into?' I slumped onto the sofa.

She came over and sat next to me. 'So, when were you going to introduce me to this Ross?' Her eyes twinkled.

Now my cheeks burned.

'Some friend has asked you to their wedding and you decided to make up that you had a plus-one?'

Avoiding her eye, I nodded.

'Kate! It's not like you to lie! And there are thousands of people every year who go to events on their own. You'd be viewed as a confident, strong woman.'

'Or as a wallflower wimp,' I said. Izzy already knew bits — about the teasing; me not fitting in with the popular crowd. However I'd never really talked about what exactly had happened between me and Saffron and how she'd ditched me as soon as we left primary school. How we'd once been friends but then, for no apparent reason . . . I cleared my throat and again tapped on my laptop. 'Sorry for going on,' I mumbled and tucked a strand of hair behind my ear. 'I know I should be over the whole high school thing by now.'

'I don't think people ever get over that teenage stuff, Kate. It's fifteen years ago for me and I still remember the knots in the pit of my stomach when the older girls used to corner me in the toilets. I've always loved cooking and used to hang out in the food technology department at lunchtime and read up on new recipes with my favourite teacher. I didn't smoke, drink or snog . . . guess I was an easy target.' She shrugged. 'But those experiences don't need to define our whole life, right?'

I nodded.

'So, why don't you just forget this whole Poldark thing? Tell Saffron you and Ross split up. Or, even better, don't go to the wedding at all. She's not even a friend. You've nothing to prove to anyone and you don't owe her a single thing.' Izzy got up, headed over to the tiny, open-plan kitchenette and, seconds later, a cork popped. She picked up two clean glass tumblers from the side of the sink and came back. Izzy sat down and our glasses clinked. As tiny Prosecco bubbles tickled my tongue, heat spread through my chest. I put down the glass.

'But why did she invite me? I'm curious. And if I say Ross and I broke up it will seem suspicious. No . . . ' I sat upright. 'My original plan remains. I need to find a Poldark looka-like and I'm hoping an online dating site can help.' I sighed. 'If only Johnny were here.'

'But he's not, Kate. And I really hope you are trying to stop messaging him,' she said gently. 'You know he won't respond.'

My ears felt hot and I swallowed, suddenly experiencing the biggest urge to do exactly what she'd advised against. Apart from Guvnah, Izzy was the only person who knew I'd obsessed with my late boyfriend's social media platforms for the first few months after he'd gone. Now, the need to check out his profiles was less overwhelming, less compulsive, and yet proved to be a hard habit to break.

'But if you are adamant that this pretend plus-one plan is the way to go, I'm here for you,' she said more brightly, 'and I'll do whatever I can to help — starting with making us something to eat. I brought chicken and stir-fry veg. It won't take me long.'

\* \* \*

While ingredients sizzled in the kitchenette, I dived, broad mind first, into a search engine, looking for appropriate dating sites to join. Wow. What an array. I found one for dog owners, another for ramblers, several for naturists and even for grisly fans of *The Walking Dead*. I couldn't help glancing at the

28

profiles of people who'd joined that one. Most had made up their faces with plastic eaten-away skin and trickles of blood or held a crossbow or gun. Images flooded my mind regarding the perils of zombie sex and loose body parts. Ew.

But wait a minute. I moved forward and perched on the edge of the sofa. Perhaps there were dating sites specifically for fans of other shows like . . . Quickly I typed in 'Poldark dating'. I scrolled down website links offering articles about the TV pro-gramme, its stars and Cornwall and was about to give up on page three when . . . ooh: *Perfect Poldark Pairs — find your perfect brooding hero or feisty heroine. No joining fee. Could your very own Ross, Demelza or Elizabeth just be one mouse-click away?*

'You won't believe what I've just found,' I said and took another sip of Prosecco.

Izzy stopped chopping and headed over, a tea towel between her hands. She sat down and read the screen. 'Really? I mean, *really*? Can't people tell the difference between fiction and reality any more? It's fine having a celebrity crush but taking it this far . . . ?'

I snorted. 'So you wouldn't be interested in joining a site that promised to find your very own Jack Black?' Nothing attracted Izzy more than a man who could make her laugh

— apart from a Disney prince.

Izzy giggled. 'Hands up. You got me there.' She leant forward and, not for the first time, I admired the length of her legs. But then at a curvy five foot two, most people's limbs outstretched mine and certainly Izzy's as she was a willowy five foot nine. 'So, who is this Demelza?' she said.

'A feisty redheaded miner's daughter who ends up marrying Ross Poldark. Although his first love is delicate, fragile, posh Elizabeth. It's a bit of a love triangle . . . '

Izzy scrolled down the page. 'Hmm. OK, so . . . what about him?'

I gazed at the picture of a man in his, ooh, thirties, with ruffled black hair and half-shaven cheeks. My eyes narrowed. 'Nah. Read that. He reckons a date would enjoy a tour of the local mines near his house. That's making the whole Cornish dream a little too real. A romantic man, that's what I'll need to impress . . . '

Silence fell as I kept scrolling the page and we analysed profile after profile. Some photos were people in fancy dress, complete with tricorns for Ross, or red wigs for Demelza. Others were understated and belonged to people who just liked historical reading, as opposed to the hot stars of the novel's TV adaption.

'Ooh. This guy would fit the bill,' I murmured. 'He lives about an hour away. We could meet up halfway.'

'Hmm. Nice enough,' replied Izzy, as we studied the photo of a man nearer to my age, with raven hair, dark eyes and wearing a white shirt just unbuttoned enough to reveal manly chest hair. 'I mean . . . ' Izzy stared at the floor. 'Who knows, you might feel ready to . . . '

She met my gaze as I raised one eyebrow. Again I noticed the glint of the red wind spinner in the corner of the room. I shook my head. No words necessary. Izzy didn't push her point and went back to the screen.

'Marcus,' I said. 'That's a sexy name. He likes candlelit dinners, romantic seaside strolls and horse-riding.' I bit the corner of my bottom lip. 'He sounds suitable. Shall I join the site and message him?'

'You're actually going to do this?'

I wiped my forehead and perspiration dampened my hand. 'Yes. Although I feel a bit bad . . . you know, going on a date when I have no intention of starting a new relationship. But I reckon most people are just on these sites for a bit of fun. I'll pay for the meal. At least, then, they won't have spent money unnecessarily.'

In full auntie mode, Izzy pushed me out of

the way and clicked on the site's pages. 'It looks well run,' she said, a few minutes later. 'Plus they give sensible advice like not giving away too much personal information online and meeting in a public place.'

I slid the laptop back in my direction. 'Izzy. Please. I am perfectly capable of looking after myself.'

She grinned. 'I know. Don't forget, I witnessed you throw out those troublemakers the other day. Good job.'

I grinned back. I was a fearsome proposition at a certain time of the month and when a couple of teenage lads started flicking bits of doughnut around the diner, I wasted no time in getting them to pay the bill and leave — although granted, dangling their mobile phones over a large jug of Long Island Tea might have been overzealous.

'But why not look at some other profiles first?' She shrugged.

'Time isn't on my side! I've got precisely four weeks to not only meet a bed-haired, sexy-eyed guy with looks as rugged as Cornish scenery, but then convince him to accompany me to a wedding under the name of Ross.' I covered my face with my hands. 'Ludicrous, isn't it? Listen to me. Perhaps I should give up before I start.' I parted my fingers slightly to see Izzy's face.

She took my hands away and stared for a moment. 'Is it really important to you to impress this woman?'

I swallowed, wishing it wasn't. 'Yes.'

'Then go for it, even though you are super-impressive just the way you are. After dinner, I'll help select other suitable men to contact.'

My hands fell away and I gave her the biggest of hugs.

'Let me breathe,' she squeaked eventually and, as she leant back, I grinned.

Whilst Izzy finished off the stir-fry, I tapped a message to Marcus, having carefully selected my profile picture. Tempting as it was to use one of my airbrushed, Instagram snaps, I chose an un-Photoshopped head shot of me after a gig where I'd sung fifties and sixties music. I wore one of my smarter black bop dresses, with a slim belt around the waist, and updo hair *à la* Audrey Hepburn.

I pressed send, just as Izzy called me to the breakfast bar. Mmm. Sliced chicken fried with veggies, ginger and garlic. I was just about to top up our Prosecco tumblers when I heard a ping and hurried over to my laptop.

'Aarghh! He's replied already!' I said and unexpectedly my hands shook.' I clicked on the message. 'He wants to meet tomorrow night. Eight o'clock at a pub called the Dog and Duck, in Winbury.'

I ran back to Izzy and held her hands as, laughing, we jumped up and down on the spot (that was our thing, and agreed, totally inappropriate for our age group).

'You are one crazy woman,' she said, face split into a smile. She shook her head. 'I think I've seen that pub when I visit one of our suppliers. It's about forty minutes away.' She stared at me for a few seconds. 'OK. Fine.'

'Um, excuse me, I wasn't asking your permission!'

'Meet your Poldark,' she continued. 'And who knows, despite . . . despite what you think, you may be ready to . . . He could be a lovely guy.'

I fiddled with my bead bracelet.

'But either way,' she said brightly, 'I'll be lurking in the background, just in case your romantic hero turns up wielding a machete instead of a scythe.'

But he wouldn't be wielding a heart wind spinner, so however much charm he oozed, it would be lost on me.

# 3

Deep breaths. In and out. And again. Anyone would think I was about to give birth. Well, Saffron would, seeing as my waist measurement was more than twenty-four inches. I smiled. Dear Johnny had well and truly extinguished any teenage insecurities I might have still harboured about not being a size zero. Curves were his thing — on the hips, on the lips — so I always said it would be rude not to maintain my womanly look — code he understood for always giving me the last slice of a pizza.

I took one last breath and headed across the car park into the Dog and Duck. Not that I was anti-slim women. That was the difference between Saffron and me. I didn't care what anyone looked like as long as they were kind. It was hard to think of Saffron as a teacher now. I grimaced, just imagining her having class favourites, all the popular kids with the best phones, coolest rucksacks and doting hangers-on.

I stopped in front of wooden swing doors. It was an olde worlde Tudor pub, the slightly wonky white-and-black front somehow inviting me in. I'd managed to convince Izzy not to come — that at the grand old age of twenty-seven I didn't need a chaperone. As a compromise, she'd insisted on ringing one hour into the date, at nine, to give me a reason to escape if needs be. She was back at Donuts & Daiquiris, feeling inspired by all this Cornwall talk, experimenting with a new recipe for doughnuts filled with jam and Cornish clotted cream.

My mouth went dry and I fanned my face with my beaded clutch handbag, before smoothing down my dress. As the sun set, the heat of the day abated. It had been the hottest July for a long time and with August on the way the shops had already sold out of battery-run hand fans. Craving an iced drink, I pulled open the door and headed in — and almost about-turned and left as my stomach knotted really tight. Marcus and I had messaged briefly today. He said this pub served a great fish pie and we'd both laughingly agreed to have the Cornish dairy ice cream for dessert, as a homage to the *Poldark* series.

Curling my free hand into a fist, I sternly told myself not to be a wimp and stepped onto laminate floor. I gazed around, bending forwards and backwards to study tables, in between wooden black beams. One family, a young man on his own, a retired couple . . . The grey-haired woman dropped her phone and I scooted forward to pick it up. As I got up and returned her thanks with a smile, I surveyed the pub again and . . . Ooh. On my left, his back to me, was a man with curly black hair, wearing a white shirt. Stomach now tighter than an eighteenth-century bodice, I strode over and walked around his table.

'Marcus?'

He looked up and I almost peed my pants. God. It *was* him, but an older version. His picture must have been heavily photoshopped. Stupid me. Wrinkles surrounded his hooded eyes and his hair was clearly dyed black. It was thin on the top and — Aarghhh! Combed over. And out of his open shirt poked grey hairs.

I know. Listen to me. Shallow or what? OK, so he wasn't what I expected, but I was heading towards thirty, a mature woman, I should be above writing off potential romantic partners for superficial reasons — not that I was on the lookout for love. I gazed more intently . . . he could be over fifty which meant he might be the same age as my dad. Noooo. On so many levels, this was wrong.

Yet I was curious. The sweetest expression had crossed his face and he stood up until I sat down.

'Kate,' he said. 'Er, cool to meet you.' He winked. 'Finally I get to meet my very own

Demelza. Now I just need a horse to whisk you away.' He ran a hand through his hair, but it didn't seem like a natural movement. I couldn't help smiling. Only a few seconds in and he was trying really hard. 'So, what'll it be?' he said, in a bright voice. 'Vodka shots or one of those trendy ciders?'

'Just a Coke please. I'm driving. But I'll get it.'

'No. Let me,' he said and darted up as quick as you like, as if I had a contagious disease.

I watched him, at the bar, thinking back to my first date with Johnny, in a pub not unlike this. He'd seen me singing on one of my modern music nights, where I'd performed some Ed Sheeran, Joss Stone and James Blunt. He came up to me afterwards; said my voice had a unique quality he'd never heard before; wondered if I'd like to accompany him to a jazz pub the following evening as a friend had let him down. Not that we'd heard much of the bass and piano the following evening as we talked non-stop. And just before we parted, outside, he'd leant forward and kissed me oh so gently on the cheek, ever so close to my mouth, lingering for just a bit longer than expected, millimetres away from my top lip. I was hooked.

I cleared my throat as Marcus returned to

the table. He sat down, with two Cokes.

'Thanks, Marcus. Um . . . nice to meet you.'

'Wicked!' he said.

Cringe. What a painful attempt to appear younger. He'd realised it too. Marcus sighed and looked down at himself.

'I don't normally wear tops wide open like the Bee Gees, but thought I'd better make an effort — you know, for the sake of *Poldark*.' He eyed me up and down and I squirmed in my seat, sensing my cheeks pink up.

'So, obviously you're a big fan of the series,' I said.

Now my eyes roved his frame. He must have been quite an eye-turner a decade or so before. In fact there was something about his face — the dark shadows under the eyes perhaps — that made me think he looked even older than his actual years. As we chatted about our love of the programme, my shoulders relaxed and I leant back in my chair. So did he. In fact, Marcus was good company. Funny, in an understated way. Polite. Witty. What a shame he wasn't young enough to impress Saffron. Yet, I was pleased at not having to dupe him. What a lovely guy. It made me realise I'd have to be upfront with whoever I took to the wedding. Hurting people's feelings wasn't part of the plan.

We both ordered the fish pie. Looked like I'd be logging on to the dating site again tonight, to find another candidate.

'I watch the programme every week with my daughter,' said Marcus. He studied me again. 'Sorry,' he blurted out. 'I don't mean to stare, it's just . . . Please don't take this the wrong way, Kate, but from your profile picture I thought you'd be older. Like my Ruth, you can't even be into your thirties yet.' He shot me a sheepish look. 'And I expect my appearance was a bit of a surprise.' He shook his head. 'Bet you think I'm a right arse, trying to be younger than my years.'

'Erm . . . '

He grinned, chestnut eyes twinkling as he touched his hair. 'I let Ruth dye this for that profile picture. Big mistake.'

Aw bless. What a superstar. So he definitely wasn't some creep lusting after women half his age. Although I'd already worked that out after the way he'd talked about how satisfying he found his job as a care worker. Clearly he had strong principles — so why did a man with such integrity and passion need the help of an online matchmaking service?

'Ruth means well and also insisted on putting that photo through Instagram first so that I looked 'my best'.' He gave a deep chuckle. 'Always a generous child, she's been.'

I smiled. 'And I posted a photo, warts and all, with bad lighting. How old did you think I'd be?' Marcus's cheeks flushed a deep maroon and I burst out laughing. 'Don't worry. No need to answer. My classic black dress probably didn't help.'

'It's what attracted me to your profile,' he said. 'My mum used to dress like that. What I mean is . . . ' He groaned and I couldn't help giggling. 'Lord,' he said, 'I am useless at all this stuff.'

'I love all that movie-star glamour, with long cigarette holders and classic clothes. It is such a distinctive era. And you can pick up some great bargains from charity shops.' Oxfam had been my lifesaver during the teenage years. A fifty-pence vintage top from there felt newer than any hand-me-down from my older sisters. 'Guess we've paid the price for using a niche, smaller dating site. I imagine the bigger dating sites require you to enter your actual age.'

The waiter delivered our pies and we ate in silence for a few moments. Mmm. Creamy subtle flavours washed over my tongue. I ordered us another couple of Cokes.

Marcus stared at me. 'Do you think it's sad, Kate? A man of my age doing online dating?'

'No. I think it's hard for lots of people to meet that special someone in this mad,

41

modern busy world.'

He clasped his hands together. 'That's just it though. Ruth means well but I . . . I'm not ready to meet someone else yet. My wife . . . Sandra . . . She passed away two years ago and I still miss her.' He rubbed his forehead. 'Sorry, Kate. I shouldn't bore you with — '

My throat felt scratchy at the way his voice caught and those dark eyes glistened. 'No, Marcus, honestly, it's fine. Tell me about her. How did you meet?'

'At university, during the Fresher's Week fair. My new friends joined the cheese and wine club because lots of female students had signed up. But I really wanted to try potholing, and joined that club first. So did Sandra. A slow dance to Whitney Houston at a freshers' disco sealed our attraction that went on to last for life.'

They had two kids. And now four grandchildren. Then Sandra got early-onset dementia and died no longer knowing that Marcus was her soulmate. Marcus started to eat his pie again and shook his head. 'Ruth would kill me for sitting here, on a date, talking about my wife — her mum.' He looked up. 'Devastating for her, it was, watching Sandra lose all the aspects of her character, one by one. We cried more at the diagnosis than the end which, by then, was a blessed relief.' He shrugged. 'I wish my daughter wouldn't worry about me.'

I patted his arm before glancing at my watch. 'And talking of people worrying — '

On cue, my phone rang. And so did Marcus's! Five minutes later, each of us had hung up and we were laughing. Both Izzy and Ruth had rung bang on nine o'clock to give us get-outs from the date, if required.

'Enough about me,' said Marcus, as our ice creams arrived. ''Fess up', Kate, as my grandson would say. What is an attractive, personable, intelligent young woman like you doing on Perfect Poldark Pairs?'

I wasn't going to mention Johnny. That subject matter was still so . . . raw. And I'd become unused to talking about him with people I didn't know well. Plus my heartbreak had no relevance — I wasn't on this date to find The One. Just a plus-one. I covered my face with my hands. 'You'll think me mad.'

'Try me.'

Out poured the whole sorry story about Saffron and me trying to impress.

Marcus shook his head. 'Oh dear, and you turn up to meet me, Mr Flymo-man — I'd have no idea how to cut grass with a scythe.' He wiped his mouth with a paper napkin. 'You know I've learnt, over time, that the things you most want appear where you least expect them — like Sandra, at the potholing club. Perhaps the key for you will be to stop trying so hard to find this Ross.'

'But I don't have time on my side. The wedding is at the end of August, in just over four weeks. I need a miracle or to speed-date twenty-four-seven!'

As we drank coffees, and ate delicious crisp mints, our conversation moved on to more general subjects. How we'd both love to live somewhere like Cornwall. How the eighteenth-century lifestyle appealed because of its simplicity.

Eventually, he glanced at his watch. 'Right, Well. Work tomorrow. I'd better get going.' His eyes crinkled. 'Best of luck. I'm sorry I don't fit the bill, but keep in touch, Kate.' Marcus rolled his eyes. 'Ruth has insisted on registering me on Facebook, so perhaps we can connect on there and I'll come to one of your gigs. I love all disco music and swing. And if I stumble across any brooding heroes in the next week or so, I'll let you know. Or — ' he shrugged ' — you could forget trying to impress this Saffron; skip the wedding . . . '

Mature me knew he was right, but lurking aspects of Katie Golightly just wouldn't let me turn down the invitation.

Singing some Frank Sinatra, I drove my slightly rusty but cosy car home. Belting out a song had been my escape, as a youngster, from my hectic family life and from the challenges of school. I'd hole myself up somewhere private, like the back garden or bathroom, close my eyes and for just a few moments, whilst singing, felt important, felt unique — until Mum called me to do my chores.

I parked up, on a busy high street, outside Donuts & Daiquris — Izzy had insisted I call in for mock Mojito, before going home, to give her the low-down.

I got out, locked up my car and headed into the building, squinting at pretty neon lights and circumnavigating busy tables until I reached the bar. James informed customers that it was last orders. Me and Izzy headed out back, to the quiet, whitewashed staff room. We sat down on wooden chairs and she raised a neatly pencilled eyebrow.

I gave a huge sigh. 'Nice night. Nice evening. Nice bloke. But old enough to be my dad.' Cue twenty minutes of describing my date.

'So it's back to square one?' she said, eventually.

My mouth drooped. 'Let's face it. This plan of mine is never going to work. It takes long enough to hook up with someone when you've no particular type in mind, let alone when you have a list of criteria.' I raised my hands in the air. 'What with this and having to leave my flat and my Stanley Hotel gigs being cancelled, I'm just so fed up.' Another big sigh. 'Why can't James have curly black hair and brooding looks. I bet he'd look fab in a tricorn.'

Izzy smiled. But not one of her normal smiles. It had a hint of smugness to it as if she knew something I didn't. Last time she'd worn it she'd snagged me a party booking, singing at a silver wedding anniversary bash, by praising my talents to one of the customers.

'What?'

Izzy cleared her voice. 'Next week. You know I've been feeling restless.'

I nodded. Donuts & Daiquiris earned more than my boss could have ever imagined and now Izzy, being a straight-A student, needed a new challenge. She'd been university material but couldn't ignore her passion for food and now those grey cells clearly needed stretching some more.

'I've decided this place needs a makeover. Plus, I need to take a trip — to get inspired by food. I'm thinking of expanding the menu.'

'Wow. When did you decide all this?'

'A couple of weeks ago. I didn't want to say much in case I couldn't book everything in time, but I've managed to find a decorator who gets my new concept, and found a last-minute holiday deal online — I've booked a gold lodge at a spa resort. Quite a bargain it was, for a summer booking.'

'So, no work for two weeks from next Monday?'

'You'll get paid of course.'

My smile widened. 'Well, that is a good piece of news. It'll give me chance to carry on looking for a new place and, while I'm disappointed about the Stanley Hotel, I'm determined to find another regular gig. Plus — '

'Or — ' her eyes sparked ' — come with me, Kate. You deserve a treat.'

I gasped. 'Izzy, that's really kind, but I couldn't possibly afford to share the rent.'

Izzy folded her arms. 'When I say a treat, I mean exactly that — my shout. All you'd need is spending money. I'll drive.'

'Izzy, that is so kind, but — '

'Go on . . . even if it's just for one of the weeks. And, if you don't find a flat in time, when you get back, you can move in with me.'

'I don't need charity,' I said and folded my arms. 'I appreciate the offer but — '

'Kate Golightly! Lose the pride! I'm your friend. You could stay with me permanently for all I care — but a few weeks, that's not charity, it's just a mate being a mate.'

I thought for a moment and then grinned. 'OK.'

'And you deserve a holiday. We both do. Plus, I'd enjoy the company.'

We stared at each other.

'It'll be fun,' she said softly. 'Saunas, facials, walks — it's just what we both need. The outdoor life. Plus . . . ' Her eyes sparked more strongly, like a poker player who knew his hand of cards couldn't be beaten. 'All your *Poldark* talk got me thinking and I figured there is nowhere more inspiring for food, in Britain, than the South-west, what with pasties, scones, ice cream, fudge, and the White Rocks holiday resort just happens to be really close to . . . Port Penny!'

My heart raced. 'Guvnah! Oh my days!' A comforting chat with her was just what I needed. We'd not seen each other since Christmas. 'Oh, Izzy, really?'

She nodded.

My mind raced and I clapped my hands. 'You know what else this means?'

Izzy chuckled. 'You seem almost more excited at the prospect of a holiday than me.'

'Yes! Because this break couldn't have come at a better time. It gives me the perfect opportunity to meet a genuine Cornish Poldark. All it will take is a few days scouting fishing villages or — '

'For goodness' sake.' Izzy gave a belly laugh and shook her head. 'And there was me thinking you were simply so thrilled about going away with a good mate.'

'No. Yes. I mean of course.' I felt my face break into a huge grin. 'The best of mates.'

'Here's the brochure,' said Izzy and pushed a catalogue across the table.

I grabbed it and my eyes devoured the photos of cliffs and seashores and romantic skylines. I pictured them in my mind as I drove home, a couple of mock Mojitos later, having phoned my very excited gran.

The earlier heaviness in my chest had lifted. Good friends meant everything. I was one lucky woman. And hopefully by the end of two weeks in Cornwall, I'd be even luckier and would have bagged one authentic hot guy with dark brooding looks and a killer seductive smile to bring women to their knees.

# 4

'Wow,' I mumbled, as we drove into White Rocks resort.

'Looks great, doesn't it?' said Izzy and shot me a sideways smile from the driving seat.

I loved her Beetle car, with a bobbing pink rubber flower stuck to the keyboard. Katy Perry blared out from the CD player and a sherbet-scented air freshener swung in time, dangling from the driving mirror.

I smiled back. 'Can you tell it's a while since I've been on holiday? These bags under my eyes are because I couldn't get to sleep last night for imagining coastal walks, pasties and ice creams. Talking of bags, what on earth have you packed? I've brought one black Speedo swimsuit, compared to your three fluorescent bikinis. Plus a few pairs of pedal pushers and — '

'No one calls them that any more!'

I chuckled. 'OK, three-quarter length trousers, plus some T-shirts and a couple of dresses — how many have you brought?'

Her cheeks tinged pink. 'Almost as many as my different pairs of sunglasses.'

We both laughed and I gazed around the

resort. A girlie break in the sunny South-west? Bring it on . . . Cute lodges. Greenery. A spa signposted in the distance. So far this holiday park was living up to the brochure, except . . . I peered closer at one accommodation as we drove by. It could have done with a lick of paint. The decking at the front was worn and the surrounding grass needed a mow. Not that it bothered me — I was just grateful for the vacation — but it surprised me, seeing as White Rocks marketed itself as de luxe. And the cars parked outside each lodge weren't the BMWs and Audis I'd been expecting, but old family saloons and budget hatchbacks.

We parked up outside reception and a group of parents and young screaming kids bustled past, carrying inflatables and towels.

'I thought this place was for adults only?' I said.

Izzy switched off the ignition and gave a big yawn. 'I know. Weird. It was advertised as luxury online, although I did think the price was a bit low.' She pulled the brochure out of the glove compartment, turned to the right page and squinted at some small print. 'Ah.'

'What is it?'

She shrugged. 'Something about the possibility of the park being at the beginning of a rebranding period.'

'Who cares — it's a holiday, right?'

'Absolutely! As long as we still have a hot tub.'

We jumped out of the car and both stretched as if we were about to compete in the Olympics. Izzy headed off to the reception to check in, whilst I decided to take a look around. She entered a huge white building, with the spa and pool signposted in its right-hand side wing. The left of it housed a restaurant called . . . I squinted at a sign: 'Fisherman's Delight'. Swatting away a fly, I headed up a path, with lodges either side, and eventually came to a nine-hole golf course — at least that's what the sign said. It should have said rabbit sanctuary, as the sweetest fudge-coloured bunnies hopped around. You could hardly see the putting greens as the grass everywhere was so long it sashayed in the breeze. I gazed into the distance, at dipping and rising hills. A group of swallows swept across, near a flag, and I walked forward to get a closer look.

' 'Ey,' said a loud voice. 'That area is out of bounds, r-right.'

Ooh. A strong, sexy Cornish accent. Rolled 'r's made me break out in a sweat. And if the loud assistant at the petrol station was anything to go by, Cornish men thought most people were deaf.

I turned. Out of the bushes appeared a frowning man, around my age, wearing beige chinos and a tight red shirt. Gosh. I swallowed. For some reason his appearance made an impact. Was it the toned arms that held a pair of garden shears as he walked up to me? Perhaps he'd used them on his head, I thought, as his fawn brown hair was shaved shorter than the hair on my legs. Cheeks hot, I forced my arms to stay vertical, as I experienced a sudden desire to run a hand over his short hair and around the back of his neck. My eyes scoured his solid frame, which looked kind of reliable. Something about his stance, the line of his jaw, shouted that he'd be there for you, in an emergency. And those leaf-green eyes . . . once I met them I found it impossible to turn away.

We stared at each other, with intense eye contact. It wasn't awkward nor embarrassing. And the oddest sensation washed over me. As if I knew this person. Or understood him. Or, somehow had a deep connection.

I know. Stupid. And, at the sight of me, his expressionless face didn't look fazed.

'Apologies,' I said and smiled, finally managing to avert my gaze. I pointed to the sky. 'I just wanted a closer look at the swallows.'

'Not swallows,' he said. 'Try 'ouse martins. Their forked tails are shorter.'

'Ah . . . and there's me thinking you only found albatrosses and eagles on golf courses,' I said, quite proud of my sporting pun and loving the way he dropped that 'h'.

Still expressionless, he walked forward and pointed to a sign: '*Golf course out-of-bounds due to ongoing renovation work*'. 'Those party shoes of yours would cause divets, or dents at least, in the turf. You'll do better 'ere if you keep to sensible footwear.'

My cheeks flushed. Party wear? Um, no, these were just my favourite platform sandals of the moment to give my legs a bit of height. I gazed at him, in his soily slim-legged trousers and walkers' boots, then down at my strappy shoes and baggy patterned harem pants. Our style couldn't have been more different.

'It just needs a good mow from what I can tell,' I said, accidentally thinking out loud. I read his name badge: Tremain Maddock.

'And you be an expert on all things 'orticultural?'

Oh. What a shame. His rudeness quickly overrode his curious wow factor.

'I own indoor plants,' I said airily. 'And you don't need a degree in biology to know how to keep a lawn short. Rabbits alone won't do the job.'

'Really? And there's me coming over all

Snow White, thinking that birds and critters would do my work.'

His mouth twitched and I couldn't decide if that was sarcasm or a joke.

'No. Above all you need time,' he continued. 'And that costs money when you've lodges to keep clean and entrance ways to keep smart.' He pointed to a crisp packet on the ground. 'That yours?'

'Excuse me, I'm no litterbug,' I said and folded my arms.

He raised an eyebrow.

'And I resent you — '

'Please. Don't,' he muttered, as if . . . he was already the most resented person in the world.

He broke eye contact and picked up the packet, before heading back in the direction of the reception building. I had to force myself to stay rooted to the spot, in order to fight an overwhelming urge to rush over and wrap my arms around those broad shoulders.

I shook myself. Well, I couldn't see what damage it would do, just to have a tiny walk forwards and look at those sweeping, beautiful birds. Plus, I thought I saw one of the bunnies limping and my soft centre wouldn't allow me to leave until I'd checked that it was OK.

'Oi!' called that voice again, as I took a step

in the forbidden direction. I turned around.

'I told you. Keep off that grass.'

'Look, I just want to check on one rabbit. It looked as if it had sprained its foot.'

'And if it 'ad, what would you do? Catch it? Impossible. So scare the lot for the sake of a pointless mission? Plus, they'd all look the same once they scattered.'

'Cold or what?' I muttered under my breath.

He flinched. 'No. Just practical. Sometimes you have to act for the good of the majority, even if that means sacrificing an individual.'

I should have felt like laughing at such a dramatic statement, but the way his top lip quivered made me stop. Within seconds, his deadpan face returned.

'Anyway, what's the big deal?' My mouth upturned, more and more curious about him and therefore determined to get a reaction. 'Management will never know.'

'I am management,' he muttered.

'In that get-up?' I gazed at his grass-stained top. 'Don't get me wrong — I couldn't care less what anyone wears, what I do care about is people lying.'

He opened his mouth as if to speak, but then shook his head and stalked off.

★ ★ ★

'Jeez! No wonder this place is struggling with that level of customer service,' I said to Izzy later, in our gold lodge. And worth its weight in gold it was, to me, with the pine furnishings, lush green view and cute floral curtains. OK, so the kitchen worktops were chipped and the sofa was just a bit too squishy, but it was a little bit of heaven for someone, like me, whose last holiday had been a weekend in Blackpool three years ago, in a creaky caravan, with an elder sister and three adorable but super-active small nieces.

'And what sort of name is Tremain?' I said as I lay across the sofa. Izzy was in the kitchen area, putting away the last of the food. I'd carried our suitcases into the rooms and hung up Johnny's heart wind spinner above my bed. From the first moment I'd met him, Johnny had been nothing but polite and attentive. Not qualities I was used to after my bustling childhood. One-to-ones were rare with anyone I loved. The most time I had with Mum was when she took me to the dentist. I smiled. Yet, truth be told, I wouldn't have had it any other way. Oh, I loved my independence now but my memory bank was stocked full with happy images, of Christmases full of hugs and laughter.

Yet Mum always drilled into me one thing: never rely on anyone else. Unexpected tears sprung to my eyes. What a great lesson, which had steered my way through life — until Johnny, my one and only serious boyfriend. I'd come to depend on him for that sparkle in life. And then he left one night, to fetch me a takeaway, and fate decided he should never come back. I gazed at the wind spinner. Oh, Johnny. I miss you. I'd sacrifice anything to feel your warm breath against my neck, one more time. I gave a wry smile. Hardly romantic was it, that my last words to him were 'make mine a large portion of chicken tikka'.

Forcing my attention to switch, I flicked through the information pack, mentally noting the opening times of the pool and spa. I sat more upright, scanning lots of handy details about fishing villages in the area.

'Tremain?' said Izzy. 'It's Cornish. He must be the son. This is a family-run place. His mum, Kensa Maddock, handed me the keys.'

My cheeks burned. So, he was management. 'What about the dad?' I said.

'Dunno. Wasn't mentioned. Perhaps he up and left.'

'Why?'

Izzy came over and sat on a nearby armchair, smoothing down her banana-milkshake yellow skirt. 'The stress? Kensa apologised for the rundown appearance of the resort — said that's why the price was lower than usual. Apparently the place's bookings have really plummeted in the last few years, with people either struggling financially and choosing cheaper holidays, or doing all right and going abroad. She said White Rocks seemed to fail to bridge the gap. They have one year to turn things around.' Izzy shook her head. 'You should see her — such deep rings under her eyes and as thin as a cocktail stick. She said they are trying to appeal to the budget family market and next week, with August arriving, they'll have their first full-paying guests with children. The ones here at the moment won a competition, to stay here for free but give feedback.'

'But that's mad — it still looks like a couples' site to me. Where is the fun cafeteria, or ball-play area, or crazy golf site?' I'd spent enough holidays on cheap caravan sites as a child to know what was needed for a fab family break when money was tight. Who needed foreign sun if the resort had children's entertainment, a fun pool and plenty of drinks?

Izzy took off her pumps and rubbed her feet. 'Apparently her accountant and the bank dropped the bombshell only a few weeks ago — that things were so bad.' Izzy smiled. 'I really liked Kensa. She seems honest.

Upfront. Hoped we'd enjoy our stay, despite any building work going on or noisier, younger guests.'

'Yes, well, you make sure you do take a break, Izzy. I really appreciate this holiday. Leave the cooking to me. I'll drive us everywhere if you want. Do any washing . . . '

'Me? Take it easy?'

I grinned. 'True. Mission impossible.'

'It's enough to have your company,' she said. 'Anyway, you can return the favour when you're a famous singer — I'm thinking a cruise in the Bahamas or shopping in LA.'

'Dream on!' I gazed back at the laminated information pack. 'It says in there that the park belonged to her parents. That must make the place harder to give up. Still, we all have stresses. There's no need for her son to be quite so rude.' I glanced out of the window, as a random cloud offered a brief respite from the sun. The plan was to unpack and then head to the resort's restaurant, as a treat after our long, sticky, journey south. My shout, of course. Perhaps we'd enjoy a couple of cool beers. Much as I loved cocktails, it was nice sometimes to drink something simpler. Although I'm not sure whether alcohol went with an all-day breakfast, the meal Izzy was obsessing about since the receptionist mentioned it. Apparently, the resort's cooked breakfast was legendary and making it available all day was the chef's first baby step towards tweaking his highfalutin menu to give it a broader appeal.

As if on cue, my stomach rumbled and I tapped away on the laptop, planning tomorrow's trip to Port Penny, the first fishing village on my list to check out for any signs of a local Poldark. Gulls squawked outside. We'd left the lodge's door open to catch the evening breeze. I yawned. How did fresh salty air always manage to act like a tranquilliser?

'His only redeeming feature was the sexiest South-west accent,' I said in a loud voice to Izzy, who'd disappeared into her bedroom. 'Even if he used it to accuse me of dropping litter.'

I jumped as someone knocked on the open door and stuck their head inside our lodge. My mouth desiccated and I begged the universe to create a sinkhole under my bottom.

''Ousekeeping said the washing-machine door is jammed,' he said in a loud voice and looked me straight in the eye.

'Um, yes. I rang. I didn't think . . . I mean, cheers. Come in,' I rambled.

Izzy came in and I saw her note the name Tremain on the badge pinned onto his shirt.

Whilst he crouched down to examine the

machine's barrel, she glanced at me, eyes a-twinkle. I glared at her not to speak. She put her fist in her mouth. Oh God. Please don't let her explode with laughter. At least I hadn't talked within his earshot about his nice bum in those chinos. Annoying, isn't it, when irritating people also have appealing qualities? And even more annoying that such an abrupt man could be the first to produce a thought like that since Johnny. My face kind of scrunched for a second.

Tremain stood up, rummaged through a drawer and retrieved a leaflet. He skimmed a couple of pages before pressing a button on the machine and, hey presto, the door flew open.

'Try reading the instructions before you call us out, next time,' he muttered.

'Of course. Silly me,' I said. 'Thanks for calling by.'

'You're Kensa's son?' said Izzy and smiled. 'Lovely place, you've got. We are very much looking forward to our holiday.'

He acknowledged her words with a tilt of the head.

'Have you always worked here?' I asked.

'No.'

Clearly small talk didn't form part of his customer relations.

'How's the rebranding going?' said Izzy in

her business voice. I often teased her about how she changed her accent. It went kind of cockney when speaking to suppliers and bordered on received pronunciation when dealing with an unhappy customer.

'It's going,' he said, tilted his head again and strode out of the cabin.

Izzy chuckled. 'I see what you mean by his attitude, although what he lacks in charm he makes up for in . . . in . . . '

'I know. There is something attractive . . . a sense of . . . '

'Capability? Decisiveness?'

She'd felt it too. But I wasn't fourteen any more. Looks, first impressions, of course caught my eye but it was personality that really held my attention. Not that I was going to worry about the character of my much-needed plus-one. He could have bad breath or talk about nothing but the complex rules of cricket or his latest computer game, as long as he smouldered and made Saffron realise I was no longer in girl in the corner.

'Right, let's go. I'm starving,' she said. 'And itching to try that all-day breakfast.'

'Apart from the kippers . . . ' I pulled a face.

Izzy grinned. 'We are in Cornwall. A coastal county. It's time you tried some delicacies from the sea.'

'You're not getting me to try anything that lives in a shell or breathes through gills,' I protested. 'Unless it is covered in batter and served with chips or in a yummy sauce, like the pie I tried with Marcus.'

The two of us strolled towards the restaurant, Fisherman's Delight, and, as we approached, my stomach rumbled again. That was the other thing about sea air — it gave you a great appetite. In fact, in Guvnah's last letter she'd talked of having put on a few kilos. My chest glowed. I'd arranged to visit her tomorrow. Her village wasn't far from Port Penny and Izzy said she'd drop me there in the afternoon, following us having lunch out at a café she'd found that had a great reputation for Cornish fare — she was hoping to be inspired. Guvnah had a bicycle I could borrow if I fancied cycling back to White Rocks.

We headed into the reception building and the restaurant to the left. It had a long bar, stretching across the back. At the rear, on the right, was the kitchen with an open serving hatch. Fisherman's Delight boasted a classy decor, albeit a little worn — think uncluttered magnolia tables and walls covered with arty black and white photos of local beauty spots. Yet the clientele — a couple of families — were your average holiday crowd, in shorts and T-shirts, with wet, chlorine-fragranced hair. Kids sat eating chips and playing on their Nintendos. In one corner, a baby in a high chair screamed, its face covered in bright orange purée. Talk about a mismatch. Two waiters were dressed in formal black trousers and a waistcoat.

'Ooh, he's nice,' said Izzy and gazed at the younger waiter, who had baby-smooth skin and highlighted, gelled back hair. She gazed at his name badge. 'And his name is Greg!'

I grinned. Izzy was obsessed with the presenter Gregg Wallace from the programme *MasterChef*.

'Nah. He's too well groomed for me. I wouldn't dare forget to wax or floss my teeth if he and I went out.'

'I bet his chest is as smooth as a baby's bottom,' she said and pulled a face. 'I really *do not get* the modern woman's obsession with Poldark and his chest hair. I mean, imagine licking whipped cream off it. Ew. You'd probably get your teeth caught.'

'Izzy!'

We giggled.

'So full-paying families arrive next week?' I said in a low voice.

'Yes. These competition winners leave tomorrow, which gives Kensa and Tremain five days to do some last-minute thinking before the proper launch next Monday. The resort will effectively be shut down apart from a few guests like us who booked, regardless of the rebranding phase.' She blushed. 'Or rather idiots like me who didn't read the small print. It does warn that only a skeleton staff will be working over the next few days. This restaurant, for example, will be open but only in a casual way, while the staff do last-minute retraining for next week.'

I shrugged. 'Idiot or rather genius — means you got a cheap booking and who wants to eat in all the time anyway? We'll be out and about.'

The older waiter, George, came over and showed us to seats, a couple of tables away from the screaming baby.

'Should be a bit quieter for you here, ladies,' he said and jerked his head towards the young guests before wrinkling his nose.

'He'll have to change that attitude before next week,' I said to Izzy, once we'd ordered two beers and all-day breakfasts. I covered my eyes with my hands and then suddenly pulled them away — cue a minute or so of playing peekaboo with the baby. And cue silence. The mum shot me a grateful glance, as her small one returned to playing with his spoon.

I squinted into the kitchen. Raven curls flashed by now and again. I wondered how many chefs they had. The more I saw of the place it was obviously run on a tight budget. Not that that seemed to affect the quality of the food. All I can say is, wow, when our breakfasts finally arrived. An invitingly brown sausage lay glistening, next to a buttercup yellow egg, its plump yolk just waiting to be burst. I eyed a crispy rasher of bacon and aromatic fried mushrooms. I forked up a mouthful of shiny baked beans and couldn't wait to cut into the square hash browns, which promised a satisfying carb kick. Plus on the side was fried bread — I hadn't enjoyed that since my childhood. Two thirds of the way through, I felt Christmas-dinner-full, but kept on eating — it would have been a travesty not to, with all the different flavours and textures satisfying my taste buds.

The baby screeched as loudly as a fishing boat's horn, because his beaker fell on the floor. A tut headed its way from the waiter called George.

'Is there a problem?' said the mum and straightened her halter-neck floral top, as he shot her a disdainful look.

I tried peekaboo faces again, but this time they didn't work. George pursed his lips, while shouting came from the kitchen. Black curls flashed again across the back of the hatch.

Izzy studied the menu and shook her head. 'I can't see any evidence of rebranding so far. How on earth is this menu going to appeal to kids?'

I glanced down my menu and looked at the breakfast section — eggs Benedict, granola with yogurt, fried kippers, Welsh rarebit . . . Where were the cereals, toast, muffins and chocolate croissants? Breakfast. Mmm. Best meal of the day. Particularly in those budget hotels that served a morning buffet for ten quid. I'd have a bowl of fresh fruit, followed by a full English fry-up, then help myself to bottomless cups of coffee and anything baked. Muffins were the best — so soft and crumbly — although flaky croissants always hit the spot.

As if she had heard us talking, the mother of the baby called the waiter over. 'Eggs Benedict,' she said, brow furrowing, 'is that hard-boiled ones covered with Hollandaise sauce?'

The waiter wrinkled his nose again as if he'd never been asked that question before.

'We'd be grateful if the kitchen just did us scrambled eggs instead, mate, if we come here tomorrow morning after a swim, just before we leave,' said her husband, who wore a football top to match his son's.

The waiter straightened up. 'I don't believe

he would. Chef is quite firm about sticking to the menu.'

The husband glanced sideways at his little boy, who scribbled with crayons on a pad of paper. 'Surely he'll bend those rules for a child?'

Lips pursed, George folded his arms.

Shifting awkwardly in her seat, the mother sighed. 'Leave it, Phil love. Clearly rules is rules here. Come on, darling, this place is a disaster. It won't be getting a great write-up. We can make do with cheese on toast tonight, back at the lodge.'

I glanced at Izzy, before we both looked at the waiter, expecting him to do his best to make the family happy, like we did when — rare occurrence — a customer complained about a cocktail or doughnut. Instead, he just bowed and stood to the side. Unfortunate position as just at that moment the baby lost control of its spoon. A blob of orange purée flew through the air and landed on George's left cheek.

'Can't you control that child,' he muttered and threw his hands in the air. He grabbed a napkin and wiped his face, muttering something about too liberal parenting.

Phil stood up. 'What did you say?'

George put down the napkin, face expressionless. The mum shot me a worried look.

The little boy stopped crayoning and his bottom lip wobbled.

I stood up and shook off Izzy's arm before standing in between them. Being one of many siblings, I was used to breaking up disagreements. Mum always called me the diplomat as I preferred to keep my fists to myself and fight with my tongue. 'I'm sure there's no need to worry over a simple splat of purée.'

'Exactly,' said Phil. 'Honestly. This resort is useless. The restaurant isn't geared up for anyone under eighteen and the swimming pool is a joke — there is no slide, music or inflatables for kids and too many adult-only sessions. And, as for the evening entertainment . . . ' He shook his head. 'Last night was some operatic girl singing Katherine Jenkins. Great for me and the wife but where is the bingo or puppet show for the kids?'

'I guess it is early days,' said Izzy, now on her feet.

'There's no reason why any normal family can't enjoy this place, just the way it is,' muttered George, and Phil turned purple in the face.

Oh dear. Now tears hung in the little boy's eyes, while the baby grinned and smeared purée around its mouth, apparently enjoying the sideshow.

I glared at the three adults and jerked my

head towards the boy. 'Perhaps you could discuss this somewhere else?' I said quietly. 'I'll look after the children if — '

'Don't bother. We're leaving,' said Phil and grabbed his son's orange juice to knock back. Except the glass must have been wet and, as he lifted it into the air, Phil lost his grip for a second. Liquid gushed southwards and yes, you've guessed it, right onto short me.

'Urgh!' I wiped my cheek and breathed in sticky citrus smells.

'Christ,' said Phil. 'Huge apologies. I didn't mean that to happen.'

George rolled his eyes.

'It was an accident.' Phil glared at a smug George.

'Attention, everyone!' snapped a voice. Formal Cornish tones, already recognisable to me. Within seconds, Tremain stood by my side as I spat out the citrus liquid. I turned around, slipped on spilt liquid and fell to the floor. My cheekbone hit the table on the way down and I winced. Immediately, strong arms pulled me to my feet. I flinched as Tremain touched my skin, just under the left eye.

'Keep still,' he ordered and held up his hand as Izzy approached. With a handkerchief, he carefully wiped the juice from my face. He tilted my head to the light and my heart raced as he trailed a finger across my eye socket.

Must have been the shock of the argument, that's all.

'No real damage done. You might have a bruise for a few days. You're lucky you didn't hit the table corner. That could have gone in your eye.'

'Lucky?' I stuttered and wondered why his proximity made me not trust myself. Up close, I noticed a small scar above his top lip. How many women had tried to kiss it better? Urgh! Where had that thought come from? Perhaps I was dazed from the fall. Yes. I mean nothing could persuade me to press my lips against the lips of a man who was so arrogant. Even if his leaf-green eyes, for one second, appeared full of concern. Even if, up close and personal, with his broad chest, firm arms and direct stare, he looked like a man who would single-handedly fight a whole army for you, if he'd decided you were his one.

Tremain turned to Phil and George. 'It takes a five foot woman to try to settle your argument?'

'Five foot two,' I muttered, 'and that's sexist.'

Tremain flashed me a look. Blimey. Was that almost a hint of humour in his eyes? I couldn't tell, because it disappeared more quickly than the orange juice had flown.

'This is a holiday resort not a war zone,' Tremain continued.

Phil rubbed his forehead while their baby looked on, absolutely delighted. No doubt this was even better than its favourite slapstick kids TV show. 'Your waiter was rude, Mr Maddock,' he said and briefly explained what had happened, despite George's indignant interjections.

'I see.' Tremain glanced back at me and something stirred in my stomach as he scanned me from head to toe. 'Good thing that washing machine is working in your chalet — and that the drink wasn't red wine,' he said, in a matter-of-fact way. 'Sir ... Madam.' He half smiled at Phil and his wife. 'I appreciate your disappointment in our site, so I do, and apologies — we are going through a transition period, thrown upon us unexpectedly, and are doing our best. That's why you weren't charged for this week — so that you could provide useful feedback. Please.' Tremain called over Greg. 'I'm sure Chef will be happy to cook something that meets your needs.' Tremain raised an eyebrow. 'George?' He jerked his head and the two of them headed into the kitchen.

Around twenty minutes later, after Greg had taken the family's order and Izzy and I had finished our food, the kitchen's doors swung open. George stormed out and pulled off his name badge. He threw it onto one of the tables and then hurried past us, before leaving the building. Tremain appeared a few seconds later.

'All sorted?' I said.

'Yes,' muttered Tremain and shook his head. 'George seems to have reacted to a flying splat of carrot purée, as if it were a hand grenade that might threaten your life.' He cleared his throat. 'Anyway, my apologies for this incident. I've dealt with it.'

'Perhaps he just needs time — to adjust?' Izzy said.

Tremain shrugged. 'Mother and I have made it quite clear to the staff what is expected of them now. Fortunately, so far, most of our team have proved able to cope with the rebranding. But the change in clientele has brought new challenges.' Looking suddenly tired, Tremain gently took my arm and steered me towards outside, whilst Izzy sat talking to the young waiter. In the evening light, Tremain took another look at my face.

'The bruise is blackening now. I'd get back to your lodge if I was you, and soak those clothes.'

'Thanks . . . um . . . Shame about George. You wouldn't think he was such a snob, just to look at him. He seems like an ordinary guy — a granddad type, who loves kids.'

'Then lesson learnt — never judge a person by their appearance.'

I shifted from foot to foot. 'Yes, about that, you see, with the soil on your clothes, I assumed . . . ' Urgh, rambling now.

'I've never been afraid to get my hands dirty and I'd say the best managers get down with the lower ranks,' he said and walked off.

Ranks? He made his staff sound like an army regiment. I followed him. OK, I wasn't perfect, but I never found it hard to apologise when I was in the wrong.

'Wait a minute. Look, I'm sorry.'

Tremain turned around. 'Whatever. Makes no difference to me. Gardener, handyman, management . . . ' His eyes flickered. 'There are worse jobs a man can do.'

My heart squeezed as in that brief second his eyes revealed a degree of . . . damage. Once again I felt that urge to wrap my arms around his solid frame. What was that all about? Maybe, just maybe, there was a human being below that tough, uncompromising, robotic surface.

# 5

'We go together, like ramma ramma lamma, dippety dooby dooby, sha na na . . . '

'Kate! You just murdered that chorus.'

'Don't be cheeky.' I grinned and glanced sideways at Izzy as she drove along the coastal road. Or rather chugged — the volume of tourist traffic was high, but that didn't matter as it meant we could enjoy the sea views. I never could remember the exact words to that brill song from *Grease* and turned down the volume of the CD player as Izzy pulled into a car park. On the journey yesterday, we'd played the soundtracks to all our favourite girls-night-in films — *Bridget Jones, Love Actually, Pretty Woman, Bridesmaids* . . . I might like historical series, but even I some-times needed a chick flick accompanied by, yes, what else, doughnuts and cocktails.

Cars already lined every inch of the car park on top of the cliff, just as you got into Port Penny — no surprises there, due to the eggshell blue sky and picturesque sights. So we drove down into the town and finally we found a spot in a quiet cul-de-sac, up above Port Penny fishing town on the other side.

'So, you crazy woman, what's the plan?' said Izzy, as we grabbed our rucksacks and headed downhill. I stopped for a moment and drank in the scene ahead — the masts of fishing boats visible in the distance, in front of the harbour backdrop. And, right in the distance, the flat oceanic horizon, broken only by the occasional trawler. Gulls swooping. Long grasses waving. Visitors milling.

As we walked further down, the view became even prettier. Turquoise waves dipping. A sandy, U-shaped cove. In the middle was a jetty with fishing boats moored either side, their navy, green and red paintwork standing out against the shoreline. Then higher up, on top of the cliffs either side, sat non-uniform rows of different coloured cottages. A strong breeze blew against my cheeks and I was glad to have tied my hair back. Tremain would have approved of my sensible pumps, worn with three-quarter-length cotton trousers and a ginger Indian silk blouse I'd picked up from the charity shop.

Oh, and scrub what I said about Tremain perhaps being human after all. This morning we'd driven past him and, on instinct, I waved. Yes, it was a bit of a watermelon moment, like awkward Baby out of *Dirty Dancing*. I'm not sure why I did it and the response was suitably cool. In other words, a nod accompanied by no expression at all.

'Hellooo, anyone in?' asked Izzy and, keeping her eye on the road, playfully tapped a purple, varnished fingernail against my head.

'Careful, you nearly touched my eye!' I said. Mind you, easy for her to forget. I'd managed to disguise the bruising with foundation. 'The plan? Well, to find my own gorgeous miner lookalike, of course.'

'But it's not as simple as that. How exactly?' she said, as the road narrowed into a path and we cut through the tiniest whitewashed stone cottages, with doll's house doors and uneven foundations. The roads turned to cobbled avenues and I marvelled at cute plant pots in tiny front gardens. An occasional cat crossed our path, as I pointed out funny house names like Seas the Day and Sunnyside Up. Tens of gulls squawked above our heads and, as we approached the wide harbour, I breathed in a fishy stench, which hit the back of your throat.

'You see those boats?' I said and pointed to the jetty. 'Well . . . '

OK. Between you and me, hands up, I had no plan.

Izzy squinted in the sun.

'They clearly aren't touristy ones, for taking out visitors, which is great, because, um, I intend to target individual fishermen,' I said and tried to sound confident. 'And use my charm to see if they'll take me out for a one-to-one tour. That way I'll get to know them much quicker and see if they are suitable for the job of impressing Saffron.'

'It's all rather clinical, isn't it?' she said, as we came to a large rock and sat down. Pools of seawater glistened metres away and small children ran around carrying fishing nets and buckets filled with the ocean's jewels. She slipped off her trainers and ankle socks, to reveal toenails painted lilac, to match the nails on her hands.

Johnny and I went to the seaside — to Margate — for the day, once, fingers entwined we sat on the sand, lips locked. Clinical was good, because anything deeper got you hurt.

I fiddled with my beaded bracelet. 'I know. And I feel bad for . . . using someone — you know me, my natural modus operandi is to be upfront. Eventually, I'll have to make it clear that I'm not interested in a relationship.'

Izzy scoffed. 'Tell me about it. Remember when old Mrs Lowe popped in last week, for her favourite peanut butter doughnut and asked if you liked her new hairdo?'

'It was pink! All I said was she needed to update her wardrobe as the tweed didn't really go. That's subtle for me.'

'She really appreciated you nipping across the road to the chemist to find a shade of nail varnish to match.'

I blushed. 'She's a lovely lady. Always asks about my singing.' I took my water bottle out of my floral rucksack and took a glug.

'Right. Let's do it then, lovely. Before you change your mind,' said Izzy.

'How do you do that?'

'What?'

'Read my mind.'

Izzy grinned and squeezed my shoulder. 'You? Chat up a random man? Then ask him to accompany you to a wedding before you so much as know each other's surname? It's a challenging remit for any woman. But I'm here to support you. Go on.' She gave me a little shove. 'What's the worst that can happen? I'll be right here by your side.'

I adjusted the position of my rucksack. 'Would you mind if I took things forward on my own. I'd feel less self-conscious.'

Izzy smiled. 'No problem. I've already spotted a rather quaint ice-cream shop with a large selection of flavours I really must sample — purely for research, of course.'

'Then I shall expect a full report afterwards. Two hours, yes? Leave room for lunch. With all this sea air, I'll be starving.'

I watched her head back to the shops, men's heads turning as she passed. With her striking looks and winning smile, Izzy never had a problem hooking a bloke. Plus, she was the sweetest girlfriend — baking, cocktail-making, independent and as loyal as they come. She'd already had three proposals in her life, all rejected, because she was holding out for her idyllic Disney prince. I was still waiting for proposal number one. Thanks to fate, Johnny and I never got that far.

I took a deep breath and looked around, wishing I'd taken Izzy's advice and slathered my white skin with suncream. I had an English rose complexion, according to kind Guvnah — but in reality the colour was more like that of an uncooked Cornish pasty. My eyes narrowed as I surveyed the jetty ahead. I slipped down from the rock and wandered across the sand, enjoying the sensation of my feet sinking with every step. Kids ran around in costumes and deckchairs had been set up across the beach. It wasn't too crowded as most visitors seemed interested in souvenir shopping. Plus, Port Penny was known for being more of a picturesque harbour than a sunbathing trap, without toilets or changing rooms or a beach café.

In the distance, groups of teenagers, probably locals, explored caves visible in both cliff sides. Right, I needed to find black curls. A swarthy complexion. A strong miner's frame. A man with a dollop of arrogance, but combined with enough passion and compassion to make that appealing to a modern woman.

I headed over to the nearest fishing boat. It was ramshackle with peeling paintwork, but that made it more authentic, right? Saffron's crush was on an eighteenth-century miner, so I'm thinking the best bet would be a sailing vessel all down and dirty, not modern and streamlined. A man had stepped on to it and was examining a pair of oars. He wore a bright red cap and . . . hurrah! . . . from underneath that poked black curls. I coughed. Nothing. I coughed louder. Needed to see his face, because up until now he looked suitable, with the right height.

He turned around. 'Can I help you?' he said, in a lilting voice, and gave me the warmest of smiles. Eyeliner. Soft skin. Scarlet lipstick to match the cap. Oops. Unless eighteenth-century miners had sex changes, then this fisherwoman was no good.

'Um, no thanks, tickly throat — hay fever . . .'

She gave me a sympathetic glance. Hurriedly, I continued along the jetty, feeling a little seasick as the boats either side bobbed up and down. To the left, a man in a black shirt sat examining a fishing net. Short blond hair. No good. It wouldn't grow in time. With a sigh, I continued. In the next boat stood a stocky guy, with a beanie hat on even though it was practically August, and a wedding ring glistening on his finger. Forget that. A couple of kids and, presumably, their granddad were playing in the next boat, with a supply of fizzy drinks and crisps. A smooching couple sprawled across the wooden floor of the next. The rest of the boats were empty, apart from a huge white one, right at the end. Talk about flash, with piles of nets and hooks, plus masts going in all directions and polar white sails.

But ooh . . . The owner stood on deck with dashing white marine cap, curly black hair, tanned skin and a pipe in his mouth. Old school, I liked that. Plus, he was reasonably tall and the sunglasses added an air of mystery. But would he stand up to close scrutiny and exude a sexiness rugged enough to drive Saffron wild?

I approached and pretended to be engrossed in my phone. As I neared his boat, I looked up.

'Gosh.' Innocent voice. 'I didn't know I'd walked so far.'

He turned his head to face me. 'Good thing you didn't continue for a couple of metres. You'd have been shark bait,' he said and smiled.

Oh. No Cornish accent. But I couldn't be too picky. Mind racing, I smiled back. His voice was rather polite. In fact a bit plummy and I couldn't help thinking I'd heard it before.

'Didn't know there were sharks in these parts,' I said.

'Oh definitely. Mackerel shark just to name one species. Although granted, nowhere near Port Penny. I've done my research.'

I put away my phone and pulled out my bottle of water, whilst the fisherman went back to looking at his boat. How could I get myself invited on, just to get to know him that little better, or rather secretly audition him for the part of my plus-one? Discreetly, I screwed the lid off my bottle and turned it upside down. The water ran out. Mentally, I shook my head. Was I really doing this?

'Goodness. I'm gasping for a drink and I've no water left. I don't suppose you could fill this up could you?' I said and showed him the empty bottle.

His face broke into a smile again and I noticed wrinkles where I hadn't before. Plus that hair — it kind of shifted oddly when he scratched it. Oh my God! It wasn't real!

'Come on into my cabin,' he said. 'I believe there's a bottle of champers in the fridge. How about helping me celebrate?'

'Um . . . '

He lifted up his hands, grinned and whipped off his wig and glasses. 'No funny stuff, my dear. I am just a fuddy-duddy old writer doing research for my next book.'

I gasped. Of course, I'd seen him on several TV programmes last year, that's why I knew that voice.

'Hardly fuddy-duddy!' I stuttered. 'But it's a pleasure to meet you, Dick Thrusts.'

He ran a hand over his bald head and gave an infectious chuckle. 'Trevor's the name. I may like writing erotica, but in reality most of my time is spent with a nice cup of tea and my gardening programmes.'

I grinned back, now. My shoulders relaxed. Yes, I'd seen him on a horticultural show. Dick Thrusts — Trevor — was always extremely courteous and took jokes about his work very well. You see, on the tail end of *Fifty Shades'* success he'd written a bird-watching erotic book — don't ask — called *A Flock of Shags*. For the uneducated — which included me — a shag is a bird rather like a cormorant. The book was a runaway success due to its schoolboyish humour. Think Christian Grey with whips that made farting noises and blindfolds that left black stains around your eyes.

'Come on,' said Trevor. 'It's baking hot

today. I, for one, could do with some fizz.'

'Isn't it a bit early for champagne?' I said and stepped onto the boat.

Trevor steadied me. 'Darling, it is never too early for alcohol in the publishing world — there is always something to sob over or celebrate. And today it is good news . . . I've finally made some progress with my new book.'

He left his pipe on the deck and I followed him into the small cabin and, grateful for the shade, sat down on a bench. There was a tiny sink with a cupboard underneath, a cool box, a few magazines and some biscuits. Trevor poured us two drinks.

'Cheers, me dears,' he said.

'Well done on your success,' I said. 'If you don't mind me asking, what was with the wig?'

'Huh? Oh. Just getting into character. I call it Method Writing. That's why I hired this boat. My next story is set at sea. It will be called *A Finger of Fish* — sailor erotica, if you will.'

He looked at me. I paused. Then we both laughed.

'Good for you. For not caring . . . I read an interview where you said that some of your friends had disowned you for writing sex.'

Trevor shook his head. 'Stupid, isn't it? No

one gets tortured or hurt in my books.' He shrugged. 'They are just humorous stories about the one thing we all have in common.'

'Do you genuinely not care what people think about you?' I said, Saffron and the school bullies popping into my head.

'Nope. Not now. Life's too short.' His eyes went all shiny. 'My wife left me three years ago, for a plumber. Totally unexpected. Devastated, I was. For a while, I felt like my whole existence was over. That taught me a valuable lesson — that if I still had dreams to crack on with them then and there. You don't know what's around the corner and you can't depend on anyone else for your happiness.' He ran a hand over his head. 'You have to create your own luck, your own joy.'

I bit the inside of my cheeks. But I'd liked relying on Johnny. For the first time I'd had someone who had the time to listen, really listen, to all my dreams, my worries — from my views on climate change to the Kardashians.

'You all right, my lovely?' said Trevor.

And, before I knew it, I was telling him all about Johnny's death. Perhaps it was a writer's trait to have a face for listening — a tool from Mother Nature, given to authors to help them gain stories. He had sincere eyes, a sympathetic nod and gave encouraging smiles. I told him how I understood, about his wife — how being left alone all of a sudden felt like a tight fist, squeezing your heart until it burst.

'And you still send him — or rather his Facebook profile — messages?' he said, in soft tones.

My eyes blurred. Somehow I had let that slip. 'Weak, I know. I was so angry in the beginning — at the way he threw away our future together; his actions that night, on the road. I blocked him on Facebook, WhatsApp, even Instagram at first.'

Trevor raised an eyebrow.

My shoulders bobbed up and down. 'Pointless, I know, but for a brief moment in time it made me feel better, gave me some control.' My mouth upturned. 'Johnny had hundreds of followers on social media, due to his job as an RSPCA officer, out in the field saving neglected animals. We used to joke that it was his photos of kittens that I really fell in love with.' I bit my lip. 'But, in time, I accepted his death — that the accident wasn't all his fault. I couldn't blame Johnny for ever. So then my messages to him became more . . . more loving and chatty.'

Trevor patted my hand.

'I just wish he'd come back to me,' I said, voice cracking, a lump in my throat.

'I felt exactly the same, for a long time, but the intensity of that feeling eventually dissipated,' he said. 'You just need a new passion, something — or someone — else to come along. Try to have faith, me dear. It will happen.'

We sat in silence and drank. I knew Trevor was right. I mean this clinginess wasn't me — out of all my siblings, I'd be the one reading in a corner or happy to spend an evening on my own, without playing or arguing with a brother or sister.

He cleared his throat. 'You know what, we both deserve some fun. Seeing as you are here, could you do me an enormous favour? I'm writing a sex scene, set in a cabin, and I just need to know if, strategically, the positions are possible. I've got a tape measure.'

Don't ask me exactly what I had to do, because it's a secret I shall take to my grave and I will actually kill Izzy when I see her, for shoving me towards the boats! Although, to be honest, I giggled like a schoolgirl, at one point, tears running down both our faces. If I didn't already know Trevor's creditable reputation from the media, there is *no way* I would have agreed to his very polite but athletic requests. He even said he'd credit me in the book's acknowledgements. That brought the biggest grin to my face.

However, as I left him and headed down the jetty, weaving slightly after three glasses of good old Moët, the smile dissolved. It sunk in that my morning had resulted in a mission unaccomplished. This was useless. Pathetic. Had I lost my mind? How had I realistically expected to find a suitable Cornish, Poldark lookalike, let alone one who would be prepared to go along with my ridiculous plus-one charade? It was farcical. Desperate. I pictured the red wind spinner. Behaving like this did not feel like I was following my heart.

I gazed ahead and saw Izzy wave from the other side of the sand. Yep. Meeting Trevor had been a wake-up call to my madness. I would simply go to the wedding on my own and treat the rest of my stay in Cornwall as a holiday.

# 6

There is only one thing that could make Guvnah's cottage more pretty, and that's if it were made from gingerbread, spicy dried fruit and icing. It had a thatched roof and plant pots out the front, tiny windows, low ceilings and a brickwork fireplace to die for. Geoff had lived there for years with his first wife and insisted, when Guvnah moved in, that she refurbish and redecorate every room. But my gran had never been one for doing things for the sake of it. She'd redesigned their bedroom to give it a vintage feel, but only made small changes to the rest of her new home.

Seaside paintings punctuated the walls along with ornamental shelves made out of driftwood. Cosy wasn't the word for the little lounge, with the terracotta colours, a warm oak laminate floor and mosaic rug. There was just enough room for a cherry sofa and two matching armchairs. A ginger cat completed the homely picture, as did a vase full of dried beach thistles on the windowsill.

Guvnah passed me a slice of Cornish honey cake. Geoff was a natural-born cook, his preferred method being barbecuing. No one served a hot dog like him, with home-made mustard relish and fried red onions. For years he'd run a mobile snack van, specialising in sausages, burgers and hot drinks.

'I'm not sure I can find room after the lunch Izzy and I enjoyed. My pasty was served with the yummiest home-made tomato ketchup.'

'Talking of which, Geoff has just made a batch of tomato pickle. You can take a jar. I've always wanted to live in a house with a vegetable garden.'

'My favourite spot is the bench under the weeping willow.' I sighed. 'It really is a dream home. When will Geoff get back from the garage? I can't wait to see him again.'

'Only so that you can pick his brains about being a roadie in the sixties.'

I grinned, whilst admiring her purple blouse and baggy red trousers. Flamboyant was the word to best describe my artistic gran. Her clothes contrasted her uncolourful white bobbed hair and grey eyes. Chunky jewellery hung from her wrists and the outfit was completed with a wispy silk scarf. 'I could listen to his stories all day. In fact I've got him a present — I managed to track down a vinyl single of that rockabilly band he worked for, in Leeds.'

'The Bobby Boogie Boys?'

'Yes. It's in my rucksack. Vinyls are making something of a comeback. Honestly, imagine being a roadie back in the day when fans had so little access to bands, without DVDs — not everyone even had a telly. He must have felt like a star himself.' I took a bite of the cake. 'Mmm. That's got a kick. Whiskey?'

'Ginger honey mead. There's nothing like alcohol for keeping a cake moist.' She glanced at the clock. 'Geoff shouldn't be much longer. It all depends on how difficult the carburettor was to fix.' She fiddled with her pewter and lilac-stoned bracelet. 'And talking of things being fixed, what's up with you? Your mouth keeps drooping at the corners, just like it used to when you were a little girl and in trouble. It's not like you to take a holiday. What's the matter, sweetheart?'

My cheeks burned. 'Oh, you know, just fed up with losing my flat and a singing contract. We can't all be comfortably settled in a cottage that belongs on the front of a chocolate box, gliding our way quietly and conservatively through retirement, closing the door on our busy lives.' I grinned, waiting for a repost.

'I beg your pardon! I'm busier than ever. Bowling, sewing, volunteering once a week at the charity shop and my painting class.'

I gazed at a watercolour on the wall of seagulls picking through shells, near a cliff side. 'Looks to me like you don't need any more lessons. You really should display your work somewhere — in a café or garden centre.'

Guvnah shrugged. 'Geoff says the same but . . . I don't know, there always seems to be so much more to learn. Next term I'll be studying working with graphite and charcoal. Busy, busy — although Geoff's been feeling twitchy lately and has been talking about getting a part-time job.' She shrugged again. 'Comes from all those years on the road. Then running his hot-dog van. He misses the craic. Anyway, enough about us, back to you.' Her eyes narrowed. 'Are you sure that is really all that's wrong?'

'Isn't that enough?' I squirmed in my seat, as she sipped her tea, not taking her eyes off me for a single second.

'Boy trouble?'

'I'm not at school now — you can call them men.'

Her face broke into a small smile. 'And Johnny . . . How are you coping . . . ? Are things becoming any . . . easier?'

I forced my lips to upturn. 'It's going OK.'

She raised an eyebrow.

'Honest. I . . . I've accepted he's never

coming back. I just need a bit more time before . . . getting on with my life.'

That's what I told myself anyway. I was messaging him less. Didn't look at old photos so often. But I still missed his arm sliding through mine. Still missed the giggles as he'd tickle me in bed until I begged him to stop. Teasingly, he'd only agree to if I made a deal, like saying I'd do the washing-up.

'If you need to talk I'm here for you,' she said, eventually. 'Or — ' her voice brightened ' — we can always hook up online. I'm so glad Geoff's grandson introduced me to Instagram.'

As I chuckled, the doorbell rang and she gently moved the cat off her lap. 'That will be the gardener. Nice young man, even if he does keep himself to himself. I hired him last month. The front and back lawn are a bit much for Geoff and me, especially in this heat.' She got up and brushed crumbs from her legs. 'Help yourself to another slice of cake, dear. And you can take some back for Izzy. It might inspire her to create a honey mead doughnut.'

I nodded, even though she'd left the lounge by now to open the door. A loud Cornish voice resounded in the hallway and, returning to my own thoughts, I sat back to finish my cup of tea. A higgledy bookshelf reminded me of feisty author Trevor, not caring about anyone's opinion but his own. Johnny used to love my feistiness.

'You know what I like most about you?' he'd once said. 'Your fiery spirit. That optimism. Your determination. The look on your face after a gig — it's inspiring to see you relentlessly follow your heart.'

'Follow your heart'. Those words echoed in my head again. Yes, I was still singing, but also still harping back to the past, struggling to move on with a heart that still felt like a cracked vase that might leak if anyone new tried to fill it up.

The sound of a mower started up outside and Guvnah returned to the lounge. 'We really ought to be in the garden, but I know you hate wasps when eating.'

I drained my cup. 'Why don't we go there now? I'm done.'

We headed outside and sat on the patio, at a white table shaded by a floral parasol. My eyes scanned the long garden, with the weeping willow at the bottom, and borders filled with wild flowers along the fences, either side. Not that I noticed much detail as within seconds my eyes couldn't budge from a taut torso at the end of the garden, cutting the grass. Beige chinos topped by a bare chest and . . . I couldn't see the face which was hidden under an Indiana Jones hat.

Guvnah tutted. 'I tell him every week to wear a shirt. He'll get sunburn but apparently he'd rather that than sweat.'

I managed to shift my gaze to my gran and laughed. 'Really? You really want him to put his shirt back on?' OK, I missed Johnny, but that didn't mean I was completely made of stone!

The slate eyes twinkled and she laughed. 'Sadly, yes. It's proof of getting old. Hot guys become 'nice young men' and, before you know it, you've gone all maternal with anyone under thirty. Well, apart from that new Russian professional on my favourite dance show.'

We grinned at each other and she waved at the man. 'Come and meet my granddaughter!' she shouted, and then turned to me and spoke in a low voice: 'I don't know much about him. He's not the chattiest of men, but his heart is in the right place. Last time, he insisted on pruning back that leylandii tree at the bottom of the garden for nothing — insisted it was dangerous if strong winds came. Before that he'd checked out a leak in the loft for us and would only accept a scone as payment.'

As the figure neared, I couldn't help but admire the confident gait. Each stride was measured and purposeful. Plus, he had a six-pack and . . . what was that? I tried not to stare at the long scar down his right side. It looked like he'd been involved in a knife attack. The hands hung straight by his sides and he soon approached and took off his hat. My eyes widened.

'It's you,' I said.

'Afternoon, Miss Golightly.'

'Please, call me Kate.'

'You two know each other?' said Guvnah.

'Yep. I broke up an argument she was refereeing yesterday,' said Tremain and flashed her a smile. He knelt down and tilted my face. Cornish tones rang out. 'I'm guessing without all that warrrpaint on, you're cheek is still proper bruised?'

Was that a hint of humour in his voice? I snorted. 'Warpaint? I hope my make-up is reasonably subtle.'

However, my indignation was assuaged by the softness of his touch. He looked so substantial, yet his gentle fingers on my chin felt as if they could belong to an immaterial ghost. I couldn't help laughing at Guvnah's knotted eyebrows and glances darting between me and Tremain. And he . . . he looked so relaxed. No lines on his forehead. Shoulders not tensed.

'Tremain works at, or rather, helps to manage White Rocks. Yesterday I tried to calm down an irate customer and somehow ended up falling onto the corner of a table.'

Guvnah took off her silk scarf and fanned her face. 'Oh, Kate, you could have been hurt.'

'You'd have done the same.'

'True.' She gave a wry smile. 'And, Tremain . . . I never knew you worked there. I just assumed you were a full-time gardener — you've never mentioned it.'

He fiddled with the brim of his hat. 'To be honest, it's a relief to be away from the place and forget about the resort's problems for a while. Here I can lose myself in the act of mowing lawns or pulling up weeds. I don't have to think about profits and losses or bank loans or liquidation or — '

'It's in trouble?' Guvnah reached out a hand and squeezed his arm. 'You sit down, young man, while I fetch some lemonade, and when I'm back I want to hear all about it. I used to work as a troubleshooter for a big furniture chain of stores.' Her eyes sparked as she stood up and headed indoors.

'You're done for now.' I grinned. 'My gran misses the business and only retired because she met Geoff and was moving here. She helped bring her employer's shops into the twenty-first century. Early sixties and she was still putting in over fifty hours a week, convincing bosses that thanks to Kindles, bookshelves were no longer big sellers; that tight incomes meant people upgraded what they had, instead of moving house, so were prepared to buy Jacuzzis, stylish writing desks . . . the more luxury options instead of forking out for a new home altogether.'

Tremain sat down opposite me and for the first time I noticed deep circles under his eyes. Yet the leaf-green irises filled with light. 'I'm surprised because we offered luxury but profits nosedived.' He explained how, gradually, bookings had diminished.

Guvnah returned and poured out three lemonades, ice cubes bobbing invitingly on the liquid's surface.

'The thing is, Tremain, people's homes are everything to them — important to their identity, their standing amongst their friends,' she said. 'So luxury items for the bathroom or kitchen still sell and to counteract that people might skimp on their holiday choices or the calibre of restaurant they eat out at.'

I nodded. 'Where we live, another bistro has just closed. Whereas the family pub that offers a free salad bowl to start and two-for-one menu options is always bustling.'

Guvnah reached for a notepad and pen that she'd brought on the tray. 'Tell me everything, Tremain,' she said and sat upright, eyes sparking again. 'How long has the business been suffering? What options has the bank given you? What are your ideas?'

As I sipped the bittersweet lemonade, I observed the way he spoke. His loud voice actually quietened and the Cornish accent became more of a lilt. He swallowed when he spoke of how he and his mum had to face the obvious — that the business her family had spent two generations creating was under threat. None of us mentioned his father who, from what Tremain said, was around until a couple of years ago.

As he finished speaking, I drained my glass. 'So, it's Wednesday tomorrow,' I said. 'The trial guests will have left today. That gives you five days to start a serious rebranding before paying family holidaymakers arrive.'

Guvnah sucked in her cheeks. 'That's a tall order.'

Tremain rubbed a hand across the back of his neck and, for some reason, I longed to do the same.

'Next week's guests are still getting a discounted rate, but, yep, they are expecting to see a resort that will meet their needs.'

My mind went back to my first meeting with him. The golf course. Those bunny rabbits. 'You need a mascot,' I said. 'Trust me — I spent years holidaying in caravan parks as a child. The highlight was the cartoon characters on the various logos. You need something kids can identify with.' I cast my mind back to many a vacation where I had younger siblings to look after.

'Kids don't ask for much,' I said. 'Just a pool, tasty snacks and a few activities. It doesn't have to be grand or expensive.' Over the years I became a whizz at setting up treasure hunts for my brothers and sisters and kids at the nursery where I worked. They were always happy with just some chocolate as the prize as they had so much fun trying to locate it.

Guvnah made notes. 'Yes. Kate's right. In my last job logos meant everything. They have to be memorable and relatable. In the end ours was the outline of a modern chair with a heart in its back — this told people ours was the stylish place to shop at, if you loved your home. And it worked.'

'Rabbits,' I said.

Tremain raised an eyebrow.

'On the golf course. All the bunnies. A rabbit is a perfect mascot for the resort.' I cleared my throat and stared into the distance for a moment. White Rocks. White. Rocks . . . 'A white bunny called Rocky!' I said and punched the air. 'You need to find a local wholesaler who sells cuddly toys, specifically rabbits, then order in a load, or search online.

In fact . . . ' I took out my phone and tapped the Internet icon. Within minutes I'd found a seller of white cuddly rabbits wearing T-shirts you could personalise with a name. Perfect! I showed the screen to my gran and Tremain.

They both stared for a moment and then he glanced at Guvnah.

She nodded. 'Great idea, Kate! Children would love them and 'Rocky' the rabbit could be painted around the place, on signs and walls.'

Face flushed, Tremain took my phone. 'It's a genius idea, so it is, but timing-wise . . . '

'Pay for express delivery — it'd be worth it,' I said, 'and . . . ' I beamed. 'Guvnah. Lovely, Gran . . . you're an artist above all others. I bet you could quickly come up with an image of the rabbit and paint it onto a few signs.'

'I'm not a professional!' she spluttered.

'We could change the name of the restaurant,' said Tremain and leant forward. 'What about . . . Rocky's Roadhouse?'

'Fab!' I clapped my hands. 'I'm sure we could put together a more family-friendly menu over the weekend and have it printed out in time — the Rocky burger and so on; make it fun.'

Guvnah scribbled again, while Tremain glanced at me. He cleared his throat. 'You said 'we'.'

Ah. So I did.

'I don't expect you to . . . ' He shuffled in his seat. 'This isn't your problem. You're a guest.'

I stared at him. The open expression. The stoic, raised chin. For some reason I wanted to help, despite his abrupt style back at the resort.

'I'm used to keeping busy,' I rambled. 'It would make for a more interesting holiday to get involved.'

'You'd be wise to take all the help you can get, Tremain,' said Guvnah and looked up. 'This is business. Your livelihood and heritage is at stake. It's not time to be proud.'

He bit his lip. How soft it looked, as if I'd hardly feel it brush across my skin — as if it, nevertheless, would make my nerve endings burn like sparklers. I looked away. Johnny. Johnny gave the best kisses ever. And hugs. After his death that was the first thing I missed — his tight arms around me at the end of a long day, me losing myself in the feel of his breath, in the smell of his neck . . .

I shook myself. 'Then there's the entertainment you offer — that will have to change. You need a twenty-first century format.' I thought for a moment. 'What's current? Let's see . . . Celebrities. Reality shows, like *Britain's Got Talent*.'

Guvnah nodded. 'Hold a talent competition — it could be anything, singing, fancy dress lookalikes, telling jokes . . . And bake-offs are popular — perhaps the chef could offer cookery afternoons for adults and kids.'

'Yes! Great idea!' I hugged my gran. 'And what have you been offering in the form of musical entertainment?'

'Tribute singers for Katherine Jenkins or Frank Sinatra have always proved popular in the past,' said Tremain.

Guvnah jerked her head towards me. 'You need to provide music for a wider audience. Kate's here for two weeks — hire her. She's a singer. She can wow an audience with anything from Michael Jackson to Adele.'

I sat more upright. 'Yes, we could have a seventies disco night, a jazz evening, country-music line dancing . . . I'm pretty flexible.'

'You'd really do that on your holiday?' he asked.

I beamed.

'I . . . I don't know what to say.' Tremain swallowed.

'You could end one of my nights with a firework display!' OK, perhaps getting a bit carried away.

Tremain shook his head and averted his gaze. 'No . . . Mum's got a load from a show she and my dad held here when I worked elsewhere but . . . but she reckons a display would just be too much to worry about now, what with health and safety experts. We can't afford for anything to go wrong.' He made eye contact again and smiled. 'All your ideas — Mum and me . . . we've had thoughts along the same lines but . . . but I suppose we've lacked the confidence to form concrete plans and didn't really know how to make them a reality. You've both helped me see that we just need to get on with it. It may work — it may not — but at least we are moving forward and trying.'

⋆   ⋆   ⋆

Tremain and I were still discussing all the options, when he drove me back to the resort. We'd stayed for dinner in the end. Geoff was super-excited as he'd mentioned how much he missed his old catering job and so Tremain suggested he run his hot-dog stall, part-time, at White Rocks in the afternoons.

I squinted into the darkness. 'White Rocks is so isolated. It's lovely. You can see the stars really clearly without the amber glow of city lights.'

Tremain pulled up outside the big reception building and turned off the ignition. 'Yep.

I wouldn't live anywhere else. When times get tough, I head for the coast. There is nothing like a night-time walk, on the rocks, to clear your mind.'

'Or to risk your life!' I smiled. 'Well, guess I'd better get going. Do you want to meet again tomorrow then, to consolidate our ideas, talk things through again?'

Eyes serious, Tremain nodded, mouth slightly down-turned — it was as if a switch had flipped his mood now that we were back at the resort. 'Great. Thanks again. In fact, let me buy you breakfast at Fish — '

'At Rocky's Roadhouse?' I interjected.

At least that made him smile. And then . . . my heart raced. Something odd happened. His face flickered and I felt mine do the same. For a couple of seconds, I leant forward just millimetres, as he did, and the only thought in my head was what it would feel like to have his mouth pressed against mine, his body up close, my hand running over his super-short hair and solid frame. A slamming door interrupted the moment and, ears hot, I backed off, said goodnight and left. An hour later, after explaining the afternoon to Izzy, while we wore face packs, I headed off to bed.

I lay under the duvet and stared up at Johnny's red heart wind spinner, hanging from the ceiling. My eyes tingled and I reached for my phone. As I had done a hundred times since his fateful car accident, I clicked on his Facebook profile and then 'message'.

*Oh, Johnny. Will I ever find a man to replace you?* I typed. Yet I didn't press send. I didn't send self-indulgent, desperate messages like that any more, even though those words still popped into my head. Although I still secretly flicked through his Facebook photo albums and read his posts.

Sad? Maybe a little, but it made his death just slightly less brutal, to feel that he was still in my life — even though, within days of his funeral, his belongings were picked up — his favourite denim shirt, those silly Minion socks, the sexy boxer shorts . . . Although I hid his leather jacket and only very occasionally now, I slipped it on and imagined my arms were his, around my waist.

Goodness, I sound totally bonkers. I'm not. It's just been hard, having all this love to give and it not being reciprocated. I inhaled and exhaled, heart feeling lighter than usual as I remembered Tremain's understated excitement at our brainstorming session. And I ignored the little voice in my head asking, *What, you'll never, ever replace Johnny? Really? And who exactly are you trying to convince of that?*

# 7

After a sleepless night, I opened my eyes. Sunrays streamed through a gap in the curtains. I stared at the ceiling and diverted my gaze to the red wind spinner. It spun fast, which gave the impression that it pulsated. I smiled. Johnny used to thump his chest after we kissed, saying that my mouth must have a direct line to his heart. The spinner moved faster. Odd. It didn't usually move indoors. Then I noticed that my bedroom door was open. I placed my feet on the cool, wooden laminate floor and headed into the lounge. Izzy had opened the outside door and sat on the doorstep. She held a mug and, in her polka dot short PJs, yawned and squinted up at the sky.

'Another beautiful day,' I said.

She turned around, came in and, hair spiky from sleep, collapsed onto the sofa. 'The water's warm in the kettle and I wouldn't say no to a slice of toast if you are making some.'

We grinned and, quietly singing 'Walking On Sunshine', I did as requested. Izzy always took a couple of hours to fully wake up.

'You not eating?' she said, as I sat down

beside her, with just a drink for myself.

'No, I'm on a diet.'

She raised one eyebrow and I chuckled. As if.

'If you must know, I have a breakfast meeting with Tremain, to discuss the resort's rebranding,' I said with faux importance.

'Ah yes. Sounds like you have a lot to pull together. Are Geoff and Guvnah coming across?'

'Later. Tremain invited them for dinner to meet his mum and finalise any decisions. You should have seen Geoff's face at the prospect of running his snack van again. Although my gran reckons its engine will need an overhaul as he hasn't driven it for months.'

'What is he going to sell? Hot dogs, burgers?'

I nodded. 'And Tremain is going to approach the restaurant's chef today about doing a major overhaul on the menu, instead of a tweak. Apparently, Lucas — that's his name — has been resisting removing all of the fancier dishes, but after this last disastrous week he'll have little choice.'

'Tremain's the boss. He will have to insist.'

'He would have earlier but said he has been trying to reach a compromise. Says he offered Lucas a good reference if he wanted to look for work elsewhere — understood that Lucas

110

may not want to downgrade his skills. But apparently the chef has been trying to find a Michelin-starred job elsewhere for a while, with no success due to the recession.' I shrugged. 'Tremain seems like a fair boss but I guess he's finally decided enough is enough.'

'They could do with a mini Donuts & Daiquiris! That would really jolly up the place.'

I swallowed the wrong way and, coughing, set my mug on the oak coffee table. I stared at Izzy.

'What's the matter?' she said.

'Izzy . . . say that again.'

Her brow furrowed. 'They could to with a mini Donuts & Daiquiris.'

'Genius! You are absolutely right. A corner of that big, airy-fairy restaurant should be turned into a cocktail area for selling your products. If the left-hand side was somehow cornered off, as a temporary fix, you'd have a good portion of the bar. Kids and adults love doughnuts — they're fun, cheap and easy to eat on the go or after a swim in the pool. Those pizza ones you created would go down a treat. Their squishy dough and crisp, grilled savoury topping are to die for.'

'Well, they are really just cheese and tomato,' said Izzy, trance-like as if absorbing my words. 'It's all in the marketing, you know.'

'And come night-time, cocktails brighten up any evening,' I continued. 'They too have the fun factor, yet feel like a little holiday indulgence, for a reasonable price, and kids can still come in with their parents for soft drinks. What's more — '

'Kate, slow down, this is mad — what exactly are you suggesting?'

I clasped my hands together. 'Isn't it obvious? Why didn't we think of this before? You've been looking for a new challenge and I don't think simply redecorating your business and diversifying the menu is going to do it. Forget two weeks of researching Cornish fare such as ice cream and fudge. The challenge you need, my very bright friend, is to expand the whole business.'

Izzy sat more upright.

'Set up a chain of Donuts & Daiquiris,' I continued. 'A small branch here could be an experiment for you — a trial run.'

'You're crazy!' But Izzy put down her toast, only half eaten, crossed her legs and ran a hand through her hair. 'Me. Run a chain of café-bars. Employ managers. Or eventually sell franchises . . . '

'Why not? Think big!'

'I'm no Richard Branson. No entrepreneur. I'm just a girl who likes cocktails and doughnuts.'

I moved forward to perch on the edge of the sofa. 'Izzy, you are the cleverest, most hard-working, inventive person I know. Today is Wednesday. With my help, of course, you've got until Monday to set things up.'

'Impossible!' she spluttered.

My face ached, I was smiling so much. 'Nonsense. Guvnah could paint you a sign — you can show her the logo from your phone. Then it would just be a matter of ordering in glasses and alcohol . . . plus, you have the whole weekend to bake the first batches of doughnuts. I'd go with you to the wholesalers to pick up the ingredients. Obviously the furniture and decor would be a bit makeshift but . . . '

'Kate, this is all going too fast,' she said, and laughed. But she stood up. Paced the room. 'I guess the menus would be easy enough to put together and print out. Plus, I could contact Mum and ask her to pop into work for me and send us aprons and other branded bits, like the paper napkins.' She shook her head. 'I don't know . . . '

'Why? You're excited, no?'

'Yes, I mean . . . You're right, this could be just the challenge I've been looking for. If Donuts & Daiquiris was a success here I could sell the idea to another holiday resort.'

'Exactly! What have you got to lose? You

113

said yourself that you've just got money sitting in the bank, trade has been so good. You haven't got a mortgage, you're single — '

'Thanks for reminding me of that,' Izzy said and, eyes twinkling, she stopped walking around to lean against a kitchen unit.

'And you haven't got kids,' I said, ignoring her. 'This is the perfect time for you to develop your business.' I glanced at my watch. 'Look, why don't you come with me to breakfast and pitch your idea to Tremain?'

Cue the difference between arty me and logical Izzy . . .

'I don't think so! I need at least a day to put together a proper business plan. I must forecast profits, ring a few suppliers, find out what really is possible before Monday, in terms of setting up a mini branch. I would need to use the resort's kitchens to bake . . . '

'Mere details,' I muttered, begrudgingly. 'OK. Then come to the dinner tonight.'

She came over to the sofa, sat down and gave me a tight hug. 'You are brilliant, if a little bonkers — I haven't felt this pumped up for months.'

I stood up and took a bow. 'Right. This brainstormer better get ready. Tremain and an all-day breakfast await me.'

'Brainstormer? A right little super trouper you mean.'

Swaying side to side, we both sang a few lines of our favourite ABBA song.

Izzy looked sideways at me, as I finally made a move to get changed. It had gone half past eight.

'So, this Tremain . . . he isn't as bad as we both thought?'

My mouth felt unexpectedly dry and annoyingly, as I didn't know the reason, my cheeks burned. 'He's OK. Not much to say, but Guvnah insists he's a decent bloke.' I shrugged. 'Guess he's kind of interesting. He's like a book that has just the title on the cover, with no picture or blurb, and it takes a while of reading before you get a sense of the story. *The Life and Times of Tremain Maddock: struggling holiday resort manager.*' I shrugged again. 'Dunno. I just get the feeling there's a lot more to him than he lets on. Not that I'm interested. I'm only helping him because it's fun to work on a project and spend time with my gran.'

Izzy stared at me for a moment, then simply nodded and picked up her cold toast.

That was the great thing about best friends. They knew when not to say the obvious. Ten minutes later, I stood under the shower, steaming water cascading over my head and shoulders. You see, the obvious was that Tremain was the first man I'd spent more than five minutes with for the last ten months. Apart from my Poldark date, Marcus, and author, Trevor. For the first six months, anyone of the opposite sex didn't even register in my vision. Then, slowly, when out with Izzy, I might have noticed a hot guy and on the surface been able to join in with a giggle or appreciative comment. But up until now, no one had remotely caught my attention. Not that I was intrigued by Tremain in *that* way. It was just another case of Kate being curious.

And curious I was, as I arrived at Fisherman's Delight (soon to be Rocky's Roadhouse) and saw him waiting, by a table. He glanced at his watch and pursed his lips. To the right sat a couple wearing smart tailored clothes in, ooh, their mid-fifties. His face was hidden behind a broadsheet newspaper. Her made-up face looked positively miserable as she stared at the kitchen hatch. A perfect ten, with dyed brown hair and manicured nails, the only giveaway to her age were the lines on her face. A smoker perhaps.

'Have you been waiting long?' I asked as we sat down — as I tried to ignore how his round-necked T-shirt clung to the outline of subtly developed pecs.

'No. Only ten minutes.' He gave a wry smile. 'I drive Mum mad, always turning up to appointments early. But punctuality has been drilled into me since . . . ' He swallowed and sat down.

Since what? Being a kid? Perhaps it was something to do with his dad.

He passed me a menu and I grinned. 'No need for that. I already know what I'm having — it's the all-day breakfast for me.'

'Good idea. While Lucas isn't always the easiest employee to work with, nothing beats that dish of his.' He closed his menu. 'Mum will be along in about half an hour. She's just had to call out the pool maintenance people. Something is clogging up one of the drains, so it is.'

Greg, the young waiter Izzy liked, came over.

'Two all-day breakfasts,' said Tremain. 'And coffee?' He glanced my way and I nodded.

'No kippers for me though, thank you,' I said, and pulled a face.

Tremain's mouth quirked up. 'Not a fish fan? It's a super-food, you know — all those oils. Good for the brain.'

'As I demonstrated yesterday, my brain is in perfect working order. It takes a lot of grey matter to come up with the concept of a rabbit called Rocky.'

He gave me the widest smile yet and my stomach kind of tickled inside. I fought an urge to reach across the table and squeeze his arm. I tried to break eye contact, but couldn't, as we started to go over the plans we'd made yesterday. My eyes felt compelled to soak him up as if they had dried out from not seeing anything as pleasing for a long time. When our meals arrived, Tremain passed me the mustard and briefly our fingers touched. My heart raced. I ... I didn't understand why. Especially when he polished his cutlery first, with a napkin — that was seriously messed up!

I dived straight into the tangerine pile of baked beans. Mmm. Yummy. And then ... Oh dear. A sneeze started. I grabbed a napkin in time and afterwards winced as my cheekbone hurt. Tremain studied me and leant forward, brushing his thumb across my skin. As he did so, my insides kind of ... melted.

Oh my days. How could such a sensible, sober, practical-looking guy have such a sensuous touch?

'Should feel back to normal in a few days,' he said, as if world expert on injuries.

I nodded and cleared my throat. 'Your mum ... ' I managed to avoid his eyes for a second and put down my fork. 'Have you explained the gist of what we discussed yesterday? Does she agree?'

In between mouthfuls of crispy bacon and runny egg yolk, he explained how relieved — how grateful — Kensa had seemed, now that the resort might possibly have some sort of plan.

I finally swallowed the last delicious mouthful of crunch fried bread. 'Hmm. That was heavenly.'

'Perhaps you could tell our chef, if I call him out of the kitchen. I'm trying to get him in a good mood before running some more new menu ideas past him — and he did agree to cook for us this morning, even though he's flat out getting things ready for the formal launch next week.'

'Sure.' I jerked my head towards the smart couple who still weren't talking to each other. 'Are they first-time guests as well, like me and Izzy? She doesn't look very happy. Perhaps they didn't read the small print when booking, about the resort not being completely up and running until Monday.'

He shook his head. 'No. The Peppards have come here every summer for the last three years. They get on very well with the staff. They asked to come as usual — I explained the changes and that catering and housekeeping facilities wouldn't be running as normal until the launch, now that the trial guests have left, but they weren't bothered. Mr Peppard owns a few golf courses in and around London and loves visiting courses in the South-west — says they are some of the prettiest in the world. Said he understood that the resort wouldn't be firing on all cylinders while we made last-minute preparations. As it is, Lucas will probably be available to cook most of the time as he is spending the next few days in the kitchens, trialling new dishes.'

'You should ask Mr Peppard to renovate your golf course,' I said and half smiled.

Tremain gave a wry smile back. 'I'm not sure ours ranks highly in his mind, without a driving range and clubhouse.'

'Or putting greens that you can actually see,' I said coyly and cocked my head.

Tremain grinned, called over Greg and asked him to go get Lucas, while I swallowed the fact that I, Kate Golightly, for the first time in for ever, had just flirted with a man. An image of the wind spinner flashed into my mind, but only fleetingly. It was soon replaced by the sight of Tremain's soft mouth talking, as he chatted about his golf course and how he might set it up as a more fun crazy-golf activity.

I listened intently, as his plans made sense. Most families coming here would have children too young to play an adult game.

'You haven't got any brothers or sisters?' I

found myself asking.

He shook his head.

'That's a shame. I mean, it would have been an extra person to share the load of turning this place around.'

Tremain shrugged. 'No guarantee of that, though — take me, I haven't always worked here. It was only a year ago that I came back here from . . . ' A muscle flinched in his cheek and I leant forwards.

'From where?' I murmured and my stomach scrunched as his eyes turned dull, like those of an animal that had just been shot.

'The army,' he mumbled.

I raised my eyebrows. The Armed Forces? Tremain? Of course. With his super-short hair, athletic body and words he used — like saying 'the best managers get down with the lower ranks' and 'this is a holiday resort, not a war zone'. Then there was his obvious punctuality and the way he polished his cutlery. And that air of physical capability.

'Why did you leave?' I said, instinctively knowing to use gentle tones.

He stared at me for a moment. Swallowed. Took a deep breath and opened his mouth just as the kitchen door swung open. I glanced up and a man walked towards us, black curls bobbing, tight jeans showing beneath a white waist apron. He turned to look at the smartly dressed woman. The cut of the denim accentuated rugby player thighs. The top two buttons of a white shirt were open and revealed a taut, hairy tanned chest.

My eyes widened and in my mind played the Marvin Gaye song 'Let's Get It On', as the chef's gait seemed to go to slow motion, raven hair moving up and down with each step. He caught my eye. Wow. Smouldering charcoal irises with a hint of dirty intent. Chiselled cheekbones. Louche stubble. A strong, teasing mouth. Golden skin. An eyebrow raised as if enjoying a private joke.

Poldark . . . Poldark had been living at White Rocks all this time, just metres away from me. He stopped by our table and I almost dropped my cup of coffee. Miracles did happen. My fictional hero existed right here, in Port Penny.

# 8

'I thought I might actually die with excitement,' I said to Izzy, as we both put the finishing touches to each other's make-up — for Izzy that meant me applying an extra slash of glitter pink lipgloss to her mouth. For me she had to dab on a smidge more face powder and subtle brown eye shadow. I glanced in my compact mirror and gave her the thumbs-up. 'He looks exactly like Poldark,' I continued, 'with that fit physique, the brooding, undressing-you eyes. The only difference is he has a smooth London accent.' We were getting ready for dinner with Tremain, Kensa, Guvnah and Geoff. Izzy carried a folder of paperwork. She'd been busy all day, putting together graphs of profit projections and goodness knows what.

'Did he talk to you?' she asked, and slipped into her high red shoes. I put on my ballet pumps and straightened my navy swing dress — a favourite for those evenings when I sang jazz. I decided to go smart, for Izzy's benefit — make her look like a viable business proposition, seeing as I worked at Donuts & Daiquiris too. She wore a lime green and chocolate ra-ra dress — sounds sickly, but on her that colour combination seemed to work.

I picked up my clutch bag. 'No. Not exactly. I told him how yummy breakfast was and he grunted in return. But Poldark is a moody so-and-so, right? This just makes him more authentic. And I've got a while to work on that distant veneer.'

'Is he cooking tonight?'

'Yes. Tremain told him, no arguments — the time had come to produce a more generic menu.' I zipped up my bag. 'Lucas sat down to chat to this couple after meeting me — regular customers of White Rocks — so he must have a friendly streak in him somewhere. Charm oozed out of his every pore. I heard him tell the woman that her new hairstyle knocked ten years off her, and he complimented the man's shirt. Perhaps having to rethink the menus is just stressing him out.'

'And how was Tremain?' she said and suddenly busied herself with readjusting the belt of her dress.

'Quite chirpy, all things considered.' Until my attention had turned to the approaching chef. Inconveniently, Poldark had appeared just at the moment when it seemed Tremain was going to open up about something important.

'He used to be in the army,' I said, as Izzy and I headed towards the restaurant.

She raised her eyebrows. 'That explains his sergeant major manner.'

We continued our walk to Rocky's Roadhouse and Izzy explained her business plan. It would mean baking solidly all day Sunday — with my help — to produce the first batches of doughnuts. The cocktails were easy — it was just a matter of buying in the liquor. Her main concern was to quiz the Maddocks over exactly how much time the bank had given them, to start to turn things around, because setting up a mini Donuts & Daiquiris, even for a trial period, would mean purchasing in a good coffee machine at least. She hoped to borrow the cutlery and crockery from the resort, but would buy in fancy cocktail glasses. Izzy didn't want to invest without reassurances that the Maddocks were determined to haul the resort back from the threat of bankruptcy.

As we entered the big white building, my stomach experienced that tickling sensation again. Not sure why. Perhaps it was the thought of seeing Poldark. My mouth upturned. If he were my plus-one, Saffron wouldn't be able to believe her eyes. We headed towards the restaurant. Tremain was already there with Geoff, Guvnah and Kensa, a neat woman with ginger, grey-streaked hair in a practical bun. Tremain stood up as we approached and we sat down,

125

me in between him and Guvnah, who wore the most gorgeous terracotta Indian silk dress. I fanned myself with a menu and hoped it wouldn't take too long to order a cool drink. Geoff winked. Loved the way he dyed what little hair he had left, plus wore a slim leather tie. 'Once a roadie, always a roadie,' he'd say. His iPod was never far away from his ears, playing the Beatles, Rolling Stones or Beach Boys.

I kissed my gran on the cheek. 'It's so good to be spending time with you,' I said. 'Have you had any more thoughts about the drawings?'

'I've done better than that,' she said and reached down to the floor, to pull a notebook out of her bag. She set it on the table and opened the front cover.

'Wow!' I looked up to see Kensa and everyone else staring at the page. Guvnah had drawn the most adorable white bunny wearing a T-shirt bearing a black flag with the word 'Rocky' written on it in white — the colours of the Cornish flag.

'Now that's proper handsome,' said Tremain.

Kensa nodded and looked around the table. 'We so appreciate this input. Geoff, Tremain says you would consider parking up your hot-dog van outside, for the lunch and afternoon trade?'

'I'd be more than happy to,' he said and

loosened his tie, beads of sweat on his forehead. The waiters had set up large fans.

'I can't tell you how much I've missed my job,' he continued. 'Chatting with customers and breathing in fresh air. Even if it rains, it takes a lot to beat the smell of frying meat against the fragrant background of damp grass and wet ground. I've been looking for a part-time job as, well, retirement, it's enjoyable enough but quieter than I thought. It just never struck me to go back to doing what I do best.'

'Are you implying that life with me is boring?' asked Guvnah archly, before shaking her finger at him in mock anger.

'Wouldn't dare, my love,' he said. 'If it wasn't for you, I'd have really gone mad over recent months, just baking, reading the paper or gardening . . . '

Kensa smiled at us all. 'Before we get started, why don't we order food and drink?' She handed around basic laminated white menus. 'Lucas came up with this today.'

I cast my eye down the dishes — lasagne, sausage and mash, fish and chips . . . that sounded more like it. Greg, the young waiter, came over and Izzy's cheeks tinged pink to match her lipstick. He was dressed in jeans and a T-shirt, having offered to help management in any way he could through this final transition period before Monday's launch. He made a joke about his 'smart' outfit. Ooh perfect. A man who could make her laugh. Guvnah ordered her usual Martini and lemonade, while young-at-heart Geoff ordered a trendy pear cider. Tremain had a Coke.

'Teetotal?' I said and jerked my head towards his drink.

'I just prefer to keep a clear head when talking business.'

Ooh. Abrupt tones. But instead of being put off, I now saw that as a challenge.

'One little drink won't sway your clarity . . . or are you a lightweight when it comes to alcohol?'

He snorted. 'I could drink any of you London jessies under the table, just like that.' Tremain clicked his fingers and actually cracked a smile.

'Careful. Izzy's a demon for downing Daiquiris.'

He pulled a face. 'I'm talking real drinks, not colourful concoctions that are more appealing to kids.'

Izzy glared at me. OK, this wasn't going to help her pitch.

'Cocktails are big business now,' I said. 'They've made a massive comeback over the last few years. You can't go near a bar on a Friday night without seeing two Angel's Tits for the price of one.'

Gosh. If I thought Tremain's accent was loud, you should have heard his laugh. It bellowed across the table. I felt all fuzzy inside to see his face truly light up for a few seconds.

Tremain shook his head. 'It's such an exclusive language. Asking for a beer is much simpler. At least I'm not likely to offend anyone.'

'I have to say, nothing quite beats a refreshing Mojito,' said Kensa.

'Funny you should say that, because Izzy has an idea for bringing business and fun times into the resort that will mean Mojitos galore.'

Izzy took a deep breath and placed a sheaf of papers on the table. While Greg brought out drinks, she pitched her idea. Guvnah and Geoff both mmmed in ecstasy at the descriptions of doughnuts. Izzy had ideas to give her menu a real Cornish theme, which included warm doughnuts filled with local ice cream and others drizzled with Cornish fudge. Plus, the mini cocktail doughnuts she would decorate with iced seashells, anchors and flags and, of course, she'd sell ones bearing an edible rice paper sticker of Rocky Rabbit.

Tremain sat with his arms folded, but

gradually let them fall apart, hand resting in his lap. Kensa's eyes remained narrowed but, as the pitch went on, they widened and her forehead lines disappeared. I was on to my second glass of red wine by the time Izzy had finished. Silence hung in the air — apart from the chat of the smart couple from earlier, across the room, who were actually talking to each other tonight.

'Thanking you so much for such a detailed presentation,' said Kensa.

'Your doughnuts sound mouth-watering,' said my gran.

'With my hot-dog van and your cocktail bar, guests won't want to go back home,' said Geoff, with a wink.

We all looked at Tremain.

'Donuts & Daiquiris?' he said. 'Hmm. You wouldn't catch me in such a sugary place. But granted, I'm not your average holiday-maker. Izzy, you've made a good case.'

Kensa's eyes glistened. 'We appreciate that you're prepared to invest in this place. Not many would. But we've every confidence that we can turn things around.' She straightened in her chair. 'I've no intention of seeing my family's heritage fall victim to the recession.'

Tremain ran a hand over his short, bristly hair. 'I could easily put up a temporary wall, coming out from halfway across the bar. We could paint your side of the restaurant a different colour, and theme it with accessories like tablecloths.'

Izzy nodded. 'And it makes sense for the front to be open-plan as the evening entertainment is just outside it, in the reception, where you have an area set aside for bands or comedians and lounging chairs.'

'Yes,' said Kensa. 'It means guests spending the night in the building have easy access to the bar.' As the meals arrived, she beamed. 'Let's talk over the details later. I don't know about anyone else but I could eat the whole of a fisherman's catch.'

My stomach rumbled, but I didn't pay much attention to the food as my eyes studied the brooding face of Lucas, looking for some way in which he didn't suit the role of Poldark. Fortunately, I found none! His dark colouring looked so much the part. With strong arms, he held the hot plates with a tea towel, dealing them out easily, as if they were playing cards.

'I hope you approve of the new selection of dishes,' he said and draped the tea towel over his shoulder.

'Sounds perfect to me,' I said and wondered why everyone else was so quiet. Briefly he nodded — the first step towards a connection between us and him saving my reputation at the wedding. Then I glanced down at my lasagne. Oh. 'Why is the white sauce in a pot by the side?' I asked. 'And the pasta sheets and lasagne filling are separated.'

'It's called a deconstructed lasagne,' he said in a bored voice and wiped his hands on the white apron tied around his waist. Clearly the first impression I made wasn't dazzling.

'I've seen this on *MasterChef*,' said Izzy as she stared at her supposed fish and chips — a delicate piece of grilled . . . trout — was that? — with sweet potato wedges and, by the looks of it, minted peas. I glanced at Geoff's plate — he'd ordered sausage and mash. The latter was orange — presumably swede.

Tremain tutted.

'What?' said Lucas and ran a hand across his stubbly chin, his inky eyes looking darker than ever. 'You said to dumb down the menu, boss. So, as a start, I've been making my breakfast available all day and now this is the next step. But I still have certain standards when it comes to the overall concept and presentation.'

Tremain pushed away his plate. 'You've got until tomorrow to change this menu again and get on-board with us fully, Lucas, or you're out. Get it? Stop pissing about. We still want quality when it comes to taste, but you seriously need to rethink your concept of what appeals to the masses.'

He snorted. 'Where will you get a chef of my calibre, at such a late stage?'

Kensa reached out and put a hand on his arm. 'Lucas. Please. Try to understand. We've got to undergo a complete image transformation. You'll still have the opportunity to use your skills — for example, we're thinking of holding bake-off classes.'

'You want me to teach snotty kids how to make fairy cakes? Could things get any worse?'

From across the room the smart man coughed. Lucas turned around then turned back.

'Whatever,' he mumbled, clearly now aware that guests were in hearing distance. 'But giving away food to these people — ' he looked at us ' — isn't a good start.'

Brilliant — at the moment he even begrudged me a free meal.

'These aren't just any people,' said Tremain. 'They might just help us turn this place around.'

Lucas raised his eyebrows. 'Really? Miracle workers, are they?' He shook those unruly curls.

Tremain wiped his mouth with a napkin and stood up. 'I think you and I would be better off discussing this in the kitchen,' he said and headed that way, followed by the chef.

'Must be hard for such a qualified chef,' said Guvnah eventually, as we all busied ourselves with our food. 'I'm sure he'll come around.'

'Perhaps I should contact the recruitment agency tomorrow,' muttered Kensa. 'See if there's anyone suitable to replace him. We've no time to waste. My son's right.'

Eventually, Tremain appeared and, tight-lipped, sat down. Not much later, with a surly expression, Lucas brought out slightly less refined desserts, including a chocolate sundae and a sticky toffee pudding. Afterwards, I left everyone discussing the new options for evening entertainment to take a brief walk outside. The restaurant's humidity didn't go well with the red wine. However, I stopped, with a jolt, as soon as I left the building. There sat Lucas, on a wall, drawing deeply on a cigarette. I hovered, not knowing whether to talk or give him space. Then he looked up. Held out his hand. His mouth quirked up.

'So, you're helping Tremain and Kensa save White Rocks?'

I went over and almost fainted as his fingers curled around mine and pulled me down to the wall. Almost fainted because, for just a split second, I felt as if I were back in the eighteenth century — a damsel about to be taken advantage of!

He offered me a cigarette. I declined. Lucas dropped his onto the floor and stubbed it out with his foot. 'Disgusting habit, anyway.' He looked back up and stared me straight in the face. Gosh. Talk about earthy and dirty yet charming, as he sat there confidently with his legs wide open — Lucas was everything I'd been looking for in my plus-one.

'It must be difficult for you,' I said. 'But what choice do you have? Things have got to change.'

'I know. And, to be fair, Tremain and Kensa have given me a bit of time to adapt,' he said and gave a big sigh. 'But I came here five years ago to serve highfalutin food. It's what I'm trained to do. It's what my dad always taught me to be — the best of the best. And it's what I love. There's no chance of a job elsewhere at the moment. Cornwall overflows with great cooks. So, I . . . I just need some time.' His shoulders moved up and down. 'At least the Maddocks agree we shouldn't compromise on the quality of our ingredients or buy in processed stuff. Do you work in the catering business?'

I told him all about Donuts & Daiquiris. Izzy's idea for expansion. He hung on every word.

'Great idea,' he said. 'In fact, I'd love to hear your take on Tremain and Kensa's plans.' Those charcoal eyes twinkled. 'Perhaps you could help me brainstorm how I might better fit in with their rebranding ideas.' Lucas flashed me a smile.

Super swoon!

'How about we meet here, first thing tomorrow? You can test out the new breakfast menu I've thought out.'

This was good, right? Operation Impress Saffron was making progress. 'It doesn't involve deconstructed croissants or omelettes, does it?' I grinned. 'I don't think I could eat a spoonful of butter or flour.'

He gave a wry smile. 'No. I promise.' He squeezed my fingers. 'Say, nine o'clock?'

'Great! OK. Right!' Feeling flustered. 'I'd better get back. Everyone will think I got lost.'

'Dig the dress, by the way,' he said. 'Classy. Sexy.' His voice went all husky and, almost tripping over I thanked him and turned to go. Needless to say, my trip outside hadn't cooled me off at all.

It felt like an eternity since a man had complimented my figure. Not that I'd needed nice words during the last ten months, as I'd lived off memories of Johnny's conversations. He'd loved my full boobs. And my small waist. OK, apologies, that's probably too much information. Yet the last couple of days,

I don't know . . . perhaps it was doing me good to get away. It was as if the trip was holding up a mirror in front of me. It was hard to see me during the last year and a half reflected back. The angry thoughts. The obsessive behaviour on Facebook. I swallowed. That time could have been much better spent.

The reception doors swung open as I approached and Tremain appeared. His eyebrows knotted together. 'Kate, Izzy wants you. We're measuring up the restaurant and she wants you to help her decide a room-plan and exactly how much space the mini Donuts & Daiquris is going to require.'

'Gosh, already?'

'No time like the present.'

Lucas came up to us. 'Er, sorry, boss. About the menu. I'll rethink it.' With that, he headed back indoors.

'I'd steer clear of him,' said Tremain. 'He's a stellar chef but has got a reputation amongst the ladies at the resort. Bit of a charmer.'

'Thanks for the heads-up, but I think I can look after myself,' I said and smiled.

'I mean it. Watch out.'

Whoa. OK. Don't take the knight in shining armour act too far.

'He seems pleasant enough to me. I'll make up my own mind, thanks. Appreciate you looking out for me, though.'

'I just don't want any upset — there's enough going on this weekend without that.'

'Don't you think you and Kensa are over-reacting a bit, considering a replacement?' I said. 'Lucas seems to be coming around and has already created a new breakfast menu. I'm testing it out tomorrow morning.'

Tremain shook his head. 'What is it about Lucas that has women falling at his feet?'

My cheeks flushed hot. 'I don't do falling.' And perhaps you'd be more popular if you smiled once in a while, just to be friendly, I felt like adding. 'Isn't it a bit cold? That man has worked for you for five years. Where's the team spirit? You can't just leave him trailing behind your grandiose plans.' And, OK, selfish moment, but I needed him to hang around so that I could get to know him better.

'You don't know what you'rrre talking about,' he snapped.

'Huh? I know better than anyone. With five siblings growing up, we had to pull together to help Mum, share clothes and housework — if one of us slacked it affected all of us, so we learnt to support each other.'

'You're saying, as I'm an only child, I couldn't possibly understand the concept of teamwork?'

'No, of course not. Just . . . '

'There is no room for sentimentality in some jobs,' he said curtly, with the slightest of wobbles, and my chest squeezed as he left me and headed back inside.

What was it about Tremain that intrigued me? His random comments loaded with underlying emotion? I guessed that no, there hadn't been much room for sentimentality in the army, but Tremain was in civvy street now. Why was he finding it so hard to chill out?

I exhaled slowly. Whatever. For the moment I was going to forget Mr Frosty Robot, as tomorrow morning I had a date with a smokin' heart-throb.

# 9

'Wow. Those croissants melt in the mouth,' I said and took another bite, tiny flakes of pastry disintegrating on my tongue. 'Did you order them in from a local bakery?'

This was me, trying hard to concentrate on the breakfast-tasting session, with Lucas just centimetres away. A lock of black hair fell over his eyes and I had to pin my arm to my side in an attempt not to brush it back. His mouth quirked up on one side and he leant back. I fixed my gaze on my plate, determined not to gawp at the chest hair that poked invitingly out of the top of his polo shirt. I could just imagine him riding a horse, or standing on a cliff side, on a rainy day, looking as moody as the landscape. Gosh, he'd look dashing in Poldark's redcoat army uniform.

'Nope. Ultimately, the resort is trying to cut costs, so Tremain and I decided if we have to compromise a little on quality — which neither of us really wants — breakfast might offer a few possibilities. I bought packets of part-baked croissants from the local super-market, then heated them up here. I'm glad they've passed the test. Now, what about this?'

Using a spoon, he scooped a mouthful of creamy Greek yogurt out of a pot and sprinkled muesli on top. Hardly able to breathe, I leant forward as he fed me.

Mm mmm. 'What's in the muesli? There is something sharp that really complements the creaminess of the yogurt.' I cocked my head. 'And a spice that reminds me of Christmas.'

Lucas smiled and took a mouthful himself, afterwards licking his lips slowly. 'Well done, Kate. It's cranberry, to give it that punch, with an underlying smattering of cinnamon. It doesn't cost much more to make your own muesli.' He pulled a face. 'And to cater for the new budget family market, we've decided to stock a small selection branded sugary cereals for children.'

I shrugged. 'That's sensible. Kids can be picky.'

He nodded. 'Plus we've invested in a toast-making machine for guests to use — Kensa's suggestion. And on some days I'll bake muffins.'

'I know it isn't easy for you, but the resort can't carry on it has been. Will you set out the breakfast buffet style?'

'Yeah. Only one waiter, Greg, will be needed in the morning, to show guests to their seats and supply them with hot drinks.' He ran a hand through his ruffled hair. 'It's an experiment — to see if guests go mad for seconds and thirds or, in the end, we make a profit.' He shrugged. 'Personally, I don't think it's going to be that popular. Most people eat in their chalets first thing and would only make the effort to go out for something special like eggs Benedict. Not stuff they can buy from the supermarket.'

I caught his eye and he laughed. 'I admit it. I'm a food snob. Nothing gets past you, does it?'

Wasn't he just charming? The complete opposite to his boss, who was probably just jealous that Lucas knew how to put women at their ease and he didn't.

'But you may have a point . . . I trust that you are still going to offer your lovely fried breakfast?'

'Yeah. Cereals, yogurt, toast, croissants, that will all be self-service, but if guests want anything hot they will have to order off the menu.' He shrugged. 'I suspect many of those out to grab a morning treat will simply head to Izzy's place next door, for a coffee and doughnut.' Lucas gave a good-humoured smirk. 'I can't believe she invented a pizza-flavoured one. Pure genius.' He gazed sideways at me, the smirk morphing into a

142

smile. My eyes scanned his face. I just couldn't get over how much he looked like the lead of mine and Saffron's favourite telly series.

'What?' he said and rubbed that chin. 'Have I got yogurt on my face?'

'No. Nothing. I was just . . . you see . . . ' I picked up my coffee and took a large glug. Oops. Big mistake. It went down the wrong way. Cue a coughing fit. Firmly, Lucas prised away the cup and then clapped me on the back.

'Hey. Never knew I had that effect on women.' His eyes sparkled.

Bet he did. 'No . . . I drank too quickly . . . you see . . . '

He took my hand. 'Kate. I'm messing with you. It's OK. Just relax.'

His fingers squeezed mine before he took away his hand. At that moment, the Peppards came in and the woman shot me the dirtiest of looks. Lucas stood up to greet them both and her face melted like an ice cream on a Cornish beach. Subtly she rubbed his arm. Hmm. Looked like somebody had a crush. But then I couldn't blame her. And her husband didn't seem the nicest of chaps. Yesterday I'd heard him criticise her tight skirt, saying it was too short and totally unsuitable for a woman of her age.

Bravo for Lucas, who discreetly moved away from her touch. Truth be told, I thought she looked great. But then I rarely thought bitchy thoughts about people, which was why I'd found it hard to accept how Saffron had changed, once we'd started high school. I'd just rather see the good in people. Plus, a kind word or compliment cost nothing. Not that I was a doormat. Growing up in a busy household, with an eternal list of chores, you soon learnt not to let yourself be taken advantage of. But people rarely got to me in a bad way. Not even the postman who always hissed at next door's cat. He just didn't like animals but would do anything for a human, including picking up one pensioner's prescription for her, while out on his round.

However, Tremain kind of proved to be the exception to the rule. For some reason I found his abruptness and quick mood changes hard to overlook. And here he came, face screwed up as if he'd just eaten one of Izzy's sage and onion doughnuts (occasionally her creations caused the gag reflex and that Christmas flavour, that never made the menu, was one).

'Why don't we hook up later,' Lucas muttered to me, 'and you could help me brainstorm further ways to make this rebranding work? In fact, why not let me take you to dinner?' Before I could answer, he picked up my dirty crockery and headed back to the kitchen.

Tremain sat down in his place. 'So, is this a holiday romance brewing? The chef and the singer who ignored my advice?'

'You may not say much, but when you do it is certainly to the point,' I said and heat surged into my face. 'Why the interest?'

Tremain gave me full eye contact and my heartbeat sped up. 'Just looking out for one of my guests — that's you. I don't trust him. Never have. I respect his cooking but he's . . . he's . . . '

'What?'

'A bit of a player, I reckon, when it comes to romance — especially with the type of well-heeled female guest who used to frequent our resort.'

'Hmm, that Mrs Peppard couldn't keep her hands off him, just then.' I shrugged and wondered if Tremain was simply jealous of Lucas's easy manner with women. 'But that's good for business, no, if he's popular with the opposite sex?'

Tremain stared at me for a moment and then his shoulders bobbed up and down. 'So,' he said, eventually. 'Breakfast? Your verdict?'

'Excellent,' I said. 'Really tasty. A good choice. And you'd never notice where you

145

and Lucas have cut costs.' I raised an eyebrow. 'As we agreed last night, today are you putting up that temporary wall and helping Izzy paint her side of the restaurant, while I put together some song lists for the music evenings and help Guvnah with the Rocky Rabbit signs and merchandise?'

'Yep. I just bought one hundred white toy rabbits, with T-shirts, each printed with the word 'Rocky'. I paid extra for the order to be pushed through quickly.' He shrugged at me. 'I hope the investment is worth it.'

'You say that as if it will be my fault if the whole Rocky Rabbit-branding concept fails.'

He swallowed. 'No . . . no, Kate, look, whatever happens, I can't tell you 'ow grateful I am. For the first time in ages, last night, my mum didn't take the books home or talk to me about something to do with work.'

'You live with her?'

He shook his head. 'We've got separate lodges. I'd just popped around to fix a wonky shelf. It was great — seeing her relaxed. Smiling.'

Oh gosh. Those intense leaf-green eyes. Pulling me in. Feel like I'm drowning.

'She's been so worried and spent every night, since as long as I can remember, at her kitchen table, poring over the accounts.' His voice cracked. 'I'm so grateful — to you, Izzy, Guvnah, Geoff . . . even if all our plans don't work.'

I welled up. If ever there was a case of someone or something being neither black nor white, it was Tremain. And no, that doesn't make him my Mr Grey. But you see, he was blunt, didn't do small talk and in several days I'd only heard him laugh once. He made no effort whatsoever to be alluring, yet there was an aura about him that I found . . . For a second I stopped breathing. Did the word 'adorable' really just pop into my head? As he chatted about his ideas for my music evenings, a volcanic heat rose from the pit of my stomach to my cheeks. What was going on? One minute my heart fluttered because of gorgeous, debonair Lucas, the next deep feelings rocked me because of his stand-offish boss.

'Kate? What do you think? How about a seventies night on Monday and jazz later in the week? I'd pay you the going rate, of course.'

Focus, Kate, focus. 'No, honestly, that's not necessary. It'll give me an opportunity to hand out my business cards — you never know, some guests might live in London.'

'I insist.' He pursed his lips. 'White Rocks isn't a charity and — '

He sounded like me when Izzy had offered to pay me more than her other staff. Perhaps I could work out a way to make him feel better, without actually being paid.

'Wait — OK, I do have a few demands, as payment in kind.' I cleared my throat. 'An all-day breakfast whenever I want one and . . . you not telling me off if I want to go to the golf course and admire the swallows.'

''Ouse martins,' he corrected, and we smiled.

'As for the seventies night, I'd simply call it 'disco'. That way I can include any modern dance songs for the younger guests, such as those by Beyoncé and Calvin Harris, alongside old favourites by the Jacksons and Bee Gees.'

'Surrre.'

'And the jazz evening . . . I've been thinking — that's probably going to alienate younger guests. Why don't we do an ABBA night instead, just to play it safe this week? Everyone has seen the film *Mama Mia* and — '

'Not me.'

'How did you miss that?'

He shrugged. 'Not really my thing.'

'Oh, come on, even husbands, boyfriends, dads loved that movie.'

'Which year did it come out?'

'In 2008,' I replied, without hesitation. 'I went for my twentieth birthday.'

'I wasn't in England that year. Out fighting, I was. The Middle East,' he said, voice suddenly monotone. He stared past my shoulder and instinctively I knew not to pry.

'Come on. We'd better get busy,' I said. 'I'll head back to my chalet and see how Izzy is getting on with phoning her mum. We're hoping she can send down some branded items for the café-bar.'

Tremain cleared his throat. 'I'll go pick up the plasterboard for the temporary wall.'

I headed back to the chalet and enjoyed the breeze, glad that the humid weather had broken for a while. White clouds fluffed themselves up proudly in the sky, which was just as well, as the day ahead made for hot work.

I rearranged the bar and tables of the new Donuts & Daiquiris, to make it stand out from the restaurant next door. Then I helped Guvnah produce some signs. Lucas made us sandwiches for lunch while he experimented with new dishes — the classics by the sounds of it, including chicken tikka masala and apple crumble with custard. Geoff parked his van up outside, having decided to clean it up on site — sixties music blaring out, of course. Tremain and I gave him a hand to polish the frying plates and wash down the outside. Then Tremain drove him to the wholesalers to buy big squirty bottles of mustard, hot-dog rolls for freezing, tins of the sausages and kilos of minced beef. Just like in the old days, Geoff insisted he'd make what he could from scratch.

'It may be fast food,' he said, 'but the preparation doesn't have to be fast too.' His next few days would be spent making his own burgers to freeze, plus chilli sauce and coleslaw from scratch.

With a yawn, at around seven, I made my way back to the chalet, leaving Izzy behind to — there is no other word for it — *flirt*, with Greg, under the guise of him taste-testing her cocktails. I felt desperate for a shower and a slug of something icy. I took out my keys and stepped onto the decking porch. Out of nowhere, Lucas appeared, looking pretty hot in a tight black T-shirt and fitted jeans. Talk about bedroom hair! He smoothed it down — pointlessly, as the feisty breeze ruffled it again. A cigarette hung casually out of the corner of his mouth, giving him a dangerous edge, like a cowboy about to draw his pistol.

'Have you forgotten our dinner date?' he said, with one of his teasing half-smirks.

I blushed. How did I manage that? 'Um, of course not.'

'Then you and I can go over any new ideas Tremain and Kensa have had and see what we can add to help turn the future of this place around.'

My chest glowed. What a dedicated employee. Clearly Tremain wasn't a very good judge of character. I mean warning me off, because Lucas was supposedly trouble with the ladies? From what I'd seen that had to simply be down to jealousy. Lucas was polite, complimentary, an industrious worker . . .

I beamed. 'Just give me fifteen minutes to shower and change.'

'No problem.' He ran a hand across his stubbly chin.

Lucas must have been in his early thirties, but there was no hint of a receding hairline. He was manly. Confident. Virile. Everything a modern woman could want. Forget this namby-pamby metrosexuality. Who wanted a guy who'd borrow your bathroom products? Whistling in the shower, I washed away the grime of the day, humming one of the cheeriest songs ever, 'Walking on Sunshine'. I couldn't believe my luck that, after the bad news of losing my flat and the Stanley Hotel singing gig, just days later I was spending lots of lovely time with Guvnah and . . . I bit my top lip. Deep breath. Yes, I was, to some degree, mixing again with the opposite sex.

151

Once dry, I yawned again and pulled a grey lacy blouse out of my cupboard, along with a white flared vintage skirt. I released my hair from the shower cap and ran a brush through it, before applying a smudge of fudge eyeshadow and slipping on my platform sandals. Even though we'd been inside most of the time, my skin had tanned a little and long-lost freckles had reappeared across my nose. I turned to leave the bedroom, just happening to spy the red heart wind spinner, hanging from the ceiling.

I stood still for a moment and realised today was the first day, in a long time, that I hadn't thought much about Johnny and the brutal way he'd been taken from me. The police at the door. My sobs as they said the words 'flooded road', 'skidded' and 'fatal car accident'. My trembling voice as I insisted I would be the one to inform his parents. His mother's wail.

I shook myself, locked the chalet behind me and smiled as Lucas jumped up, quickly ending a call. He shoved his mobile into his back pocket, dropped his cigarette onto the ground and stubbed it out with his foot. Then he placed his hands on my shoulders. A woodsmoke smell distracted me for a second. There were no guests — who on earth would be preparing a barbecue?

152

'You look beautiful, Kate. Understated but sophisticated. It's an honour to be seen out with you tonight.'

I gazed into those charcoal eyes that promised all sorts, but mainly an escape from the last ten months; from staring at the wind spinner, full of regret, wishing time and time again that Johnny wasn't dead. I swallowed. For some reason, on this holiday, I seemed to be making progress with accepting that Johnny would never, ever come back and, before I knew it, I'd leant forward, and as if on automatic, my hands wrapped around Lucas's neck. Our lips touched. Then parted. I was in the process of taking a huge emotional step when a woman's scream interrupted the first kiss I'd had for a very long time.

# 10

I jumped back and turned around to see Maria, a Spanish woman who worked for housekeeping. She pointed to the chalet to the left of mine. Smoke bellowed out of an open side window. Tangerine flames flashed from inside.

'I fetch Mr Maddock,' she said.

Lucas stood open-mouthed while this emergency extinguished the awkwardness of our first kiss. There was no time for me to analyse why it hadn't set me on fire. Talking of which . . . 'Do you think anyone is in there? I can't hear anyone shouting, but perhaps they are unconscious — we should check,' I said.

He shuffled from side to side. Surely self-assured Lucas wasn't embarrassed after we'd snogged? 'No. I doubt it. The resort is empty. I'll go and call the fire engine out.'

Before I could say any more, he'd disappeared. Odd. He had his mobile on him. Why did he need to phone from reception? No doubt there was a certain protocol to follow. Still . . . I approached the chalet and flinched as acrid smoke snuck around to its front door, where I stood.

I hopped from foot to foot and turned around again. Where *was* Tremain? He'd know if a member of staff or anyone else had been living in this chalet. Yet it was early evening and unlikely that someone was in there fast asleep. Unless they'd been drinking and passed out or collapsed due to illness.

I squinted and tried to see into the lounge, but smoke now obscured all the windows, with the occasional flicker of orange. I groaned, agreeing with my conscience — and my curiosity — that there was only one course of action now. I ran back to my chalet and, with fumbling hands, unlocked the front door. I threw my clutch bag on the floor and grabbed a tea towel, before running it under the kitchen tap. Within a couple of minutes I was back by the other chalet. Deep breaths. Then I covered my face with the wet tea towel and pulled open the front door. I stood back for a few seconds, to let smoke escape.

'Anyone there?' I hollered.

No response.

Flames licked walls on the left and mostly came from the sofa. I squinted again. Ow. My eyes stung. Crouching down, I entered. The chalet looked empty. I could see no personal belongings. Nevertheless, I had to check and, heart racing, headed for the bedrooms at the back. There the air cleared a little and I flung open two doors. All the beds were empty and not even made up. Thank goodness for that.

Chest tight and wheezy, I spun around and my stomach twisted. Flames had spread across, to the middle of the lounge. I swallowed, mouth feeling dry and scratchy, even though it was behind the wet tea towel. I gave a raspy cough that reminded me of my chain-smoking granddad. What if a flame caught my top? Or my hair? From head to toe I was highly flammable. Why oh why had I splashed myself all over with perfume? And there was now no way I could exit the way I'd come in.

I froze to the spot. Here I was alone with the gods. Alone with my mortality. Had I made good use of my life? Wasted it? Spent it wisely? Would many people miss me?

I shouted out, but my voice just gave a squeak and I realised my whole body shook. I stepped forward and could just see Tremain out of the window, on my left. We caught each other's eye before the smoke bellowed between us. A voice yelled, 'Step back.' Eyes watering, I returned to the bedrooms.

Crash. Glass shattered. Gulping with panic, I made my way back to the lounge, by feeling the walls, as it stung my eyes to try to focus. I remembered something I'd read about keeping near the floor if you were in a fire. Feeling hotter than I had at any time during the humid summer, I crouched down and slowly kept moving on my knees. A blistering sensation against my face reminded me of childhood Guy Fawkes Nights and getting told off for standing too close to bonfires.

'Kate! Kate, where are you?' called a strong Cornish accent. Tremain. Thank you, thank you. And, immediately, for no rational reason, I felt completely safe.

I pulled away the tea towel. 'Here! By the bathroom. I'm on the floor,' I croaked.

Within seconds, strong hands slid under my armpits and hauled me up. An arm swept under my legs and Tremain carried me easily towards the left-hand smashed window. Breaking glass scrunched under his feet. Lucas stood outside and stretched his arms forward, inky eyes wide. Tremain passed me through the hole to him. Moments later, I lay on the grass, surrounded by the two men, Izzy, Geoff, Guvnah, Kensa and Maria.

I rolled onto my side and coughed violently.

'Back off, everyone, give her some space,' said Tremain. I looked up. Charcoal smudges streaked his face. Gently, he sat me up and pushed an open bottle of water to my lips.

'What on earth were you thinking of,' he said gently.

I wiped my mouth and gulped, suppressed a sob and tried to control my shaking shoulders.

'She's in shock,' muttered Izzy.

'Brave Bella,' said Maria.

'She could have got herself killed,' muttered Tremain.

'I thought someone was in there,' I said and heard a siren in the distance.

'No point saving someone, if you are only going to get yourself or someone else killed in the process.' He looked at me with eyes that momentarily expressed a chink of injured depths.

'It was a split-second decision,' I said and coughed again, tears running down my face.

'And what about the people you left behind? How would they have felt — and managed? Izzy, your family . . . ?'

'I didn't realise the flames would spread so quickly.' The siren was deafening now.

'The number-one action in any emergency is risk assessment,' he said, sounding as if he still wore military uniform.

'Leave it, mate,' said Lucas and patted my leg. 'Come on. She's been through enough. You can give her the health and safety drill when she's feeling better.'

'Tremain, let's go. The fire engine's here. We must ring the insurance people. Start to get this sorted. Let Izzy look after her friend,' murmured Kensa, and the two women exchanged a look.

I sniffed and dried my eyes with my arm, at last breathing more easily. Izzy washed my face with a tissue and water. Within seconds, a paramedic knelt by my side while a fire officer ordered everyone away from the chalet.

An ambulance took me to hospital. People visited. The evening became a blur of lung and blood tests. It was only later on, when the chaos had subsided, that I realised how reckless I'd been; how lucky I was that the effects of smoke inhalation hadn't taken hold. Tremain had talked sense.

'The fireman found cigarette stubs but they think the fire was caused by a scented candle on the windowsill,' said Kensa, when she visited, bearing a box of chocolates. She sat down on the bed, her ginger hair providing a welcome bit of colour against the white, clinical surroundings. 'Seems like it fell onto a newspaper on the sofa. Once the flames reached a certain height, they reckon the net curtains ignited. Our sofas have passed all safety checks but, even so, this one couldn't stand up to the sustained heat.'

I pushed myself upwards, into a sitting

position, and jostled against the pillows behind my back. 'A scented candle? But no one lived there.'

Kensa's face flushed. 'They also found a pink leopard-print bra. Seems like a lovers' tryst might have taken place. A scrap of charred newspaper was found outside with today's date.' She shrugged. 'No sign of a break-in, though. You didn't hear anything from your chalet next door?'

I shook my head. 'I'd only just got back and had a quick shower. Look, thanks for visiting. Sorry for all the fuss. I hope it hasn't distracted people from the important stuff — three more days of rebranding the resort. I've managed to persuade Guvhah and Geoff to go home. The doctor has just got to discharge me and then, a bit later on, Izzy is going to pick me up.' I stared at the white bed covers. 'Tremain hasn't visited — not that there is any reason he should. I know how busy you both are but . . . he thinks I'm really stupid, right?' I looked up to meet her gaze.

She squeezed my hand. 'Just ignore him, dearie. Tremain . . . The whole incident reminded him of something in his past. Something we don't talk about much.' She bit her lip.

'To do with his army time, before White Rocks?' I said.

'He told you that?' He mouth fell open. 'About his experiences in the Middle East?'

'Not really. No details. I just know he used to be in the services and that he's only been here for a year.'

'Yes. A year. Almost exactly.' Her lilting voice wavered. 'And that was a year after he left the army and my husband left me.'

'I'm sorry — about your husband.'

She gave a half-smile. 'Don't be. Ultimately he was a loser. He acted like lord of the manor, all that time the resort did well, with our fancy guests. Then when the recession hit, lost interest. He left with a twenty-three-year-old pool attendant. Tremain sees him occasionally. Apparently they are expecting.'

Ouch. Now I squeezed her hand back. It had been hard enough losing Johnny, and we'd only been together for a few years.

'So . . . Tremain . . . the Middle East . . . ?'

Kensa averted her eyes. 'He did several tours of duty there, over the years. Saw things no man — or woman — should witness. Lost comrades. Killed people. Learnt to hold things in and keep on a brave face.' Her voice wavered and she gave a small smile. 'Believe it or not, I think he likes you. He never normally mentions his military career to anyone.'

A fuzziness filled my chest and, for the first

161

time in hours, I smiled.

'Tremain has avoided social contact since leaving the military,' she continued. 'He put off coming back here to work, because he didn't want to mix with people. But I struggled without my husband for a year and even though I told him I'd employ a deputy manager to help, somehow Tremain found out how tough things had been and he insisted on coming back. He's very loyal.' She cleared her throat. 'But, yes, you haven't known him for long but already the two of you have had several conversations, no?'

I nodded. Curiouser and curiouser. Why had Tremain become such a loner? Why did he feel able to talk to me?

\* \* \*

The words 'avoided social contact' rang in my ears a couple of hours later, as I lay in my own bed, back at the chalet. Izzy lay next to me having provided popcorn and hot chocolate, after painting our nails. What with setting up a branch of Donuts & Daiquiris, it looked as if our spa treatment plans were shelved, so we had to fit those essential girlie moments in whenever we could. I'd painted her hands and she'd painted my toes.

'Avoided social contact,' I said. 'What do

you think she meant by that?' I asked.

'Kate! You've already asked me at least three times.'

I blushed. 'Short-term memory loss must be a side-effect of smoke inhalation.'

'Or of being a super-hero.' She turned and kissed me on the cheek. 'Kate Golightly, you were so brave today. But don't ever do anything like that again.'

'I don't feel like a hero. I feel foolish.'

She passed me the popcorn bowl and I shoved in a large mouthful.

'Greg thinks you're super. Good thing for our friendship that he isn't your type! Whereas sexy Poldark Lucas . . . '

I stopped chewing for a moment. How would it be with him tomorrow, after our snog?

'I thought he might be my type, but when we kissed . . . '

Izzy spluttered. 'Hold the front pages!' She glared at me accusingly. 'There has been lip-to-lip action and you never told me?'

'It has been a rather busy evening,' I said and chuckled.

Izzy brought up her knees and hugged them. 'Tell me everything! Was his mouth soft? What did he do with his hands? How did he smell?'

'Izzy! Those are the sort of questions a

teenager might ask! And anyway, what about you and Greg? Did he like your cocktails?'

'Hmm. Especially the Slow Screw Against the Wall.' Her infectious laugh resounded around the room. 'Nah. Only joking. But he's really sweet. Funny, too. We, um, kissed too, this evening, just before I came out to pick you up.'

'Now who's been holding back information!' I raised one eyebrow and she twisted a lock of that short peroxide hair.

'Oh, Kate, he's adorable; took my breath away. The room spun, ten minutes passed like two, tingles sparked up all over my body . . . '

I put up my hand. 'Enough. I'm still in a delicate condition.'

A dreamy expression across her face, Izzy stared ahead for a moment. I sipped my hot chocolate. Why hadn't my kiss with Lucas felt like that? The red heart wind spinner fleetingly caught my eye. Perhaps I was just out of practise. I gazed at the shiny red metal and, to my surprise, didn't feel the urge to check out Johnny's Facebook page or study his photos on Instagram. Instead, I felt a twinge of guilt and my eyes pricked. Would Johnny think me unloyal? My throat hurt. No. Johnny always said that life was for living and rarely had lie-ins or spent evening after evening in front of the telly. Plus, I remembered my feelings of mortality in the burning chalet. I couldn't live with regrets for ever. Perhaps . . . my chest squeezed . . . perhaps it really was time to move on.

My throat felt scratchy. *Move on* — individually such innocuous words but together, loaded with significance. Johnny had been such a big part of my life, even after his death. My chest squeezed tighter. Was me thinking of other men letting him down? I sniffed and smiled briefly. No. Johnny was practical to the last. His granddad had hooked up with his single neighbour just six months after his grannie died. Johnny couldn't have been happier for him. Said that in his view, the new relationship didn't detract from what his granddad had enjoyed with his grandmother; that love gave life purpose, whether it was for a person, vocation or pet.

'Guess we'd better get some sleep. Lots to do tomorrow,' I mumbled, suddenly wanting to be on my own. 'First thing, I'm going to check out the sound equipment for Monday's disco night.' I glanced sideways at Izzy as she tidied up some stray bits of popcorn. 'So why *do* you think Kensa was so secretive about her son leaving the army?'

Izzy stopped tidying and rocked her head from side to side. 'It could be . . . Nah. Probably not.'

'What?'

She sighed. 'My Uncle Ron. Got himself into a bit of a mess a few years back. His car-selling business was doing badly. He fiddled his tax form.'

'And?'

'Ended up getting a two-year sentence. When he came out he never called it prison. Only referred to it as his 'trip away'. Maybe Tremain was thrown out of the services or even jailed.'

'But what for? I can't imagine anything serious.'

'Well, it might not be that at all,' she said and swung her feet off the bed and onto the floor. 'But it could explain why he and Kensa are so cagey about his former career.'

Tremain? With some sort of black mark against his character? I guessed that was possible. And he did have that funny scar I'd seen at Guvnah's. Perhaps he had a history of violence — but his gentle touch and my heart told me that couldn't be true. Maybe Lucas knew more about it. Hmm. Lucas. How had our kiss been for him? Was I still in with a chance of taking him to Saffron's party? Treating myself to another all-day breakfast the next morning, before checking out the sound equipment, would probably be the best way to find out.

# 11

Wow. Friday already. Three days to the reopening of White Rocks. The less humid weather suited everyone on site. What a list of tasks lay ahead of us. Kensa would go shopping for inflatables for the pool, to make it more fun for young ones. Izzy would practise the new Cornish-themed doughnut decorations plus wait for a delivery of all our branded extras — her mum had posted them express delivery. Tremain had to work on the gardens, to spruce the place up. Housekeeping would vacuum and polish and scrub. Geoff was staying at the cottage to make his chilli sauce and would later shop for napkins, cooking oil — all the little things he hadn't bought yet. And then this afternoon Guvnah and I planned to visit some of the chalets, to paint an image of Rocky Rabbit onto the wall of every children's bedroom.

But this morning? I'd sing through part of my playlist for the disco evening on Monday, to test the entertainment area's acoustics — after the biggest all-day breakfast. I snuck out early, chest back to normal after the smoke of the evening before — unlike my hair which still stank and needed three washes before it remotely smelt of the passion fruit shampoo. I wore beige three-quarter-length trousers and a white blouse, with beads hanging from the neckline and a fringe all around the bottom hem. Guvnah despaired sometimes at my bland choices, but working with a best friend like psychedelic Izzy, I figured my subdued shades helped the universe balance things out. Whistling a Michael Jackson tune, I headed for the reception building.

'Morning, Kate!' called Maria, as she passed in a housekeeping buggy. 'You feel OK today?'

'Yes. Thank you,' I called back and gave the thumbs-up. Although not one hundred per cent between you and me. Truth be told, I still felt foolish — risking my life for nothing. I should have heeded Lucas's conviction that the chalet would be empty.

'Well, I think you've got guts,' said Lucas, as he sat down next to me to eat. He'd rustled up the perfect breakfast, knowing by now that I liked no kippers and extra baked beans. The crisp fried bread felt so indulgent — a real no-no for the cholesterol-obsessed twenty-first century. And he'd grilled tomatoes so that they melted in the mouth — same for the mushrooms that had been lightly fried.

'Guts or no sense?' I said and gave a wry smile. 'Tremain was right. I could have got killed. All for nothing.'

'But you didn't know that.' Lucas wiped his greasy fingers and rubbed his hand up and down my bare arm. I waited for chemistry between us to spark. However, since the original excitement over finding my very own Poldark had subsided, I realised that this romance — if that's what it was — might be a slow-burner.

Romance. Gosh. I hadn't talked of that for a while. I chewed a mouthful of bacon and relished the smoky flavour. I stared at Lucas — that dirty gold skin, the foppish hair, that dangerous stubble, a teasing sense of humour, that hard-working ethic . . . He was the whole package, right? I'd be stupid not to consider him as more than just a companion to a wedding.

'Have I got egg on my face?' he said.

My cheeks burned. 'Sorry. I just wondered . . . has anyone ever said you're a doppelganger for Poldark?'

Lucas stretched back in his chair and burst out laughing. 'Yep. All the time. I'm used to it now. A lookalike agency even approached me last year.'

'That could have paid well.'

He shrugged. 'Cooking is what I love. And

I don't ride horses. Nor do I know the first thing about mining. I'd probably be a huge disappointment.' A tide of emotion swept through those dark eyes and a muscle flinched in his cheek — the first hint that perhaps cocksure Lucas actually lacked confidence.

'I doubt you could ever disappoint a woman — being a whizz in the kitchen would notch up a thousand Brownie points.'

'Yep, but life isn't just about impressing the opposite sex. It's about impressing yourself; having self-respect. And that earns you the respect of others like your friends, colleagues and parents.' He fiddled with his watch strap. 'My dad has had high hopes for me. Working as a lookalike wouldn't impress him much.'

This wasn't the first time he'd mentioned his father and I was about to say aren't you too old to worry about what he thinks, when I realised that I was no better trying to impress Saffron, a mere friend — and ex-friend at that — so talk about being a hypocrite.

'How about dinner tonight?' I said, brightly. 'Seeing as last night's date never took place?'

He kissed me on the cheek. 'Sounds great.' He stood up and took my plate. 'Just don't go hurling yourself into any other emergency situations, before we've had a chance to leave the resort.'

'No need to tell me.' I groaned.

'Now go and sing some cool tunes. I'll hear them from the kitchen.'

'Still creating the perfect menu?'

He sighed. 'I'm trying desperately to come up with my own quality version of burgers, and chicken nuggets that will still appeal to kids but be reasonably healthy.'

'Good luck with that,' I said. 'In my experience, nothing satisfies a kid's taste buds more than saturated fat, additives and sugar when on holiday.'

Jokingly, Lucas held his head in his hands and I grinned as he strode off to the kitchen. Humming, I went into the open area ahead, in between the reception and the restaurant. Its back glass wall gave a great view of the swimming pool. Around stood comfy leather chairs, circling low coffee tables, plus a snooker table to the back left and a fruit machine to the right.

As you entered this area, on the immediate left there was a small podium with a mike-stand and DJ turntable. Plus, a CD machine with big speakers and a karaoke machine leaning against the wall. I plugged the mike in and switched it on.

'Everything OK?' said Tremain, who'd been polishing the coffee tables. He put down his cloth. 'How are you feeling? After last night.'

'My pride's dented. I feel silly. Fine

though. This sing-through will tell me if my lungs have fully recovered.'

Tremain curled his hand around the top of my arm. It felt as if liquid lava suddenly flowed from that spot to my chest and cheeks. 'Sorry, if I was a bit harsh last night. Proper brave, you were. I just . . . '

'It's OK.' I recalled Kensa's words about the fire reminding him of something that had happened in his past. 'How are you?' I leant forward to sniff his hair and he stepped back.

'What are you doing, woman?'

I giggled. 'Just seeing if you've managed to get rid of the smell of smoke. I had to take more than one shower.'

He leant forward to smell mine. His proximity made my palms feel sweaty. Confusion washed over me. It was so long since I'd dated and now I wasn't so sure of the telltale signs of attraction. Tremain caused a physical reaction, but him and me? No. Often he was rude, untalkative, detached . . . He chuckled. 'Jeez. You smell like you spent the night enjoying a barbecue on the beach.'

'Have the firemen any more details about how the fire started? Kensa filled me in on what they thought yesterday.'

He shook his head. 'Nothing to add. The only bits of evidence are the shreds of newspaper, scented-candle holder and pink leopard-print bra — a size ten from M&S, apparently.'

'Clearly not mine, then, Sherlock Holmes,' I said and flexed my arms in the air, taking on a muscleman position.

'Nor mine,' he said and grinned before heading over to the reception desk.

Blimey. Perhaps that smoke had laughing gas as a secret ingredient. As he walked away, I admired his strong outline, remembering how he'd swept me into his arms last night. Hands up, that is hardly an alpha-female thought, but, as you know, I am an avid fan of historical romances, featuring dashing heroes on steeds.

I picked up the mike. 'Testing, testing, testing, one, two, three.' Hmm. Good quality. I wouldn't have to overstretch my voice. However, just to double-check the area's suitability, I ran through a couple of songs. 'Blame it on the Boogie' was always a sure winner, and got people on their feet to do the actions to the words 'moon' and 'sunshine'.

As my CD played, I swayed side to side. Often for gigs I was lucky enough to have a mate, Jim, play his portable piano, but, failing that, I had a good range of recorded soundtracks, minus the vocals — compilations that I'd put together myself. Like this one for a disco evening. I had another for jazz. ABBA as well. A fifties one and another for eighties-retro evenings which had been really popular over recent years.

I closed my eyes as I sang and got into the zone, so that I could exactly judge the pitch and tone of my voice for this venue. When I opened them, Lucas had come over. The Peppards had arrived and sat watching, him in baggy knee shorts and a polo-neck shirt with a designer logo on the front. She wore a tight cream blouse with a plunging neckline and shorts that showed off the fact that she must spend every spare hour in the gym. Tremain now stood behind the computer at reception, fingers tapping in time on the desk.

When I stopped everyone gave me a quiet round of applause. I smiled. This was the one area of my life where I wasn't the slightest bit embarrassed. Compliment my outfit or make-up and my ears would probably glow scarlet but clap my singing and I'd just bow my head or give you the thumbs-up. It wasn't because I considered my voice amazing — it was because the approval meant less. Of course positive reviews lit up my world for a while but bad ones would never stop me singing. It was what I did. It was me. Music ran through my bones. It gave me purpose. Singing was my past, present, future and any afterlife.

I closed my eyes again. How good it felt to be performing. A few days away from a mike made me feel like an addict reaching the point of needing a detox — singing again was the ultimate, feel-good rehab. I opened my eyes as the last notes of the CD player stopped, to see Mr Peppard shrug, pick up his golf magazine and get to his feet.

'Coming to get a coffee?' he said to his wife and jerked his head towards Donuts & Daiquris. You couldn't miss Izzy, who had just arrived in her favourite yellow tie-dye T-shirt. While the resort wasn't officially open, it made sense to serve people for early feedback.

Mrs Peppard glanced at Lucas. 'No, dear, I'm not thirsty. I'll just sit here and listen to some more music.' She gave a false-sounding laugh. 'And I'd only be tempted to have one of those doughnuts. Have to watch my figure — or no one else will.'

A meaningful comment directed at Lucas?

One more song, I thought. Something modern. I fast-forwarded the CD to one of my favourite Beyoncé tracks — suitably, for me, 'Single Ladies'. Johnny never got as far as choosing a ring, let alone putting it on my finger — although, in a funny way, it always felt as if he had. Our future together had seemed so indisputable. Or so I'd believed.

I stared over at reception. Kensa had appeared and was trying to get Tremain to dance. Oh the horror on his face. Kensa looked about twenty years younger. It was the first time I'd seen her joking since we'd arrived. She must have been feeling positive about the week ahead. Mrs Peppard stood up and grabbed Lucas's arm. Politely, he shook his head, but she pulled him nearer and placed one hand on his shoulder, leaving him no choice but to slide his arm around her waist. He shot a look backwards, towards Donuts & Daiquiris. Mr Peppard was sitting down, hidden behind his golf magazine. His wife stared intently into Lucas's face. Her crush was more obvious than ever and reminded me of a scene from *Dirty Dancing*, where dance teacher Patrick Swayze is accosted by a wealthy woman holidaymaker.

'It's embarrassing for her — and her husband,' I said to Guvnah, later that afternoon, as we sat in the bedroom of chalet number six, painting an image of Rocky Rabbit onto the wall.

Guvhah adjusted her headband. We both wore long aprons and had tied our hair back. Despite this, she'd still got a splodge of white paint on her nose.

'She must be lonely.' My gran shrugged. 'Money alone doesn't bring you happiness.'

'Agreed. Her husband has always got his head in a newspaper or magazine, or is criticising her clothes. Bravo Lucas for remaining polite. He even kissed her hand at the end of the dance and led her back to her husband. Talk about well handled.'

Guvnah's tongue stuck out as she carefully drew an 'R' on the front of the rabbit. 'Tremain seems like a lonely chap to me,' she said. 'Looks like he could do with the love of a good woman.'

'You could be right. Just before she left to buy inflatables, Kensa asked if I have five minutes for a coffee. She's got it into her head that Tremain and I get on well. Said that tomorrow — the fifth of August — was a big day for him. Bad memories or something. The second anniversary of an event he would rather forget. Kensa just mumbled something about wishing he'd never signed up. She wouldn't say any more, but asked me to keep an eye on him.'

'He used to be in the army?' Guvnah stopped painting. 'Well, I never . . . Although I suppose that explains his love of the outdoors. You said yes to Kensa, then?'

'Naturally. Not sure how useful I'll be though, without more information.'

'Just stay close, I suppose — in case he needs a friendly face for a chat.' Guvnah shook her head. 'We take our Forces for granted. I'll never forget old Mr Bartholmew who lived next to me, as a child. Fought during the Second World War, he had, and used to walk around shouting, 'Bang!' He never recovered from all the shelling he experienced.' She sighed. 'I wonder what happened to Tremain.'

We both painted in silence for a few moments and then she cleared her throat. 'You and Facebook. Izzy told me you still chat with Johnny on there. Or rather talk to. Chat with would imply it was two-way, which it isn't. Sweetheart.' She pursed her lips and met my gaze. 'This pointless messaging has to stop.'

'How *could* she? That's breaking my confidence.'

'Kate, my precious girl . . . ' Guvnah held her brush in the air and continued to meet my glare. 'It's only because she cares. We all do. Me, Izzy, Geoff, your mum . . . '

'Really? Mum never mentions Johnny on the phone,' I muttered.

Guvnah shrugged. 'No. Because we've all been tiptoeing around you.'

Eyes tingling, I pulled a face.

'Geoff and I discussed it last night. You know I adore you. But now I've got you near me for a while, I feel it has to be said. Here you are, a young woman, on holiday, with delightful young men around. You are beautiful, talented, kind-hearted . . . isn't it about time you considered moving forwards with your life?'

'In my own time, thank you,' I said tightly and sat on the bed.

She sat down too and, with her free hand, slipped wrinkled fingers into mine and squeezed. 'Your constant clicks on Johnny's Facebook page . . . It's like someone visiting a grave more than once a day.' Guvnah cleared her throat. 'Usually it's people my age saying 'who knows what's around the corner', but you know that for sure, having lost Johnny so suddenly. Don't waste another minute, darling — please.'

My throat hurt at the pained expression on her face.

'It's like when your granddad passed — what I have with Geoff will never detract from that love. It's a completely separate relationship at a different stage of my life. Equally as special but in no way denigrating my first love'.

I nodded, recalling the comment Johnny made about his grandad's new relationship.

Guvnah paused for a moment. 'How often do you message him now?'

My throat tightened further. 'Not so often.

And these last few days, I've not even read through his posts.'

'But you still . . . I don't understand. What do you get out of it, when you aren't getting any response?'

'I . . . It gave me something to focus on, I suppose, at the beginning. Helped make each day seem more normal, checking his pages on Facebook and Instagram. And then it became a comforting habit.' I sighed. 'He always used to say I was obsessed with social media. Guess I'm proving his point.' I met her gaze. 'This week has actually made a difference though. New faces. A change of scenery. The fire. I haven't even looked at my phone today.'

'Perhaps it is time to unfriend him then,' she said. 'I know it's a big step but it only involves a few taps on the screen.'

It was great having a grandmother who kept up with all things technical. I loved seeing her watercolour paintings on Instagram and pretended to get very cross that painter her had more followers than singer me.

We stared at each other.

'What? Now? Right this minute?' I said.

Guvnah shrugged, but didn't take her eyes off my face.

Sitting in this bedroom reminded me of the smoke-filled ones I'd checked last night

— the wave of panic that I might die, without having fully lived my life. Then Johnny's face popped into my mind. The crinkly eyes. That mole just above his right eyebrow. The way his cheeks crumpled when he found something funny. All the little things. Then I saw Lucas, with his manly stubble and kiss-me-if-you-dare mouth. Finally, an image of Tremain hovered before my eyes. The determined gait. That short, short hair that begged to be ruffled. Those leaf-green eyes that for very brief flashes betrayed some deep hurt.

I refocused. Guvnah had started painting again and hummed one of Geoff's favourite tunes from the sixties. I got up, walked over to the little window, took my phone out of my pocket. I tapped the Facebook icon and hit 'Search'. Johnny's name always came up first. My finger hovered over the 'Friend' button. I tapped it and then moved my finger down to the 'Unfriend' option. I inhaled. Exhaled. My chest squeezed as if I'd been strapped into the tightest bodice ever from one of my historical TV series.

Finger shaking, I closed my eyes and pushed downwards. When I opened them again, Johnny and I were no longer Facebook friends. Guvnah didn't say anything as I brushed past her and out of the bedroom. Vision blurred, I headed out of the front door and outside. Despite the occasional white cloud, the August air felt warm and cheerful. Birds chirped. The freshly cut grass smelt fresh. A particularly adventurous brown bunny lolloped across my path. I snuck around the side of the chalet, leant against its wooden wall and sunk to the ground. Footsteps approached.

'Kate? Everything all right? I was just bringing you and your gran coffees and doughnuts — Izzy insisted.'

I looked up and, with the bright sky behind him, Lucas really could have been mistaken for the dreamy Poldark actor. He crouched down and laid his tray to one side. 'You don't look well. Think you need to go back to the hospital?'

I reached up with my hand and pulled him towards me. In that second I just . . . just needed some human contact of the romantic kind. I reached up with my other hand and gently tucked it behind his neck. Our mouths met. Urgently, I kissed him. No matter that all the old clichés of sparks flying and the earth moving didn't apply. It was purely physical, although I waited for some degree of emotion to kick in, but nothing. Was it like that for him?

Eventually, I pulled away nevertheless gratified because it was as if I was emerging from a thick fog that had followed my every step for months.

'Hey. Wow. I wasn't expecting that,' he said, one eyebrow raised.

'Me neither.' My mobile vibrated in my back pocket and I ignored the sensation as I caught my breath.

I was no longer chained to my phone — to Facebook — and, for the first time in ten months, I felt in charge of my own destiny.

# 12

'You kissed him? Again?' said Izzy, her finely plucked eyebrows practically disappearing into her hairline. We were setting out cocktail glasses in the bar. Saturday morning. Two days to go. We'd all achieved so much yet had so far to go. So much for a spa holiday! There was no time for beauty treatments. However, we had managed to get up early, have a swim and sauna.

'What's the big deal?' I said. 'I bet you've kissed Greg for literally hours by now.'

Her face broke into a broad smile. 'When I'm not laughing at his bad jokes, yes, but that's not the point. You can't compare. For you, Lucas is practically a celebrity! Just a peck on the cheek is a huge achievement! We should dye your hair red like that Demelza's.'

'Idiot,' I said and smiled. 'Next you'll expect me to get his autograph.'

She grinned and for a few moments polished a glass. 'But honestly, Kate,' she said eventually, in soft tones, 'it's great to see my best mate dipping her toe into rocky romance waters again.'

'You talked to Guvnah about me,' I said.

Her cheeks pinked up. 'Only because I've been so worried. I take my role as your auntie very seriously,' she said brightly, eyes nevertheless glistening.

I put down my tea towel and gave her a quick hug. 'I know. And I'll never be able to repay the support you've shown me over the last few months. I'm sorry you've worried. But I honestly feel I'm . . . moving on now. Bit by bit.' I stood back and rearranged glasses into orderly lines. 'I'm so thrilled that this place has given you the challenge you've been searching for,' I said, keen to change the subject. I wasn't ready to voice out loud the fact that I'd unfriended Johnny. It felt right but telling Izzy made it seem so final. I just needed a little more time to fully get my head around that and ignore the occasional jab of guilt. *Unfriend* was such a brutal word. 'Lucas is really interested in the reasons for your success.' I said. 'Last night he quizzed me all about your business secrets.'

'Like what?'

I picked up a bottle of superior vodka. 'The fact that you use only the best ingredients. None of this cheap stuff from the wholesalers. Plus the finest fruit to use as a garnish and good quality mixers. As for the doughnuts, they speak for themselves. All hand-crafted, with detailed decorations . . . Like the way, for this outlet, you've created flavours themed to Cornwall.' I shrugged. 'He wanted me to go into such detail, it's almost as if he's thinking of setting up his own bar. Perhaps he's planning ahead, in case White Rocks' rebranding doesn't work. He couldn't give up cooking though — maybe he'd open a bistro.'

'Are you going to tell him about Saffron's wedding and your need for a Poldark plus-one?'

'I will, but not quite yet. We're only just getting closer. I don't want him to think that's the only reason I'm interested in him.'

Izzy's face lit up. 'So it isn't?'

I sighed. 'Oh, Izzy, I just don't know. When we kiss, it's nice, and exciting because, well, obviously, it's been a while. But it doesn't feel how I remember, with Johnny. You know — a whirlwind of sensations spinning through my body.'

'*Nice* is a good place to start.'

I nodded. And I was heading for thirty. Johnny and I were in our early twenties when we first met. Perhaps this was 'mature love'.

'He is charming. We could chat easily for hours. He wanted to know all about my singing as well. Last night he got me to show him how the mike worked and looked through my CDs. He even wanted to borrow them to play at home.' I could just picture him in one of Poldark's foppish eighteenth-century blouses, singing Adam Ant and coming over all eighties New Romantic.

She grinned. 'Greg and I don't do much talking.'

I smiled back, but just with my mouth, not my heart. That's what the first few dates — the first months — should be like, right? But then, perhaps I was expecting too much. No two relationships were the same. I chewed on my top lip. And I may have unfriended Johnny on Facebook, but didn't have the strength to take down his red heart wind spinner. Not quite yet.

'So . . . ' I rubbed my hands. 'Are we starting to bake today? We can freeze some basic ring doughnuts — take the pressure off next week? Just tell me how I can help.'

'Yes, I just want to check through all my ingredients. Make sure I've got enough yeast, flour, butter and oil at least. And I've got a second-hand deep-fat fryer arriving from eBay this afternoon so I won't have to keep mithering Lucas to borrow his.'

'Did your mum remember to post us the injection nozzles?' Not a lot felt more satisfying than injecting cream into dough-nuts, plumping them up.

She nodded. 'Plus I've ordered edible rice paper stickers bearing the Rocky Rabbit logo

— they should arrive Monday or Tuesday.'

'It's all falling into place.' I gazed around. 'Get you — a doughnuts-and-cocktails magnate.'

'Couldn't have got my bigger plans started without you, clever girl,' she said. 'Wouldn't even have thought of this expansion idea.'

'What's this? A mutual appreciation society?' Lucas's face appeared around the temporary wall and he gave one of his teasing smirks. 'I can hear every word in my restaurant. That's plasterboard for you.' Greg appeared by his side. 'We were thinking,' continued Lucas, 'do you two fancy a double date this evening? Could be the last chance we get to go into town at night. Tomorrow is going to be hectic and once guests are here we'll probably all be working twenty-four-seven for a while.'

Tremain couldn't complain at Lucas's dedication. Twenty-four-seven? I gave him the thumbs-up.

'A double date sounds like a great idea,' said Izzy. 'Shall we all meet here at seven? Kensa told me about a great Italian restaurant with sea views.'

'It's a date,' said Greg and winked.

'Right. I'd better get on reorganising the kitchen,' said Lucas. 'Tremain's discovered a line of cheap crockery with pictures of rabbits on, for children's meals. He's off into Port Penny to pick them up from the local potter, who managed to order them in at cost price; in an early staff meeting this morning he said something about having an errand to run as well, and not being back until late.' Lucas shook his head. 'All sounded a bit mysterious to me. You'd think he'd rush back here, what with us being so close to the re-opening. And his face . . . ' Lucas sucked in his cheeks. 'We're all stressed, but Jeez, he looked downright miserable this morning.'

'Who did?' said a loud, Cornish voice.

Lucas rolled his eyes and turned around to Tremain. 'Er, Mr Peppard. His wife was trying to persuade him to go for a peaceful swim, before all the families arrive next week. I don't think he's the sporty type.'

Ooh. My curiosity had risen at the mention of Tremain running an 'errand' and Kensa's words about today being difficult for him. My stomach scrunched as I noticed the way Tremain's shoulders slouched. His face looked pale, with circles darker than ever under his eyes, as if he hadn't slept for a week. Mind you, he probably hadn't with all the strain he'd been under, plus he had been in a fire . . . perhaps I was worrying about nothing; maybe this was my curiosity magnifying thoughts in my imagination and

189

causing trouble, as it often did.

'Heh, Kate,' said Izzy, in a low voice, while my attention was still focused on my promise to Kensa, 'why don't I innocently mention Saffron's wedding tonight, when we're all out? Mention that you are looking for a plus-one? I bet Lucas jumps in and offers to accompany you. I get the feeling he likes posh dos.'

I turned to her. 'Huh? Tonight? I . . . don't know. I was going to wait a while.' Tremain. I needed to find a way to shadow him today.

'True, but you can't spring it on him at the last minute,' she said.

'Yes, I suppose so,' I said, not really listening. I strode over to Tremain. 'Fancy trying a mocktail?' I owed it to Kensa to try to find out more about his plans for the next few hours.

'You think I've got time for *that*?' he snapped. Without saying goodbye, he stalked off. I ran after him. 'Whoa. Hold up. What's the matter? Where's the man who shared a joke with me yesterday?'

He gazed at the ground. 'Just a lot on my mind, so I have — you know, like the future of my family's business riding on how things go next week.'

I touched his arm but he shook it off and looked up. 'Haven't you got doughnuts to make or scales to practise?'

Ooh. He'd really grabbed my attention now. I thought we'd bonded a little after Thursday's scorching life and death situation.

'I . . . need to go into town; wondered if you could give me a lift.'

'Nope. Stuff to do. Anyway, what do you need at this late stage?'

'Cocktail sticks,' I said, remembering that Izzy had to pop out for them later. I could save her the trip. 'And paper coasters. We forgot to order everything, so rang around a few bars in Port Penny. One called the Cocktail Hour was particularly obliging.'

'Ah, rrright — the owner, Tim Watson, knows my dad.'

I studied his face. Perhaps this errand he was so cagey about had something to do with his father and the imminent baby. That would explain not talking about it. He wouldn't want to upset Kensa. Or was Izzy right, he had been in trouble in the army . . . perhaps he *had* been jailed and had some kind of parole officer to visit? But then what did that have to do with today being the anniversary of something bad? Kensa said it was two years ago his dad had ran off with the pool attendant. Could today have been the day he actually left? That might make sense. They say divorce is traumatic for a child, be them an adult or young kid, I stared at him. Not that I'd know. My dad left a month after I was born. The father of my younger siblings came in and out of our lives, but we knew he wasn't reliable so I'd got used to thinking that just having one parent was pretty normal.

'Surely small things like coasters can wait a few days?' said Tremain.

'Nooo. Giving guests a supreme doughnut and cocktail experience is all about the detail. We need that from the start.'

He threw his hands in the air. 'Order them express delivery off the Internet. They'll probably be cheaper.'

I folded my arms. A promise was a promise and Kensa had enough on her mind without her son going AWOL. And the more fuss he made, the more I thought Kensa was right, he shouldn't be alone. 'Don't you think it's the least you can do? Since arriving I've been bruised around the eye for breaking up a fight and done my best to save people from a fire.'

'No one was at risk,' he muttered.

'I'm sure you jumped into situations like that, at some point during your army career,' I said and eyed him closely.

His shoulders drooped. 'Yes. And I learnt the hard way that it doesn't always end well.'

I held my breath. Was he about to confide in me? Share his big secret? No. For several moments he just stared into the distance.

Eventually, I raised my eyebrows. 'Look. I've agreed to be paid for my singing in breakfasts. All I'm asking for is a ride.'

'I also gave you permission to walk on the golf course, to watch the 'ouse martins.'

'Swallows, you mean,' I said.

Nearly. He nearly cracked a smile.

'Oh, for God's sake. You're a rrright pain. So go on, get in my van — I'll be there in a minute.'

A minute? More like twenty. A waste as there was so much to do today. But I bit my lip when he got into the driving seat. No point in complaining, he might change his mind about letting me tag along.

'You'll have to get a bus back,' he said. 'I'm going to be out a while.'

'We could meet for lunch?' I said.

'No time.'

Back to being a robot, huh? I shot him a sideways glance and longed to curl my arm around his shoulders to give him a hug. His abruptness didn't niggle me so much now. I was beginning to realise, there might be something serious — painful — at the root of it. I swallowed, thinking back to myself, over the last year. Some days, I hardly spoke to my colleagues at work, due to mooning around, missing Johnny. When I was in one of those moods, Izzy always knew a quick fix. As soon as six o'clock arrived, she would make me a strawberry Daiquiri and order pizza for us to eat, out the back, without any questions or judgements. That meant a lot to me at the time. I'd repay the favour by treating her to a cinema trip. Ever so hard I tried, to be cheery and not bring other people down, but Izzy always saw straight through a brave face. I glanced at Tremain again. So, I was trying not to judge his impolite manner.

'Such a gorgeous view,' I said, as we drove along the coast. Little fishing boats bobbed on turquoise water. Smooth scone-coloured sands contrasted the rugged cliffs. 'You must have loved growing up here. The most sand I ever saw, as a child, sat in Mum's egg-timer — apart from on our caravan holidays, when I'd spend every moment possible rock-pooling. A pretty shell seemed like treasure, back then.'

'It gave me a love of fresh air. Every summer was spent crabbing and swimming, when I wasn't helping out at White Rocks.' He shrugged. 'I guess holidays were rare for you, what with five siblings.'

'Too right. Guvnah and Granddad were always generous and helped us out, but I never went abroad until Jo — until my last boy-friend bought me a trip to Paris, as a surprise.'

'The girlfriend of one of my mates from my

last job originally came from Paris, moved here as a little girl. Her family gave him fancy ideas about art and music, we always said.' A brief smile crossed his face. 'I met her parents once. They couldn't understand a word I said.'

'No surprise there, even I have trouble!' I said and chuckled. 'Are you still in touch?'

Tremain's fingers tensed on the steering wheel and he shook his head.

We headed downhill, intermittently queuing behind tourist traffic or tractors, angry horns beeping from time to time. As we descended into Port Penny, I once again admired the narrow, cobbled roads and little cottages either side. Seagulls squawked and swooped as we neared the town, no doubt hoping to find scraps of last night's fish and chips. Expertly, Tremain navigated the tiny avenues and visitors, only having to brake once when a dog broke free from his leash which was tied up outside a café.

Eventually we turned into a small car park, opposite the harbour, belonging to a shop called Port Penny Pottery. I climbed out of the van and breathed in. Fish. Seaweed. 'Ew! What a stink!'

'You get used to it, over the years,' said Tremain.

'Good thing I'm just here for a holiday.'

He gave me the strangest of looks before jerking his head towards the back entrance to the pottery. 'Right. Business to do. The Cocktail Hour is just up the hill. Go out of this car park, turn left then left again at the boatshed. It's next door to the pharmacy.'

'Thanks,' I said and shivered. Grey clouds had come in and, for the first time in weeks, it looked like England was going to experience rain.

Tremain opened the van door and fumbled in the glove compartment. He straightened up and threw a small, floral umbrella across the van's roof to me. 'Here,' he said, gruffly. 'Mum left it last time I took her shopping.'

I smiled and took off my little rucksack to shove it in.

With that he was gone. Right. The Cocktail Hour first. Really quick so that I was back here to see where he went after collecting the crockery. My detective work would be stumped if he got in the van to drive elsewhere. Hopefully this errand was in the town and I could follow him on foot.

I shivered again, wishing I'd brought one of my cardigans. After turning left at the boatshed, I headed up the hill.

Children ran around eating fudge and carrying buckets. Sunglasses and caps had disappeared in favour of raincoats and umbrellas.

Not that it affected the number of people shopping and taking photos. I tapped on the window of the Cocktail Hour — Tim had said it would be closed but he'd be waiting for me to call. What a lovely man. He gave me plenty of coasters and cocktail sticks — the colourful, plastic ones that Izzy was so fond of, but couldn't be found in your usual supermarket.

Twenty minutes later, I was back on the cobbled avenue and hurried back to Port Penny Pottery. And just in time. When I arrived and stole carefully into the car park, Tremain was packing boxes into the boot of the van. OK, I admit it. I watched for a while, admiring his strength and those subtle biceps, as he easily lifted the cardboard boxes. His blue T-shirt pulled over his tight body in all the right places. His determined face wanted me to kiss it in an attempt to smooth out the frown lines. Mmm.

Gosh. Did I really just think that? Nah. Must be overtired. I mean, my fantasy figure was a long-haired, eighteenth-century Cornish miner, who wore loose clothes and was more athletic than stocky and firm. Tremain looked up, as if he knew he was being watched and I scuttled behind a bush, almost getting caught with my rucksack. When he'd gone back into the shop, I headed out to the front of the shop, crossed the road and stood behind a red letter box.

Fortunately, I'd had my sun cap in my bag and put that on. A spot of rain fell onto my arm. Great. I'd look really obvious if I put up his mum's umbrella. After what seemed an age, Tremain walked out of the car park. He turned right. Grateful for the crowds that had braved the threatening bad weather and disguised me, I tracked him, at a distance.

We passed a row of shops and then he veered right, up a hill, past a fish restaurant and a post office busy with people buying postcards and stamps. Finally, he stopped outside . . . a florist's? I stood outside a souvenir shop, opposite, hiding amongst shelves of swimming costumes and surf-boards. He disappeared inside and came out carrying a bunch of one, two, three . . . twelve red roses.

A sensation of nausea rose up the back of my throat as I stepped back. Oh. Tremain must have a girlfriend. Perhaps his errand today was nothing to do with the so-called sad anniversary. But why be so secretive about her? And why . . . why did I mind? Tremain meant nothing to me. I'd leave him to meet his lover. Yet, as I studied the scene where he stood, something didn't fit . . . his face. It didn't bear the expression of a man about to spend the afternoon enjoying a romantic tryst. The mouth drooped, to match his shoulders. He took a deep breath then started to walk back, in the direction of the harbour.

I followed him down the hill and the fishy smell became more pungent. Fishermen called out to each other and I saw the female one I'd mistaken for a man, on my first trip down here. I weaved my way in between holiday-makers on the beach and kept my distance from Tremain, glad for bodies to hide behind. And bless the stoic British, many of those bodies wore bikinis or Hawaiian swimming trunks, despite the drop in temperature. Children built sandcastles with moats. The most sensible person I saw lay fully clothed, behind a windbreaker, enjoying a steaming drink out of a flask. Seabirds swooped to pick up uneaten halves of sandwiches and, as we headed towards the right-hand, rocky side, tots stood holding fishing nets, squealing if they thought they'd seen a tiddler or a crab. Tremain pressed ahead, carrying the bouquet, now climbing larger rocks. My brow furrowed. He'd arranged to meet a girlfriend *here?* The imminent storm wouldn't make that very romantic.

And, of course, this hike had to be on a day I'd decided to wear my platform sandals. I climbed onto a large stone, covered with green seaweed and . . . Yes. You've guessed it, slipped and fell, right onto my bottom. Just as well. Great padding. As two nearby children giggled, their dad helped me balance as I stood up. I slipped off my shoes and put them in my rucksack, pushing them in carefully, so as not to bend the boxes of paper coasters. It was probably safer to climb with bare feet. By the time I'd thanked the dad and admired the kids' buckets full of the smallest fish you've ever seen, Tremain had disappeared.

I narrowed my eyes. Trickles of rain had turned into fat drops, but I was still loath to ruin my disguise and put up the conspicuous umbrella. I scanned the wall of rocks, squinted and right at the end was a stocky man, in a blue T-shirt, carrying something red. The bouquet of flowers. How on earth had he got there so quickly?

I pushed on, crouching as I crossed slippery stones, other people finally giving up and heading back to cover, off the beach. Noisily, I breathed, as the rocks got larger and I had to jump a couple of gaps. Tremain disappeared around to the right, at the furthest point of the cliff side and I crept up to the edge, clothes wet now, face soaked, wishing I'd tied my unruly hair back. Slowly, I peered around the corner. Huh? Tremain stood right at the edge of the water and one by one threw the roses out to sea.

Palms feeling sweaty, I squinted once more. Surely he wasn't about to do something stupid? My mind raced. My chest squeezed. No. Not Tremain. First, Johnny, and now ... I wasn't ready to go through losing anyone else I remotely cared about again. I stuffed my fist into my mouth as I gagged and the tide swept a couple of the flowers back, past me. I bent down to pick one up and smelt it, then put it back to continue whatever journey Tremain had intended. When I raised my head back up, Tremain sat on a rock and hugged his knees. Thank God. Thank God. He'd stayed on dry land.

My throat tightened. I blinked rapidly. He started to rock to and fro, hands covering his bowed head. Quietly, I clambered over, balancing as best I could on the slate-grey, wet rocks. The waves became bigger and pooled across to my feet as their crests broke. The smell of salt replaced the harbour's fishy stench.

'Tremain?' I said softly, as I stood behind him. He didn't turn around. Perhaps he hadn't heard due to the rising wind and rough water. 'Tremain?'

His face lifted. He turned and deep, sorrowful eyes met mine. He opened his mouth to speak, but changed his mind and looked away again. My chest ached, as I crouched down behind him. His body rocked forwards and backwards again, like an animal locked in a cage.

'Oh, Tremain,' I mumbled and slid my arms around his shoulders. Rain pelted now, as I leant my cheek on his shoulder and rubbed my hands up and down his arms. Slowly the rocking stopped and Tremain sat still, despite waves crashing near his legs.

'It's OK. I'm here. No need to talk,' I said. Many a lost moment I'd had like this, when Johnny first left, and talking had been the last thing on my mind. 'But we can't stay here for ever. If the storm worsens it could get dangerous.'

'But it ended so badly and was all my fault,' he said in a strangulated voice.

'What was?' I said gently and rubbed his back. A relationship? His career in the army? However, no more words came from him, so I scrambled to my feet, walked around to his side and held out my hand. Tremain looked up, took it and unsteadily got to his feet. He wiped his eyes. I stood on tiptoe and wrapped my arms around his neck. For what seemed like the longest time ever, we just hugged, despite the pelting rain, my racing pulse — and one heart-wrenching gulp from Tremain.

# 13

In a conventional relationship, with a normal person, connecting, like me and Tremain did, on the rocks, would make you closer, right? Not that I was looking for thanks from him but a bit of friendship, well, a girl can never get enough of that. But no. As soon as we were back on the sand, he shook away my arm.

'Thanks for nothing,' he muttered. 'I wanted to stay out a bit longer.'

'Would that really have been a good idea,' I said, softly.

'That's for me to decide.' He shrugged, as my teeth chattered. 'Anyway, you haven't the skin for the extremes of Cornish weather. Kensa has enough to deal with at the moment, without me being responsible for you coming down with pneumonia. You should have left me there. Minded your own business. Let me do what I'd been planning all year.'

My jaw fell open and a wave of nausea hit the back of my throat. 'You weren't thinking of . . . Things are never as bad as you think, over time, Tremain. Please tell me you haven't considered . . . '

'Jumping into the sea, to end it all?' He

snorted. 'Of course not. I would never do that to my parents.'

Yet he looked away, out to the ocean, which looked ash-coloured, as the afternoon started to head towards evening. His wet T-shirt clung to the firm contours of his chest. Broad shoulders. Slim waist. A person who'd led an active life.

'What is it with you,' he finally said and turned back. 'Saving imaginary people from fires, rescuing me from a supposed suicide attempt — your safety would fare better, so it would, if you lived in the real world. The average person doesn't thrive on drama.'

'Nor do I.' Count to twenty, Kate, like you used to with toddlers in your old job. 'I think you'll find it's called having a bit of humanity.' Something a cold, insensitive zombie like him would never understand. How it drained me. The ups and downs. One minute the expression in his eyes warmed me up, the next they shimmered all frosty, with as much heat as in today's sea. My teeth chattered again. Tears pricked my eyes and I was grateful for the continual pelt of rain on my face to disguise my frustration. I wouldn't call it hurt. No. Because that would imply I cared about him and . . . I sucked my top lip in between my teeth . . . and with him that was clearly pointless.

The cold, the wet, exhaustion — all three

overwhelmed me. That was it. I'd had enough of Tremain. Why was I wasting my time being nice? He clearly didn't give a jot about me or my life. 'Don't worry. I won't bother you again. Just drive me home. Izzy, Greg and Lucas will be waiting. I'm out on a date tonight.'

He flinched. 'Fine. But don't say I didn't warn you about that loser.'

'What do you care?' I said and threw my hands in the air. 'Clearly my feelings are of no importance.'

He flinched again.

'And thanks for the perspective. I've tried to be friendly. Put up with your rudeness. But you know what? I haven't got the word 'doormat' written across my forehead.'

'No. Just 'fool', if you let my head chef anywhere near you.'

'Too late,' I said, whole body shivering now. 'A romance is already on the cards.'

Urgh. Why did I say that?

A muscle twitched in his cheek and he stared for a moment. 'Right then. We'd better get you back.'

I sighed. 'Look, Tremain, I don't want us to fall out, but . . . ' Ouch! I glanced down. One of my bare feet had stepped on a washed-up red rose. I bent down and held it out to him. 'This is one of yours.'

He snatched it and stared at it for a moment,

before gently throwing it back towards the incoming tide.

I sighed. Lowered my tone. 'Perhaps if you talked about . . . whatever it was that ended badly.'

Without replying, he trudged on; didn't even bother to pretend not to have heard my words.

★   ★   ★

We drove back to White Rocks in silence, the fan heater filling the vacuum that should have been filled with chat. At the reception area I jumped out of the van, slammed the door and half ran to the chalet, with half an hour to get ready before going back into Port Penny. Except . . . My heart sank at the prospect of the evening ahead, as I made my way in, even though faint rays of sunshine now shone through the windows. A note lay on the kitchen work-top. Izzy had got ready early and was at reception with Greg, having a pre-dinner cocktail — or, snog more like. I pictured Lucas's smoulder-ing face, tried to get excited, but at the moment all I could think about was wounded, infuriat-ing, exasperating Tremain.

You see, a combination of strength and vulnerability had always been a killer combina-tion for me. On the outside, he looked like a superhero, with his triangular torso and obvi-ous strength . . . yet, like Superman, he revealed occasional glimpses of an insecure Clark Kent.

I hurried into my bedroom, changed into dry trousers and a T-shirt, with a cardigan, socks and my pumps and grabbed a waterproof that hadn't been used for weeks. Despite the struggling sun, it was still raining. I glanced in the mirror. My hair hung is soaked twists. I shrugged and put up my hood before heading into the kitchen for a speedy glass of orange juice. My stomach rumbled as I went outside and locked up. I reckoned Tremain would still be outside, in the fresh air.

*Really sorry. I can't make tonight. Will explain later*, I texted to Izzy and Lucas before heading down to reception building. Tremain's van was now parked up. Kensa could be seen through the reception window, polishing the desk. I spotted Izzy, Greg and Lucas in Donuts & Daiquiris and, urgh, Lucas gazed out of the window at that moment, stared and then waved. He came to the door and headed outside.

'Kate? Babe. I just got your text. What's going on?'

'Sorry, Lucas. Just . . . '

'You look rough! I mean . . . What on earth has happened?'

No one ever said Poldark was chivalrous.

'I ended up on the beach in Port Penny today — long story — and . . . and . . . saw someone in trouble. I won't bore you with the whole saga, but, to be honest, I'm exhausted. I've just got back. All I want is some soup and an early night.'

'Can I help with that,' he said with a half-smirk.

'No! I mean, thanks, but . . . '

He kissed me on the cheek. 'No problem. But at least let me make you breakfast tomorrow morning.'

I smiled. 'That's becoming a bit of a habit.'

'Do you think Izzy and Greg will mind if I still go out with them tonight? I'd love to quiz her about running her own business.'

'Thinking of branching out on your own?' My eyebrows raised.

'Who knows what the next few weeks will bring. I've grown up knowing I can't rely on anyone else.' He swallowed hard and the light disappeared from his face for a minute.

'No, of course Izzy won't mind,' I said. 'Although with those two snogging, you might not get much conversation.'

He smiled and rolled his eyes. 'Maybe over some bacon tomorrow you wouldn't mind filling me in a bit more on detail of the Maddocks' plans for next week. We had that staff meeting this morning but they might have told you some extra details that could prove useful to me. I'd like to make sure I'm helping with the relaunch as much as possible. It's all our futures at stake.'

See, I thought to myself. Tremain was wrong. Lucas does have a heart. Tremain. I scoured the grounds filled with chalets ahead of me. Where could he be? Out in the open, probably, and the biggest expanse of land nearby was the golf course. I headed that way.

On reaching the edge of an overgrown putting green, I stopped dead. What was that noise? The wind had dropped and raspy, thick breathing wafted over to me. In the distance, I spotted a figure running as fast as he could, with a hoody over his head. He was shouting. Angry yells, bloodcurdling ones, in fact. I stepped back. Then he rested by a tree and punched the trunk several times, before shaking his hand. Again he ran, in circles, letting rip with his voice one more time. I squinted at his fists, ever so tightly curled. He changed direction and paused for a moment, clearly having seen me. He slumped to the ground and his hoody slipped off. I focused hard. *Tremain?*

Without thinking, I ran in his direction. Panting, I reached him and he stood up and looked at me to reveal those leaf-green eyes drinking me in.

'Tremain. What's the matter? You're messing with my head.'

We looked at each other. His face kind of

squished. My body felt compelled to feel the warmth from his. He stepped forwards and put his hands on my shoulders and kind of leant on me for a moment.

'I want to help,' I murmured, 'but I'm so confused; don't know where I stand. I had to come looking for you, even though I knew you might reject any sympathy or kindness. What were you talking about on the beach? A bad end? Blaming yourself?'

'Someone died. Because of me. I let them down.'

'Oh, Tremain,' I mumbled, chest squeezing at the anguish in his eyes. Izzy was wrong. This man could not be a criminal. Goodness and sincerity emanated from his whole being. So, who had lost their life? A girlfriend perhaps, what with the red roses he threw into the sea.

He stared hard at me. I stared back, unable to break my gaze. He bent down. Our lips met. Oh so soft, at first, and then more persistent. My heart raced faster than ever. He must have been able to feel it against his pecs. My hands reached up and slid around his shoulders. I ran my fingers across that short hair, bursts of heat igniting places that had been sooo cold for such a long time. Urgently, he kissed me as I pushed against him and his mouth explored mine. Eyes closed, I sank into a dark, warm, exciting, pleasurable abyss.

'Oh God,' I gasped, as our kissing became more gentle and his lips trailed the curve of my neck. I leant up against him as hard as I could and wished my body would melt into his. Then . . . My phone rang. I opened my eyes. Reality returned. What was I doing? Most of the time Tremain treated me like an irritating girl next door. And then there was Lucas . . .

I stood back and pulled the phone from my waterproof pocket. I cleared my throat. Waited a few seconds, to catch my breath.

'Izzy. Hi. No . . . I'm fine.' And breathe. 'I just didn't feel up to it. Yes, later . . . Honestly. You have a good time.'

Tremain and I looked at each other. He sat down on the ground.

'Running around . . . shouting . . . Why were you behaving like that?' I sat down next to him and ignored the wetness of the grass. Ignored how my heart still beat as if it were accompanying a fast Scott Joplin ragtime song.

'Dunno. Just made me feel better. No one ever walks up here. Didn't think I'd have an audience.' He grimaced.

'Don't you go all surly on me again.'

'What about your date?' he muttered.

'You've cancelled it.'

'Yes. I promised your mum that I'd keep an eye on you today and I intend to do as I said.'

Tremain turned to me and groaned. 'I was hoping Mum had forgotten about today. She's got enough on her plate at the moment — doesn't need to be fretting about me.' Dull eyes met mine. 'What did she tell you — about today?'

'Nothing. Just that it was the second anniversary of something bad that had happened.'

He shrugged. 'Well, if that's all this is — keeping me under surveillance for Mum's sake — then consider your job done because I'm fine. I can cope and she doesn't need the extra worry. OK?' His eyes widened. 'Please, Kate.'

'Of course I'm not just here because of Kensa. Honestly . . . ' I rolled my eyes. 'Are you determined to keep any potential friends at arm's length for the rest of your life?'

'I didn't just then.' He gave a small smile and stared into his lap. 'Perhaps it's safer, though. That way I don't get hurt — and nor does anyone else.'

I took his hand and tenderly slotted my fingers in between his. 'Listen. Something bad happened to me too, ten months ago. I've felt no hope at all for a long time. Very, very slowly the edge of the pain became blunter but a dull ache took its place that nothing would ease. However then I came away with Izzy to Port Penny and . . . it's given me perspective. Perhaps you need a change of scenery? You could — I don't know — go abroad once the holiday season is over.'

He snorted yet didn't pull his hand away from mine. 'Abroad? I've done enough travelling to last me a lifetime. I like it here. It's familiar. No one takes any notice of me.' He looked up. 'So, ten months ago . . . ?'

My breathing quickened. With his eyes wide and fingers still in mine, somehow I felt unable to avoid the implied question.

'My boyfriend. He — '

Right at that moment, my phone rang again. I wasn't sure if I felt relief or disappointment. I'd taken the step to unfriend Johnny on Facebook. Perhaps now was the time to talk about exactly what happened.

'Sorry,' I muttered and pulled my mobile out of my waterproof's pocket. 'I'm Miss Popular tonight, for some reason. Hello . . . ?' A few seconds later, I ended the call. 'A cold caller. No, I don't need solar panels.'

'So . . . for whatever reason you aren't with your boyfriend any more.'

'Gets lonely sometimes, doesn't it,' I said, 'not having anyone to just do nothing with? I mean, Izzy's great for the cinema or a meal out, and for a heart-to-heart chat. But I miss having someone to chill alongside me, just lazing in front of the telly, not watching anything particular — I miss the familiarity. The closeness. The security.'

Tremain shrugged. 'Not sure I've ever had that.'

Oh. No close relationship. So maybe what happened a couple of years ago wasn't anything to do with a deceased girlfriend. But why the red roses? His lips pressed together in a firm line. I wouldn't ask any more questions. Not tonight.

Tremain shook himself. 'I'm guessing by the way you wolf down those all-day breakfasts that a woman with your appetite is starving, after an afternoon on a rainy beach.'

'Don't be cheeky!' I said. 'But who could blame me? We haven't even had lunch.'

He jumped up. 'Come on then. Let's go to the Rocky Roadhouse kitchen. I haven't got the cooking skills of Lucas, but can make a mean omelette. They'll go well with a couple of beers from the bar.'

'Sounds like a date,' I said and got up. 'I mean, obviously it's not, you see — '

For the first time today, Tremain laughed. 'No . . . You're definitely not my type. Too inconsiderate by far. Any woman with half a

214

heart would have left me by the golf course to wallow in self-pity. Not . . . given me the best kiss I've had in a long time.'

My cheeks felt hot, a voice in my head begging for a repeat of that lip action. 'I've spent months doing that,' I said quietly.

'What, kissing?'

I smiled. 'No. Wallowing in self-pity. I tried to put a normal face on it. Ever punctual for work. Paid my bills. Still helped out my elderly neighbour and looked after next door's kids whenever their babysitter let them down. I've been shopping. To the cinema. Laughed with customers. I've only really felt true to myself out on stage at a singing gig. There is no pretence there. And people who know me well have been able to tell inside, the hurt, it's still raw. Yet just lately, they've prodded me into change . . . I'm so grateful I've finally seem to be waking up to the fact that life has to go on — and it's up to me whether it does that in a miserable way or with fun.'

The wind tousled my damp hair. He tilted my head. 'Glad to see that bruising from the orange juice glass is almost gone.'

The pulse of my heart rang in my ears.

'And by the way,' he said, eyes not leaving my face, 'you give great hugs, Kate Golightly. Really. On the beach today . . . just now . . . it meant a lot; was just what I needed. I haven't let anyone hug me like that for a long time.' His voice broke. 'Didn't feel I deserved it.' He swallowed and then looked at me, smiled and crooked his arm for me to slide mine into. Side by side, we walked back to reception, as if we we'd known each other for years.

Such an innocent gesture felt good. Comfortable. One hundred percent right. And — unnervingly — ten times more of a turn-on than getting hands-on, snogging Lucas. Lucas. Oh God. What a mess.

# 14

How adorable. The first guests on Monday afternoon were the Jones family — meet Shirl, Earl and Pearl. That is a mum and dad with a seven-year-old daughter who had the cutest choochy cheeks and tightest black Afro curls. Big smiles. Thumbs-up. Lots of thanks to reception. Just what we needed. 'Best of luck with the rebrand, mate,' Earl said to Tremain, who was personally taking them to their lodge. He and I smiled at each other. We'd barely had time for a chat since Saturday night. Yesterday he'd darted around the resort with a clipboard, helping house-keeping and updating the information folders in each chalet with the week's activity and entertainment plan, plus Rocky Roadhouse's new menus. We'd caught each other's eye occasionally, me getting the tickliest sensation in my stomach.

I spent most of the day to-ing and fro-ing from Guvnah's, deep-frying, filling and decorating doughnuts and delivering them back, on site, to Izzy. She'd stayed at the resort, using the second-hand fryer she'd bought. Between us we made a great array, most of them in Tupperware boxes for the week, but some on display. When I'd returned from Guvnah's last night, Tremain was apparently snowed under, in the office, doing last-minute updates to paperwork. Kensa cornered me. Squeezed my shoulder. Said that to her amazement, since Saturday, Tremain had seemed more cheerful. She'd probed me to see if Tremain had fully explained what happened two years ago and I made it clear that he hadn't. Curious as I was, I didn't want to trick Kensa into revealing his secret. Tremain had to tell me himself. If he wanted to share, he'd do it in his own time. If not, I could understand how sometimes, despite what counsellors said, the only way of coping was to internalise stuff.

Geoff was already outside, frying onions for his hot dogs. I exited the reception building with Tremain and the Jones family. Oh my, what a savoury, caramelised smell wafted our way.

Earl patted his generous belly, which slightly overhung the top of his shorts. 'We didn't have time to stop off for lunch and don't really want to wait to make sandwiches.'

Shirl smiled and peered out from under her black dreadlocks. 'Guess a burger or a hot dog wouldn't hurt. After all, we are on holiday.'

'Yay!' said Pearl and punched the air,

looking cute in a mini version of her dad's red football shirt. Earl took the site map from Tremain. 'Don't worry about showing us the way.' He jerked his head towards the drive. Four cars had pulled up. 'Looks like you're in for a busy few hours. We'll go and suss it out on foot, while we eat, and then come back to pick up our car.'

Tremain nodded and took me to one side. 'Everything all set for the disco evening? It kicks off at seven, right?'

I gave him the thumbs-up.

We smiled at each other. Both of us cleared our throats. I couldn't help staring at that little scar above his lip. It reminded me of that scar on his torso. Was that anything to do with the roses on the beach?

'Right. So. Perhaps I'll see you later,' he said.

'Why not pop by for a doughnut?' I forced myself to look away from the lips that had reawakened parts of me on Saturday night. 'Made by my fair hands. Payment, if you like, for that omelette after our wet day on the beach.'

'About that . . . we're good, right? You . . . you don't think I'm some kind of nutter? Roses . . . yelling on the golf course?'

I leant forward and kissed his cheek. 'Nuts are good. You ask Izzy. Our peanut-butter crème doughnut is the top seller.'

He took my hand and looked down at it, before raising it to his mouth. His kiss sent hot waves of pleasure to places that I'd almost forgotten existed. 'Thanks, Kate. I don't think I said that at the time.' Shyly, he looked up. 'I'd like to get to know you better, if that's all right? Guess it takes one nutter to know another.'

I swallowed. Squeezed his fingers and then grinned. 'Speak for yourself! I'm one of the most rational, logical people I know.'

He raised one eyebrow. 'I don't know many people who eat omelette between two slices of bread or pour their beer into a wine glass.'

With mock disapproval, I pulled away my hand. 'Clearly I am way too sophisticated for you.'

However, I grinned back at him; felt all fuzzy inside. On closer inspection, those leaf-green eyes had such a depth of colour — shades of pine, moss and seaweed. Whereas Lucas's charcoal irises seemed more one-dimensional. Oh, my days. Listen to me. What a difference one weekend can make.

A lightness entered my chest as the realisation dawned on me — impressing Saffron, finding this plus-one for the wedding, now wasn't as important. Lucas was charming. Broody. Would no doubt be seductive as hell if shirtless and brandishing a scythe. But the appeal was on the surface only. Whereas kissing Tremain had moved the core of me. I wanted to know his past, his present, his regrets, his dreams . . .

'See you later then — for one of those peanut-butter beauties.' Consulting his clipboard again, Tremain headed back to the reception building.

As it happened, there were hardly any doughnuts left and for the next day we'd need to thaw out more trays than planned. Many families arrived at around 3 p.m., in between lunch and dinner, so that when they spotted the doughnut counter it seemed like the perfect snack. Those with a less sweet tooth, stopped at Geoff's van before checking out their chalet. By the time six o'clock came, in other words cocktail o'clock, there were no doughnuts left decorated with anchors, flags or Rocky Rabbits.

'I see you've already taken a dip in the pool, Pearl,' I said, as she sat in the café-bar, eating the mini pizza doughnuts their mum and dad had ordered with their Mojitos. Her wet hair curled tighter than ever and wet armbands lay on the tiled floor. In her hands, she clutched one of the white Rocky Rabbit cuddly toys. Shirl looked down at her towelling sarong.

'Not the usual outfit I wear when I'm out

for a drink. And I don't think I've ever been to a specialised cocktail bar before. Wait until the girls at the office hear about this. They're all youngsters, out every weekend — this will give me some much-needed street credibility.'

She grinned and then took a sip. Shirl glanced at her husband. Ooh. Usually customers closed their eyes or made some appreciative noise. Instead she put down her glass and grabbed a mouthful of savoury batter.

'Could have made one of these better myself,' said a snooty voice from across the room. Mrs Peppard. I turned to see her nose wrinkling as she put down a Chocolate Martini and straightened her tight cerise skirt.

'I'm not sure the cocktails are going down well,' I said, back at the bar.

'What?' Izzy stood up. She'd been bent over, having just stacked away some clean coffee cups, ready for tomorrow morning.

'The cocktails — people aren't raving about them like they do back at home.'

Izzy showed me her watch. Ten to seven. 'Shouldn't you be setting up? And, as for the drinks, I wouldn't worry — people are probably tired from long journeys. It'll take them a good night's sleep to get into full holiday-mode. Chill, my lovely.'

Perhaps she was right. And Mrs Peppard always was fussy — apart from when it came

222

to Lucas. She never found fault with his food, but last week complained about the wet floor in the swimming pool changing room and even though the resort wasn't officially open, moaned that the grass outside was too long for her stilettos.

As for the Joneses, Shirl had said herself that cocktails were a real treat — perhaps she'd never had a Mojito. The first time I ordered a Grey Goose le Fizz, talk about bitter. It tasted like the saltiest lemonade. And *never again* would I order a Smoker's Cough. To you that's Jägermeister with mayonnaise. Gunky or what?

Mrs Peppard shot me a critical glance, as I passed her table, and pointedly pulled at the collar of her exquisite silk blouse. While her style wasn't mine, it shouted 'quality' from a mile off and her blouses reminded me of the detailed vintage pieces I picked up from charity shops. Yet as I exited the café-bar, and entered the open-plan entertainment area, I took stock of my own outfit: a grey fifties jive dress with a slate silk scarf around my neck. Smart enough — even by Mrs Peppard's standards. Perhaps there was something else about me that she didn't like.

'Let's have Michael Jackson to start, babe,' said Lucas, holding a tea towel. He smiled. 'I've just popped out to wish you luck, and to take a break from making nuggets and burgers.' He half grimaced. 'At least children are eating my healthier versions, although I have to hold back on any sauces and garnishes. I'm wondering if I'll ever use my full set of skills here again.'

'For the moment, I'd just do whatever keeps the customer happy,' I said. 'Especially the kids — if they're smiling, so are their parents.'

He looked serious for a second. 'Let's hope your performance goes as well as — if not better than — my cooking. And if not, well, just remember that despite my overall success, one kid just vomited up on one of my home-made breaded fish goujons.'

He patted my shoulder and hurried off. I glanced at the reception clock. One minute to seven. A few families sat in the comfortable chairs, holding drinks. Children played cards on the coffee tables, or drank Coke while playing on Nintendos or phones. Kensa passed through and beamed at me. The Joneses came over, carrying their cocktails.

'Right. Great to see everyone here,' I said, into the mike. 'Let's kick off this disco evening with one of my favourite classics . . . 'Can You Feel It' by the Jackson Five!'

I flicked on my CD player, knowing the exact order of the songs. Hmm. It was way too quiet. That was annoying. I'd set it to exactly the right volume during my sound-check, earlier in the afternoon. Cheeks flushing, I turned it up. When I faced my audience, phew. No one seemed to have noticed. Someone, probably Kensa, had dimmed the lights. Feet started to twitch. Shirl and Earl swayed in their seats. As I reached the first chorus, the Peppards came over to the lounge area. Mr Peppard seemed oddly interested and for once wasn't taking refuge behind a newspaper. They sat at the back and stared at me intently. Next up was 'We Are Family' by Sister Sledge, followed by 'Crazy in Love' by Beyoncé for the teenagers, who were just starting to lose interest.

Shirl got up with Pearl and danced by their chairs. My chest glowed. Nothing gave me more pleasure at my gigs than watching little ones build their dancing confidence. Usually, like Pearl at the moment, they would start off just sidestepping their feet, one two, one two. But often, by the end of the evening, they'd allow an adult to twirl them around and start creating their own rhythmic hand movements.

I couldn't imagine being an only child; having one parent to myself, let alone two. My siblings would have found it lonely, but I had my music and books. Although — and much as I loved having my own flat — I would have missed the giggles and hugs, the inside jokes about Mum, the back-up in the playground if someone teased me about my hand-me-down clothes.

An hour in and I was getting a great round of applause after each song — apart from the Peppards. Clearly disco wasn't their thing. Someone tapped me on the shoulder. Lucas brought me over a pint of water.

'You're doing great,' he said. 'Well done. If you get hungry, there's a couple of those fish goujons by the CD machine.'

I swallowed. That was sweet. I hoped he'd understand when I backed off from our romance — if you could call it that — which I'd do after tonight's gig. Even though I had no guarantee of any future with Tremain, the sensations I'd felt, with fingers running through his hair, meant I didn't care, the thirst in me was so urgent to really start living again — not carrying on some pretend love affair, just to impress an old school friend, who, actually, wasn't even a friend.

I devoured one of the goujons, the home-made breadcrumb disintegrating deliciously on my tongue. Then glugged back a mouthful of water. I turned on the CD machine. 'You Sexy Thing' by Hot Chocolate came on. Except that my mike wasn't working. I fiddled with the buttons. Nope.

'I'll just be a moment, folks,' I said and tracked the cable back to the wall. Everything looked fine to me. Izzy appeared and took a look. She couldn't find a problem either. Deep breaths.

'Slight equipment malfunction everyone, but no matter. I have the loudest of voices.' There was no way I'd let Tremain and Kensa down. Forcing my lips upwards, I turned on the CD again, just turning the volume down.

'Ace voice!' shouted Earl. What a great guy. The track came to an end and I prepared myself for 'Shake It Off' by Taylor Swift — not exactly disco, but a great dance track for all ages. Except that a heavy-metal tune suddenly blared out of the player. Huh? Everyone — even the Joneses — pulled faces and I hurriedly fast-forwarded the music, but that's all that played for the rest of the CD. I took out the disc. It didn't look any different. My heart sank. I'd left my other disco mixes back home, while trying to keep my luggage for the holiday to a minimum.

I turned around to my audience, a quarter of whom had already left.

'What a shambles,' muttered Mr Peppard as he and his wife stalked past. You'd think, as regular customers, they'd have been more loyal.

Earl Jones took Pearl off his lap, stood up

and came over. 'Anything I can do to help, love?'

I shrugged. 'It's a mystery. This is one of my most popular CDs. Nothing like this has happened before.'

'Ah well, never mind,' said Shirl, who came over, carrying Pearl. 'These things happen. We enjoyed ourselves. My little one adores singing, you know.'

'I'll give Pearl some tips, before you leave White Rocks. Let her use the mike. We can have fun singing scales.'

Shirl's face broke into a smile 'That's kind of you. She'd love that. And try not to worry about tonight. I reckon most of us guests are knackered after travelling here today. They'll probably be grateful for an earlier night than planned.'

I made my apologies to the guests — none of whom looked grateful as they filed out or headed to the bar. Earl asked reception for a screwdriver, and they eventually found one in the handyman's cupboard. He insisted on staying behind, as Shirl left to put a very sleepy Pearl to bed. He wanted to take a quick look at the mike. The hand piece was fine, so he dismantled the socket.

'Look.' He held it out in his chubby hand. 'The wiring's messed up. Never seen anything like it.'

'Well, it's not the newest piece of equipment.' I sighed, so having wanted tonight to be a roaring success for the Maddocks. 'Thanks, Earl.'

He skimmed a hand over his balding head. 'Chin up. Early days. We enjoyed the evening.' He handed me the screwdriver and socket and went on his way.

Yes, but not enough to finish your cocktails, I thought and headed over to their table. I picked up one of the glasses, smelt the liquid inside and shrugged. Perhaps today was just jinxed. At least Tremain hadn't been around to see the disaster.

'Bad luck,' said Lucas. 'Come on. Take the weight of your feet for a moment.' He led me over to the comfortable chairs and, with our backs to reception, we sat down. 'I might have some news that will cheer you up.' He beamed. What a dazzling smile. Such dark, rakish looks but . . . nope. Nothing. My heart beat steadily. I didn't long to press myself against that athletic chest. Instead, I imagined being wrapped up in Tremain's solid embrace. 'Izzy's just been speaking to me — about something she forgot to mention when we were out, Saturday night.'

My brow furrowed.

'She said you were going to a wedding in a couple of weeks and needed a plus-one.'

Oh . . . crap. I remember now. I'd been distracted by trying to work out a way to shadow Tremain on Saturday and Izzy had rambled on about mentioning the wedding to Lucas — said she could do it subtly, without letting on that the invite was only because he looked like Poldark. I hadn't really listened therefore she didn't know I was having doubts about this dashing man.

'Not much fun, is it, going to that sort of event on your own? I'd be happy to oblige. I mean, that's what friends are for, right? Helping each other out. And by then I could probably do with a break from this place.'

'No! Really! I mean, I couldn't possibly . . . '

He grinned and . . . oh dear. Actually knelt on the floor before me. He took my hand. 'Lovely Kate, I would be honoured to accompany you to your friend's wedding.' He kissed my fingers.

What could I say now? Sorry. I'm not going. Because I've met someone who makes my heart sing as loudly as my voice?

'Kate?' said a loud voice from behind me. The hairs stood up on the back of my neck. 'I believe there was some sort of problem with the electrics.'

I turned around and looked up. Tremain. Face expressionless.

'Catch you later, babe,' said Lucas with wink. He got to his feet and headed off.

I stood up. 'Tremain. It's not what you think. You see . . . '

'On my way over I heard disgruntled customers talking — the mike and your CD didn't work, right?'

He went to move away, but I put my hand on his shoulder. He shook it off.

'Don't be like this!' I said. 'Lucas . . . You see tonight I was going to say to him that . . . '

Tremain held up his hand. 'It's no business of mine, Kate. It's not as if you and I are a couple. I'm sure Lucas will make the perfect plus-one for this wedding or whatever it is I heard you talking about. Anyone else might be a little . . . complicated. I hope my antics over the weekend provided you both with a good laugh.'

'Don't do that.'

'What?'

'Put words in my mouth. Push me away.' I took his hand firmly. 'And assume things you don't know anything about.'

His fingers slid out of mine and he forced a laugh. 'Honestly, Kate. Thanks for helping me through a difficult couple of days but — Well. This is your holiday. I get it. You just want a bit of fun.'

I folded my arms. 'Right. So you think I'm the two-timing type? I cancelled my date with him. You think I risked pneumonia just to get a snog?'

'Does Lucas know what happened between you and me?'

'No, you see I haven't had time but — '

Tremain shook his head and stalked off.

I didn't follow. What was the point? The more I made excuses the worse it all sounded. I sat down again as my stomach cramped into tight knots. A couple of hours later, it still hurt and, having muttered something to Izzy about being tired, I went to take refuge in my bedroom.

'You OK?' she said.

I forced a smile. 'Yes. Just frustrated about the mike and everything going wrong this evening.' I stood up from the sofa and yawned. 'Good movie. Nothing beats *Brides-maids* when you're in need of a laugh.'

Izzy stood up and gave me a hug. I guessed she was doing that mind-reading thing again; she knew I was down, but knew better than to push me to find out exactly why.

'And how about, to end the perfect evening, I make two hot chocolates?' she said and ran a hand through her short hair.

'With marshmallows on top?'

Izzy pretended to look shocked. 'Is there

any other way to drink it? Please. That question is sacrilegious.'

'Thanks all the same, Izzy, but I really am shattered. Think I'll go straight to bed.' I swallowed. 'You're the best. This holiday . . . it's done me good.' I cleared my throat and smiled. 'And, as a thank-you, perhaps in a day or two, when things have settled down, how about I finally book us a couple of spa treatments? For starters, I bet we could both do with a massage.'

She gave me the thumbs-up and headed towards the kitchen while I went into my room and shut the door. I gazed up at the red heart wind spinner, with the realisation that I hadn't thought much at all about Johnny for a couple of days. And..and I felt all right with that. No guilt-tripping. No memories flooding back. No yearning to friend Johnny again on Facebook and have a one-way chat.

I stood up. What a mess. Yet mess was good, right? It proved you were living. And whether I left here single or not, it didn't matter. I knew that the moment had come to say goodbye to Johnny and move forward, just as me or as part of another couple.

I stood on the bed and took down the spinner. It glinted under the lampshade. I sat on the bed and gazed at it on my lap. Slowly, I pushed its metal curves back to the flat position and then ran my hand over it. A tear trickled down my cheek and, vision blurry, I lifted it to my mouth and kissed it as gently as I could. Then, with a sniff, I pulled my suitcase out from under the bed, lifted the lid and placed the wind spinner inside. After one last look, I pushed it away, under the bed. Then I wiped my eyes, cleaned my teeth, changed and got into bed.

# 15

After a fall-out in the playground, I'd sometimes been blanked, but Tremain took blanking to a whole new level — forget sending someone to Coventry, it was as if he'd sent me to the International Space Station. Two days later, on Wednesday, he'd still avoided all my attempts to chat and explain my position. Lucas didn't help by continually popping up by my side, always full of questions about Kensa and Tremain's latest plans, searching for any extra feedback I might have received, outside of the staff meetings, on how the rebranding was going. I admired his enthusiasm. It must have been hard catering for the tastes of us normal folk, after years of serving people who knew that scampi is actually langoustine — one thing, if nothing else, that I have learnt from my time with my Poldark lookalike.

Take today. Tremain and I were both travelling in a hired mini-coach to take a group of guests into Port Penny. Lucas came up with the idea yesterday. He had a fisherman friend who could offer a decent rate to take ten holidaymakers out to sea.

Tremain agreed to trial it and hastily spread word amongst the guests to sign up. If it was successful, then it would become a regular excursion. Kensa asked if I would accompany her son. Her eyes looked lined. She didn't need to say why. I knew. Since our argument, Tremain had gone into himself again.

Now, as he drove and I sat in the front passenger seat, the metre between us could have been a mile. If I asked a question he simply replied, 'I'm concentrating on the road.' I'd given up. When we'd clambered on the white twenty-seater van, before the guests arrived, he muttered a few details of the day out, but hardly lifted his head from paperwork.

We pulled up into the pottery shop's car park. Apparently, Tremain had rung ahead and, as a favour, the owner let him park there. And then . . . Ah OK. Perhaps I'd been a bit rash. While the guests got off, begging for a quick look at the local ceramics before we headed towards the harbour, Tremain sat down next to me. He slid off my sunglasses and looked me straight in the eye.

'Sorry. For being an arse.'

'Oh. Um . . . '

'Seriously. Treating you like that after you'd been there for me, on the beach. There's no excuse.' He shrugged. 'Your private life is just

that — private — so you and Lucas
. . . whatever. It's fine by me.'

'It is?'

'Yep. Of course. He's surprised me, actually, this last week, working extra hours. He's always asking Kensa if there is anything he can do to help. Perhaps Lucas is one of those people who only show their best side in a crisis.'

Ex-army Tremain sounded as if he'd had experience of meeting people like that.

'You and him . . . go for it. Life's too short, right?'

I swallowed. 'But us . . . the golf course.'

His face flushed. 'I guess we both got carried away with the emotion of the moment. Plus, we were tired. Wet. Both those things can skew judgement, no?'

He gave me a penetrating gaze making me wish my sunglasses still covered my eyes. Could he see the truth? I hoped not, because clearly his version of events was different to mine. My chest ached. So that's all our kiss had been to him — a misjudged decision.

'Friends again?' he said and held out his hand.

My fingers curled around his. I longed to hold tighter. Pull him near. Not to let go. Feel those soft lips on mine. Lose myself in his closeness.

'Of course. Friends.'

Tremain gave me back my glasses. 'Right.' He cleared his throat. Let's round up everyone and find our fisherman.' He grabbed an anorak from the driving seat. 'I hope Lucas is right about hearing a last-minute weather forecast saying this storm had changed course. I almost cancelled the trip this morning, as torrential rain was due. And, in my opinion, these clouds now don't look as if they are about to budge. I don't think you'll need to wear those shades.'

I gazed at the windscreen, now covered in spots of rain. No matter. I didn't feel like strolling in sunshine. Everything felt a little shady after Tremain's announcement that our kiss had, effectively, meant nothing.

The day got shadier still. Talk about a washout. Guests had come prepared with waterproofs, but one little lad couldn't get warm and spent the walk down to the harbour wailing that he hated Cornwall — despite Earl Jones's attempts to get everyone to join in a sing-song. When we arrived at the jetty, we discovered that a demonstration was taking place by animal-rights protesters. They held up placards bearing gruesome photos of injured fish and were shouting out insults to our group, as we headed for one of the boats.

A skinny woman in combat trousers and a camouflage-patterned T-shirt grabbed the arm of a curvy, female White Rocks guest. 'You should be ashamed of yourself,' she hollered. 'If you must fish to enjoy your holiday, follow a catch-and-release policy. Feed our waning seas by putting your trophies back. Don't feed your stomachs that are probably already full of fudge and pasties.'

The woman's husband squared up to the protestor. 'Mind yer own business. We're here to enjoy our holiday.'

'By torturing innocent fish with lines and hooks?'

The face of the couple's small daughter scrunched up. 'I'm not eating fish any more,' she said and burst into tears. Her parents glared at Tremain as rain pelted down.

'The police and local newspapers are here,' muttered the dad. 'Shame White Rocks didn't plan ahead to find out what was going on.'

As it was, we found out afterwards, none of the tabloids had been interested in this demonstration before. One protester moaned that it had only been reported, the week earlier, in the local *Port Penny Express*. Then, to top it off, when we finally pushed through the noisy crowds and got to the boat of Lucas's friend — on time, of course, despite the protest, thanks to determined,

239

ever-punctual Tremain — there was a simple note taped to the cabin window: '*Apologies. Due to illness, fishing excursions will resume tomorrow. Please call the number below to rebook.*'

'This is a joke!' said a man in a drenched anorak.

From beneath her rainhood, his wife nodded and pointed to her kids. 'We were promised a taste of Cornish life and fresh fish for tea.'

'I want my money back,' said another mum. 'We'd have been better off spending the day at the pool.'

'It's not White Rocks' fault the weather didn't clear,' said Shirl and looked apologetic when Pearl announced that she wanted to go back to their chalet.

What a day. Would misfortune hit every effort to make White Rocks a success? It was with trepidation, that evening, that I set up for my ABBA show. Tremain insisted on working on reception, so that if there were any technical problems he'd be there to help.

'That's very considerate of him,' said Izzy, as I grabbed a small Coke before I was due to start and sat up the bar. She mixed a couple of Long Island Iced Teas. As I'd walked in, I noticed that several customers had left their drinks, half drunk.

Heat surged into my face. 'Yes. He's been very good — not shown his disappointment about Monday's disco evening. I hope tonight's show goes better.'

'You OK?' Izzy smiled.

'Uh huh.' I forced my lips to upturn.

'How are things between you and Lucas?'

I put down my drink and placed my head in my hands. 'Oh, Izzy. Everything is so screwed up. Lucas is nice. A great guy. Saffron would be spitting to see him on my arm. But Tremain. When we kissed . . . '

'Whoa!' Izzy stopped mixing the drinks. 'More snogging secrets kept from me? Just when were you going to tell me about that?'

'Long story. It happened over the weekend.'

'Was that why you couldn't come out Saturday night? You've still not really told me what that was all about.'

'I know. It's been mad busy, hasn't it? When was the last time we had a proper girlie chat? I want to hear all about Greg, for starters.'

Izzy blushed. 'He's got the cutest habit of staring at the floor, right after he pays me a compliment. His aftershave is the muskiest, sexiest smell ever and his jokes are so awful, I haven't stopped laughing since we met.'

'Aw.' I squeezed her arm. 'You deserve no

less, Izzy. He sounds the best.'

She grinned. 'You're right — a girlie get-together should be on the agenda. Let's try to take time out together soon, like you said, maybe a facial or that massage. Until then, my advice for you is — you know what Johnny always used to say . . . ' She studied my face.

'Follow your heart,' I murmured.

Izzy nodded. 'You'll work out what's right. Hearts are funny like that — much cleverer than brains when it comes to the really important stuff.'

Talking about following your heart . . . 'Look. Izzy. Those glasses people have left are still half full. I'm convinced something is wrong with our cocktails.' I went over and picked one up, bringing it back. I smelt it. 'Not very strong.'

Izzy took a sniff. 'True. Could just be that the ice melted quickly.' She turned around to the array of liquor bottles, hanging upside down at the back of the bar. Izzy prepared a shot of vodka, took a sip and gave it to me. We both pulled faces.

'Not as good quality as ours back home, is it?' I said.

'Wait a minute.' She bent down and came up with three bottles.

'Well, they certainly open more easily than

the ones we usually buy,' she said with a puzzled face and poured out a gin, tequila and whiskey. We tried all three separately.

'None of them taste right,' I said.

Izzy's face flushed. 'Tomorrow I'll be ringing the suppliers. This is outrageous, especially considering they weren't the cheapest option. They must have swapped the labels with a cheaper brand.'

Lucas appeared at his side of the bar. 'Problem, ladies? You look as if you've just drunk a glass of seawater.'

I explained. Lucas grimaced. 'That's wholesalers for you. Sometimes I don't think they even know the origins of their stock.'

I shrugged. 'But they weren't from there — remember, I told you, we only used good-quality products. Izzy sources her suppliers very carefully.'

He pointed to his own bottles. 'Use the Rocky Roadhouse's for tonight. Beers and wines are always more popular than shorts anyway, on our side, with meals.'

'Thanks, Lucas,' I said and my face broke into a genuine smile, hoping it wouldn't hurt him to know he and I had no future.

As Izzy remade the Long Island Iced Teas and took them over to a young couple with twins, I almost reached for my phone, for the first time in a while feeling an urge to message Johnny. But that's all it was. An urge created through habit. During tough emotional times, over the last year, my way of coping had been to tell him everything, even though I knew he wouldn't read my words. But I felt comfortable with not re-friending Johnny on Facebook. Plus the red wind spinner would stay locked up in my luggage.

However, to follow your heart was good advice and had served me well in the past. Johnny's parents had wanted him to go to university and become an accountant — they said that all children naively dreamt of working with animals, but Johnny said he'd always known, deep inside, that it was his vocation.

I could do this. I could sort out my life without having to chat to Johnny. As I stood in front of my audience later, and started singing 'Waterloo', I remembered how he had pushed me to pursue my dream of becoming a singer. Whenever possible, he'd attended my gigs, even if it meant craftily gatecrashing a wedding.

As my voice soared and, thankfully, the mike worked and the music kept playing, I cast an eye across the crowd. The Peppards sat at the back, staring at me intently. Lucas appeared at the side of the room and tapped his foot. We smiled at each other. Then Mrs

Peppard hand-signalled him to join them. Tea towel over his shoulder, he headed their way and after about five minutes chat the couple quickly left. Lucas winked at me on his way past and went back in the direction of the Rocky Roadhouse.

As time passed, I worried less about things going wrong. Tremain sat behind the computer at the reception desk and every now and again I caught him watching me. 'Supertrouper', 'Dancing Queen' and 'Voulez-Vous' all went well. Fully in the zone, I closed my eyes and swayed side to side. My brow relaxed. My shoulders dipped. This was the best stress-buster in the world. Like a hot bath with masses of fragrant soap bubbles and . . . I gasped.

My eyes snapped open and my heart pulsated with jolts as if it were punching the inside of my chest. Children screamed and jumped up from their seats, followed rapidly by their parents. Loud bangs and crackles came from . . . from somewhere and, at the same time, a piercing smoke alarm rang out across the whole of the reception building. The walls reverberated. I could have sworn the floor shook.

'Kate! You OK?' Lucas appeared at my shoulder, eyes wild, searching the room. 'What the hell are those bangs?' he shouted.

'It sounds like a war film.'

I swallowed, thinking of the obvious after recent months of terror attacks around the world. Deep breaths. No. Get a grip, Kate. International terrorists weren't interested in a struggling holiday resort in Cornwall. Yet mums and dads hurtled out of the glass doors, carrying their kids. Izzy and Greg came over.

'It's coming from the storeroom,' shouted Greg and pointed to a door in between the open-entertainment area and the Rocky Roadhouse. Dirty, dark grey smoke wafted from under the door. He made to go in but Izzy pulled him back. 'No. Wait for the police. It could be dangerous. I think we should check that the building is clear and then head outside.'

'Has anyone rung the emergency services?' I shouted and gazed around. Where was Tremain? Perhaps outside, checking all of the guests were all right.

'I have.' Kensa appeared. 'Where's my son?'

I shrugged as Izzy and Greg went off to check the building. Lucas said he would search the pool area, even though it should have been empty for a couple of hours. I went to take a look around the kitchens. Perhaps there was a problem with the gas.

But Kensa pulled my arm. 'No. Don't. I think it's . . . fireworks.'

'Huh?' I thought for a moment. 'I remember now. Tremain told me you had a load left over from a couple of years ago, when he didn't work here. But he said you wouldn't put on a display because of worrying about the health-and-safety issues, that you had enough concerns without that.'

'And it's true. I never got around to selling them off. Stupidly — ' she shook her head ' — I shoved a boxful into the bottom of the storage cupboard. Yet I don't understand how they caught fire.' The banging stopped and she wiped her eyes with the back of her hand. 'But the real reason I wouldn't have a display, Kate, is because Tremain . . . he can't bear the loud noise. The army. Bad memories. Please. Go look for him. I must see to the guests but I'm really worried about him. Oh, Kate. Please. Do your best. The bangs. He must not be alone.'

# 16

Together, then push arms out . . . together then push arms out . . . same with the legs, think frog-like, keep going and breathe . . .

As I did breaststroke to and fro across the pool, my eldest sister's words came back to me. She'd taught me to swim — Mum had no money for lessons and was too busy to take me to the pool. Despite my longing for tranquillity and independence though, often over the years I'd learnt to appreciate the hustle and bustle of my chaotic youth. You see, I couldn't find Tremain last night and he still hadn't returned. I couldn't help thinking again what if he'd had a sibling? Someone he could have confided in? A person who knew him, his history, and all the places he would have run to if life's problems suddenly seemed insurmountable? I'd searched the golf course. Wandered around all the chalets. In the end I'd even persuaded an obliging Lucas to drive me to the beach. I didn't divulge what had happened with the red roses — that was private to Tremain. Not that it mattered. Lucas seemed pretty shaken up by the fireworks and was keen to help me find his boss, even though they were hardly the best of friends.

And then, late last night, after returning, the strangest thing happened. For the first time in ten months, I put pen to paper and wrote a song. Inspiration had left me this last year. At one point I wondered if I would ever write my own material again. Johnny had always encouraged me. Our love inspired me and once he'd gone my creativity lost its spark, despite several feeble attempts to relight it again. But finally, due to the hurt, the passion, the anger . . . all those emotions I'd experienced with Tremain this week . . . finally those feelings had morphed into lyrics and notes. Rough ones, but creative scribbling nevertheless.

I ducked under the water and bobbed up to find Mrs Peppard poolside. Full make-up still on and hair stylishly twisted up. She sneered at me and stood for several minutes as if wanting to show off her cellulite-free, bikini-clad body. So, I had to smile when a child water-bombed a metre away from her and soaked her legs.

I clambered out of the water and headed for the changing rooms, feet smacking against the cold tiled floor. Just before I went in, Kensa appeared, carrying a pile of white, fluffy towels, from the laundry room, no doubt on her way to stock up at Reception. Unlike Mrs Peppard, she hadn't got a scrap of make-up on. Her puffy eyes looked red. Loose strands of hair hung down from a tight bun.

'Still not back?' I murmured and pulled my towel around my practical black swimming costume. A couple of small girls, wearing colourful armbands, exited the changing room and pushed past, followed by calls from their mums to slow down.

We stepped out of the way. Kensa shook her head.

'Have you informed the police?'

'No.' She shrugged. 'He wouldn't want me to and . . . this happened once before. Six months ago. He came back the next day.'

'Did you know where he'd gone?'

She shook her head again and turned as a phone rang out from Reception. 'Look, I know it all seems very strange, Kate. And you've been brilliant. I'm sure he'll be all right. I . . . I'll ring the police if it goes past twenty-four hours and he hasn't even called.'

Biting my lower lip, I headed into the changing rooms. I realised it was too early for Tremain to be listed as officially missing, but what if something terrible had happened? And yet, like Kensa, I had a sense that he would be all right. There was a profound sense of strength about him, despite the fact he'd clearly been through some sort of trauma.

Stomach rumbling, I dried my hair. I'd grab a doughnut on my way back to the chalet — Izzy was doing the early shift and I would help out after lunch. I couldn't face an all-day breakfast with Lucas. The false jollity and affection — it was all too much. Today I would definitely fess up about the real reason I'd thought him the perfect plus-one for Saffron's wedding and would tell him that a relationship between him and me . . . ? Uh uh, that was no longer going to work.

I peeled off my dripping swimsuit and picked up my knickers from the bundle of clothes in front of me, on the brown slatted bench, humming the tune that I had written last night. Hurriedly, I slipped them on and then glanced sideways at a folded pile of tiny, designer clothes. No doubt they belonged to Mrs Peppard. What a surprise that she hadn't locked them away in a Louis Vuitton holdall, although she probably wanted to show them off to other swimmers and could easily afford replacements.

I was about to look away, as I struggled to put on my bra over slightly damp skin, when something in the pile caught my eye. I pulled on my T-shirt and double-checked I was alone in the room, then lifted up the blouse on top to investigate a centimetre of pink leopard-print material that was sticking out.

My jaw dropped. Underpants. The label indicated they formed part of a matching set. I squinted. M&S size ten — just like the bra found in the chalet that caught fire. I searched further through the pile and found a plain blue bra — Mrs Peppard struck me as the kind of woman who would wear matching underwear if at all possible, so the other half of the set must be missing.

Oh my days. It was her. Mrs Peppard, the scented candle, the burning sofa . . . She was one of the people enjoying a lovers' tryst. So who was her lover? Or did she and Mr Peppard get kicks from having sex in forbidden places? I shuddered at the thought of her critical, standoffish husband doing anything other than checking his shares in the paper or talking about golf. I pulled on my fifties halter-neck blouse and three-quarter-length cotton trousers. Before heading out of the changing rooms, I neatened Mrs Peppard's pile of clothes and slipped on my pumps.

In the reception area, Housekeeping were cleaning up black smudges from the walls near the storage room. The smell of smoke still haunted the air. Earl Jones sat in Donuts

& Daiquris with his family and waved before I went over. I glanced at the reception clock. A quarter to ten.

'Not having cocktails for breakfast, are you? How decadent!' I said and smiled. 'You didn't fancy a Rocky Roadhouse fry-up?'

He grinned and patted his stomach. 'Shirl wouldn't let me do that every day — although I suspect, caloriewise, a couple of your doughnuts are no better.' He ran a hand over his receding hairline and clasped his hands together. He opened his mouth to talk and then closed it again.

'Everything OK?' I said, and smiled at Pearl. 'You and I really must have a singing session together. Do you like, let's think . . . the band 5 Seconds of Summer?'

The little girl nodded enthusiastically and took a big bite of donut.

Earl pointed to a couple of comfy chairs near the poolside window, away from the busy housekeeping staff. 'Look, can I have a chat for a moment?'

Oh dear. You didn't often see a serious look on his face. Perhaps he had a complaint to make and would rather approach me than stressed Kensa. We went over and sat down opposite each other. He sucked in his cheeks and leant forward.

'You know, I lost my job last month. That's

why we took this discounted holiday. Normally, we would have gone abroad.'

'Oh no. Sorry to hear that. I'd never have guessed.' I gave a half-smile. 'You are one of the cheeriest guests we've had here this week.'

He shrugged. 'No point wallowing, is there? Especially when you've got kids. Reality will hit when we get home. I'll have to find another job quick-smart.'

'Is there much likelihood of that where you live?'

He shrugged. 'Nope. We'd be happy to move, though, if it was the right job, with prospects — Pearl is young enough to change schools.' He exhaled. 'But the reason I mention it is . . . Look, I don't want to speak out of turn, but — '

'You've been nothing but supportive and helpful since arriving — please, go on.'

He cleared his throat. 'That's kind of you — and one reason, I guess, is that I understand what White Rocks is going through. You see, until last month, I managed a hardware store. I've always been good with my hands — thanks to my dad, I grew up knowing about electrics and plumbing. It didn't take me long to work my way up to management and, a few years ago, I was offered a top position at one of the stores biggest outlets.' He shrugged. 'But, as White

Rocks has found, the recession hit us and we needed to rebrand to pull in new customers. I did a lot of research on the Internet, and on my feet, visiting the competition. I made lots of suggestions — like the company expanding into garden ware and perhaps opening a small café . . . '

'Didn't they like your ideas?'

'No, because someone else just beat me to putting the same solutions forward. Long story, but I eventually worked out it was my deputy, John. Good friends we were, or so I thought. He passed off my ideas as his own. He's a good ten years younger than me. No kids. Not even married. The company saw him as a better prospect for managing the new-look store.'

'That's awful!'

Earl's face flushed purple. 'Yes, and I'm still trying to manage the anger, am trying not to let it eat away at me. Anger at John. Anger at my bosses. Anger at myself for being so naive. The recession has made everyone look out for themselves . . . All I'm saying is . . . ' He lifted his hands in the air. 'So many things have gone wrong here since we arrived, do you think someone could be ambushing the Maddocks' plans on purpose?'

'No!' I said and let go of my holdall. I stared at Earl. 'Seriously. Everyone here has pulled together as a team. Even Lucas . . . '

Earl raised an eyebrow.

I smiled. 'Let's just say, after years of serving highfalutin food, he wasn't completely on-board for serving convenient kids' grub.'

'Well, I'd never have guessed — he couldn't have gone to more trouble with our picky Pearl. One of the few meals she'll eat is fish-finger sandwiches. He made a special batch of his fish goujons just for her, with the cod shaped into perfect rectangles. Shirl was well impressed. She works part-time as a chef in a local pub, cooking food like Rocky Roadhouse's and said they'd never make that much effort.'

'There you go! Also the housekeeping staff has worked extra hours and the local pool attendant even charged Kensa a discounted rate, until business improves. Why would anyone actively encourage White Rocks to go bankrupt?'

★   ★   ★

I was still asking myself this question, back at the chalet, an icy orange juice in my hand. I had an hour before my shift was due to start and couldn't think of anything else, not even my new song, which I was really excited about. Take those fireworks — apparently a candle had set them off. Been lit on the shelf above and fallen into the box. The storage-room light wasn't working, and Kensa thought a member of staff must have lit the candle to see what they were doing, and was now too afraid to own up that they had accidentally left it burning.

But what if it was part of an underhand plan to ruin the ABBA evening? I shook my head. It would have to be someone pretty ruthless — or stupid — to risk that. Or . . . I shifted in my seat. Someone, at the moment, a little off-balance. I mean, wouldn't it have been easier and more sensible to use a torch instead of the old-fashioned way of lighting wax? Perhaps Tremain had had enough of running White Rocks? Would it suit him better if the place actually failed? What if Izzy was right after all, and he'd maybe been in prison and had a track record of underhand behaviour? Yet I'd find it hard to believe that he would risk anyone's safety, after the way he rescued me from the chalet fire. And he knew how much the family business meant to his mum. No. That theory made no sense at all.

So what if Earl was on to something and an outsider was trying to sabotage Kensa and Tremain's plans?

I put down my orange juice and headed

into the kitchen. I grabbed a notepad and pen off the work unit. Carefully, I peeled off the sheets bearing my musical scribbling from last night, and darted into the bedroom to stash them in a drawer. Then I came back, opened the door and went out to the decking. I waved at children playing and then sat down, enjoying the warm glow spreading across my body, due to the sun.

Right. First up. Make a list of everything that has gone wrong.

The mike at the disco evening. I remembered enjoying the goujons Lucas brought over for me. Then when I went back to sing it didn't work. Eating those tasty morsels had distracted me and I wouldn't have noticed someone crouching down in the dark. Earl said the wiring was really messed up — surely the mike would have sounded faulty, over the time, if the wiring was wearing? It wouldn't just not work without a hint of something being wrong.

Next was the CD on that same evening the disco tracks suddenly turned to heavy metal. Talk about a mystery. Lucas said all my CDs had been fine when he'd borrowed them — could one of the guests, an outsider, have switched it while I wasn't looking? Perhaps a teenager who hated cheesy music and wanted something more to their taste? No. It was definitely my disc.

I scratched my head and stopped writing for a second. So many questions and no answers. Deep breaths. OK next. The trip to the beach had been a total disaster. The weather forecaster Lucas had listened to had got it wrong about the storm moving away. We didn't know about the demo. Then Lucas's fisherman friend cried off ill.

What a day that turned out to be — in the evening, we had the fireworks, which set off the smoke alarm. Oh the irony — Kensa had been so grateful to Lucas for pointing out, a few days earlier, that the smoke alarm in the cupboard was flashing to indicate the batteries were low. Shamefaced, she said she'd always been proud of putting guests' safety first. Tremain then checked the whole building. Fortunately, it was the only one.

Anything else? I thought hard. Geoff's van had been a success and the kids loved Guvnah's paintings and the Rocky Rabbit toys. But then an image of Mrs Peppard's disapproving face popped into my head. Ah yes. Our cocktails. I recalled Lucas asking me how Donuts & Daiquiris had become so successful and my answer had been proved true. It was all down to quality. When it came to the little affordable luxuries like cocktails, people didn't seem to mind paying a little more if the product was fab. Yet drinks had been left this last week. No one had seemed impressed. Just before I left Earl this morning Izzy had caught me to say she'd rung the drinks suppliers. They hotly denied any of their bottles were swapped for cheaper versions before sale and suggested she came over to examine their current stock for herself. So Izzy looked at some more of the bottles and worked out why they were so easy to open — the seals had actually been discreetly broken. Someone must have tampered with the bottles by pouring out some of the good stuff and watering down the rest. Thank goodness for Lucas letting us use his bar's supplies. They would last for a while until we sorted out this mess.

I put the pen down on the decking and stared hard at the list, trying to find a common element. But the harder I stared, the more impossible it became to find a link. I tossed the notebook down next to me, and got up to brush my hair and change. When I came back, it was almost time to leave for work. I shook my head. *Work?* How did this happen? I was supposed to be on holiday! Or at least be carrying out my mission to find the perfect plus-one for Saffron's wedding — yet that had turned out to be far less straightforward than I thought.

With a yawn, I picked up the notebook again and stood up, pacing the wooden slats beneath my feet, only stopping to help turn over a ladybird that had got stuck on its back. My eyes scanned the points I'd made and . . . Oh. I focused hard. This time one word jumped out at me. It appeared in each of my descriptions of things that had gone wrong. My stomach scrunched. No. I had to be wrong. It didn't make sense. What would be the point?

The hairs stood up on the back of my neck and I swallowed hard. You see the word — or rather the name — the common link . . . was *Lucas*.

My mind raced through the events of the last days . . . surely not . . . but, but . . . what if . . . ?

No. How could I possibly think the worst of my seductive charmer? Or was that smoothness all part of his guise? Tremain had never trusted his chef. Did his charisma shield an ulterior motive?

Briefly, I noted, once again, that I had no urge to message Johnny and ask his opinion. Instead I followed my guts, followed my heart. With a flourish, I tore off the sheet of paper and, holding it tightly in my hand, left the chalet. There was only one thing for it — I had to confront my Poldark lookalike.

# 17

'Kate! What on earth is the matter, babe?'
Lucas's brow furrowed as he looked up from
his cookbook. The restaurant was empty.
Hardly anyone had ventured into the
reception building after the fire last night.

'I need to talk about something with you.
Urgently. In private,' I said just as Greg came
in for more cutlery. Ever optimistic, he was
setting tables for lunch. I'd quickly popped
next door and told Izzy I had something
really important to do before my shift and
would explain later. Business was practically
non-existent so she was happy to carry on
working or, rather, researching new doughnut
flavours.

'Kate — babe. I know we're empty at the
moment, but I can't just leave my station, and
what's so important that you can't speak in
front of anyone else?'

Greg winked. 'No worries. I'll busy myself
out the front. If you both stay put here, at
least Lucas will be on hand if we get a
customer.'

'Sorry,' I mouthed to the waiter and gave a
small smile before he pushed back through

the swing door. Such a nice guy. What a pity he and Izzy lived so far away from each other.

Tea towel over his shoulder as usual, Lucas leant back against the cooker, raven curls framing his face. Those charcoal eyes stared at me, one eyebrow raised. Yes, on the surface he could pass as the bloody-minded, passionate and sensitive-when-he-wanted fictional Cornish mine-owner of my dreams. But deep down had he also got those really important qualities of mine and Saffron's hero, namely an inane sense of integrity and loyalty?

I rubbed my chin. One question above all had popped into my mind on the way over. I remembered how disinterested in me he'd been, at the beginning, him fawning over Mrs Peppard, but barely acknowledging me. There was the time he'd explained to me, in a bored voice, the concept of his deconstructed lasagne. But as soon as Tremain had explained I would be helping with the rebranding . . .

'Lucas.' I blushed. God, this was awkward. 'I'm going to ask you a series of questions that might sound weird, so just humour me, yes?' I forced a laugh. 'My friends know me for my mad sense of curiosity and I just can't rest until it is satisfied.'

He shrugged and gave me one of his

263

caddish charmer smiles. 'Fine. It's not like I've got anything better to do, at the moment.'

I stared at him. Strange thing to say, really, at the beginning of a relationship. I'm sure, alone in a kitchen, Greg and Izzy would very quickly have found a way to keep busy. Mind you that wasn't just his fault — I . . . I'd rather he didn't. Whereas, Tremain . . . My heartbeat quickened. I hoped he was OK. Why oh why had he disappeared?

'OK. Right.' Urgh. Best to get this over. 'Why do you like me?'

He raised an eyebrow again. 'Huh? What sort of a question is that?'

'I warned you this was going to be weird. It's just — you see, I seemed to make little impact when we first met. The first time we had dinner here, in the restaurant, clearly you didn't care who I was. Yet later outside — after Tremain had introduced me and explained I'd be helping him turn this place around — you couldn't have been more agreeable and complimented my dress.'

A twinkle in his eyes, he snorted. 'Kate, what is this? You don't strike me as needy. And you're old enough to know that most people aren't struck by love — or even lust — at first sight.'

My cheeks flushed hot. Really? I'd had

annoyingly indecent thoughts about Tremain from the off. 'Of course, I don't expect to make an impact on every man I meet. But your change of heart . . . it intrigues me.'

'And that, dear, sweet Kate, is the secret to any man's success with women — keep them guessing.' He grinned and leant forward to kiss me on the cheek.

'Idiot!' I said and playfully punched his arm before looking at the torn-off piece of paper in my hand. 'But you always look genuinely pleased to see Mrs Peppard — have done from the word go. Dancing, all touchy-feely . . . Why waste time with another woman, that is, me, if you enjoy *her* company?'

'Er, apart from anything else, because she's married! And, of course, I like you. Look Kate, what's this really all about?'

Good point. She wasn't single. 'But the two of you get on so well.'

'She's a regular customer. Got a bit of a crush on me, to be honest. I'm only buttering the old bird up.' He shook a finger at me and took on a masterful Poldark tone. 'What's with the interrogation? I never had you down for the jealous type.'

'I'm not! But bear with me. Now, next, all those questions you asked me about how Izzy's business is so successful — what was the point? Are you thinking of setting up a bar?'

Lucas took down a tea towel and twisted it gently in his hands. 'No. I just think, with my job in jeopardy, it makes sense to find out as much about the catering business as I can.' He smiled. 'What's that got to do with what I think of you, babe? I'm not sure I see the point of this conversation. Come on, let's have a drink before you start your shift. I think after all the excitement yesterday you're still a bit dazed.'

'It's just . . .'

'Yeah?'

I took a deep breath. There was no subtle way to do this.

'Lucas. I hate to ask, but please be honest. Did you have something to do with the poor quality of our cocktails at Donuts & Daiquiris? I'd understand if you're worried about Izzy becoming so successful that perhaps Tremain offers her your job or — '

He burst out laughing. 'Have you been out in the sun all morning? I think you need to sit down and have a rest.' Mouth twitching, he shook his head. 'Why on earth would I feel threatened by Izzy — she's a great baker, but I'm a cordon bleu chef ?'

Like the cloth in his hands, my insides twisted. 'Sorry!' I said. This was awful. Poor Lucas. He'd tried so hard to embrace all the changes — even making perfect fish fingers

266

for little Pearl — and here I was, accusing him of being a traitor. 'I know you didn't, but I just had to ask. Thought it better to be upfront.'

'Why? Do you think someone wants your café-bar to fail?'

I sighed. 'Or perhaps the whole resort — there has been so much bad luck this week.'

'And that's all it is. I mean, as far as I know, no one has anything against the Maddocks. Tremain's a right moody bugger, but everyone loves Kensa — even the bank manager. He came over here personally last week, to see how the set-up for the rebranding was going and to offer more advice.' His mouth down-turned. 'But I'm hurt you'd think me to blame for the watering down your supplies.'

'Sorry. Honest. I . . . I'm just trying to fathom things out. There aren't many people working here, not many suspects.' Lord. Listen to me. What was I like, coming over all Miss Marple and . . . Wait a minute. My throat constricted. I only found out myself this morning that the drinks had actually been watered down and not just replaced with cheap booze bottles. How did Lucas know that detail?

'Have you seen Izzy, this morning?' I asked innocently.

Lucas shook his head and rubbed a hand

through his unruly waves. 'Not seen anyone — not Kensa or Tremain.' He stood straighter. 'So, any more questions, babe, or can I stand down from the witness stand?'

I stared at him for a moment. Was he really innocent? If not, I was going to have to be more clever, to catch him out. Upfront wouldn't work.

I covered my face with my hands. 'Of course. Apologies. Call it a temporary moment of madness. But I guess it just proves we don't know each other at all well. How about we have that quick drink and play a game I took part in at speed-dating once? I ask a question, answer it myself and then you do the same. It'll be fun!'

Lucas grinned. 'Give me a few minutes. Two white wines coming up.'

And, sure enough, five minutes later, we stood in the kitchen drinking, out of the sight of management or any potential customers.

I slipped the piece of paper into my back pocket. 'Great. OK. First up . . . um, what is your favourite type of takeaway?' Best to start with something innocuous. 'Mine is pizza.'

'Sushi. Guess that comes from living near the coast. Just love fresh fish.'

I pulled a face and he laughed.

'Right, next — fave music. I love jazz and classic disco.' I studied his face, to see if he suspected why I was asking.

He took another sip of his wine and swilled it in his mouth. 'Yeah, I have to admit, after a few beers, nothing beats a bit of Motown music.'

Yay! Lucas had nothing to do with my disco CD playing the wrong tunes.

'Although,' he continued, 'I hate jazz. It's way too laid-back. Too quiet. Life is for living. No, if you really must know, my favourite is anything that promotes headbanging.'

My chest squeezed. 'You mean like, um, heavy metal?'

He gave a thumbs-up.

Heavy metal — the music that had been taped over my ABBA music. Quick. Another really trivial question.

'Um, favourite type of clothes on the opposite sex . . . ' Ideally, of course, my answer would be a frock coat and tricorn hat. 'Jeans and a white T-shirt for me.' Just like the guy in the Diet Coca-Cola ad.

'Animal print,' said Lucas. 'Crocodile, leopard, zebra even — you name it.'

Well, I always did think Poldark had a dangerous animalistic quality about him.

'OK, next question . . . Do you know how to wire a plug? I'm useless at any kind of DIY.'

Lucas nodded. 'Of course. My dad was an

electrician. I used to watch him work, as a kid. I could wire or unwire a plug, in the dark if I had to, within minutes.'

I swallowed. Not the answer I wanted.

'Favourite reading material,' I said weakly, choosing another random question while I asked myself if I was jumping to too many conclusions. 'I like historical reads, from crime to romances.'

'Newspapers,' he said. 'Especially local ones, like the *Port Penny Express*. I read it from cover to cover as soon as I get home on a Friday, without fail. It's great for helping me keep up with local restaurant trends.'

For some reason that answer made my brain twitch, but I was still trying to work out why, whilst asking another innocent question.

'If you were on Death Row and ordering your last meal ever, what would it be? Mine? Ooh . . . difficult question. Garlic mushrooms with dip, followed by chicken stir-fry and finishing off with sticky toffee pudding with custard.'

As he replied, in my mind I carefully worded my final question.

'So, thinking ahead, where do you see yourself in five years' time? Me . . . perhaps married. With a regular singing gig. Or, in my ultimate fantasy, producing an album of my own written music.'

The new Lucas, who'd suddenly got on board with the rebranding, if genuine, would be bound to include one goal of helping White Rocks go from strength to strength.

'Easy,' he replied. 'My heart is with customers who enjoy their food and know how to have a good time.'

My chest eased. Well, his new menus included everything Cornish tourists loved with the fish 'n' chips and Cornish sausages with mash, plus no one could have more fun than when they were on holiday.

'Running my own gourmet restaurant,' he continued. 'Having stakes in the place so that I am more than a skivvy. Serving people who know the difference between claret and red wine. In other words, moving on from here and, on a fantasy level, earning megabucks as one of those celebrity chefs on the telly.'

I stared at him.

'What's the matter, babe?'

And then the penny, or rather *Port Penny Express* dropped (sorry for the pun, I'll explain in a minute).

'Oh my God. It really was you. *You* messed with the mike plug, didn't you?' I blurted out. 'And when you borrowed my disco CD, you taped over it with your heavy-metal rock.'

Eyes bulging, he gasped. 'Are you crazy? Love, don't ever give up the day job to

271

become a detective, because you *stink* at finding the truth.'

'No one told you that the drinks had actually been watered down. As far as you knew, from your last conversation about it, with me and Izzy, we'd just been given cheap stock.'

He snorted. 'Not this again. Swapped cheap booze or watered down — what's the difference? For God's sake, Kate. This is annoying now.'

'And you must be one of the few people on the planet who reads the *Port Penny Express*,' I said. 'In your words 'cover to cover'. There is no way you wouldn't have known about the animal rights protest taking place — it was practically the only newspaper that covered it.' I threw my hands in the air. 'Is that why you insisted Wednesday would be the perfect day for the trip out, even though the weather was going to be bad?'

'The forecast I heard said the rain would stop,' he snapped. 'I thought we were friends. Do you accuse everyone you kiss of some evil plan?'

'OK then — so on which imaginary radio channel did you hear the supposed good weather prediction?'

His oh-so-dark eyes narrowed and *my* eyes tingled because my gut told me I'd got it right.

'And tell me. What exactly was wrong with your fisherman friend?'

Lucas rubbed his nose. 'God knows. I'm a chef, not a medic.'

'Why couldn't he take us out, Lucas?' I folded my arms. 'He must have told you.'

'He had . . . flu!' said Lucas in a raised voice. 'Jeez. Give the guy a break.'

'Strange time of year to have flu,' I said in clipped tones. I couldn't believe it. All this time I'd fallen for Lucas's charm. 'I bet you asked him, on purpose, to let us down.'

'Now just a minute.' His face flushed darker. 'You'll be accusing me of setting off those fireworks next.'

'Yes, that's a strange one — I mean, why would you want to check the smoke alarm was working first? You made sure Kensa examined the batteries and guaranteed it was in tip-top condition. Unless that's all you wanted to set off. With the candle. Perhaps you didn't know the fireworks were there. Perhaps you aren't that reckless. You certainly looked genuinely shocked when it all happened and guilt might have made you so agreeable when I asked you to help me look for Tremain.'

The swing doors opened and Greg appeared, apologetic expression on his face. He must have heard our voices.

'Everything all right? Mrs Peppard is here. Says she wants to see you, Lucas.' He looked at me. I nodded and he disappeared.

'And what is it with you and the Peppards?' I hissed and glanced through the hatch. There she stood in a little leopard-skin patterned top and a cream skirt. She didn't look so old that Lucas would need to butter her up.

Leopard skin . . . again my brain twitched. Of course. The bra in the chalet that caught fire. It was Mrs Peppard's — and Lucas loved women in animal print. Surely not? I gazed at Lucas and his face had lit up as he saw her in the distance and waved. I recalled how he'd run off to call the emergency services when we'd spotted smoke. If he'd been in there with Mrs Peppard earlier, he'd have known there was no one else inside. Lucas might be a traitor, but I reckoned he'd have stayed and helped with my rescue attempt if he'd thought the chalet was occupied.

'Why are you sleeping with her?' I said, in a casual tone.

Lucas spun around, eyes sparking. 'What. With who?' he spluttered.

'Don't deny it. You and Mrs Peppard. The chalet that caught fire. That leopard-print bra they found.'

Lucas shook his head, his top lip rising into a sneer. 'Good God, woman. How low will you go? I've had enough of this rubbish. I thought you and I had something, Kate, but you're just a jealous, suspicious, obsessed psycho.'

'I haven't got any proof but I know you and the Peppards are linked in some way, to make sure White Rocks' branding isn't a success.' I thought for a moment. 'That night — the fireworks . . . they called you over to talk. Soon after they left early. Then all hell kicked loose. It's almost as if you'd warned them what was about to happen. Are they in on your plan too, for some reason?'

'Yes,' he said sarcastically. 'The whole resort, the whole of Port Penny is in on my Machiavellian plans. I'm after world domination.'

I dropped my voice and stared at him for a moment. He stared back, shoulders finally drooping a little. 'Lucas. Cut the crap. Come on. Tell me. You aren't a bad person. I know that . . . Is this something to do with your dad?'

He tossed down the tea towel. 'What would you know about him? I've hardly ever mentioned my old man.'

'But you have and, when you do, it's always in terms of being a failure or a success.'

He swallowed and for a second his eyes looked all shiny.

'He was an electrician, you said? Good job. Did he enjoy it?'

Lucas snorted. 'No. Hated it, every hour of every day. His brother had the brains and went to university. My dad was told by my grandfather what he'd do. Given no choice, if he wanted to live under their roof. They were practical people. Wanted a cut from his wages as soon as possible to pay for my uncle's education.'

'Harsh. And was your dad as equally harsh with you?'

Lucas sighed and slouched back, against a kitchen unit. 'He took me swimming as a kid. I'll never forget the first time. I must have been six. He got in the pool first and held out his arms. 'Jump,' he said. 'I'll catch you.' I did and he stepped aside and let me sink under the water.'

'Oh no!'

'I thought I was drowning; swallowed so much water. Eventually, he helped me to the side. Said he hoped I'd learnt a lesson — never to rely on *anyone*, even those closest. That if I wanted to achieve my dreams I had to look out for myself, look out for number one.'

'So the Maddocks . . . this place . . . You feel no loyalty. But why try to ruin their business?'

'You've no proof of that,' he said, tightly.

'Agreed.' I bit my bottom lip. 'So tell me anyway.'

He held my gaze for a minute and then sighed. 'Kate. It's just . . . I don't want to let Dad down. He never had the support of his parents to follow his dream. He's been tough but only to fuel that ambitious fire in my belly. While he's proud of my cooking achievements, I can tell that working in a resort, cooking nuggets . . . it's not where he saw me ending up.'

'But what about you?'

He shrugged. 'I've nothing against White Rocks per se. But I would like to use my cordon bleu skills. I liked the resort the way it was.'

'With guests like the Peppards?'

'Mrs Peppard and me — we've always had a laugh. And what I said about buttering her up, it's not true. I like her — not just because she's persuaded her husband to offer me another job . . . '

I raised an eyebrow. 'On one of his golf courses?'

'Kind of. A new one.'

'Where is it?'

He said nothing.

'Lucas! Please. This has gone on long enough. Just tell me everything.'

Lucas cleared his throat. 'It's not built yet. But it will be. Right here.'

I gasped. 'You mean . . . Of course! He wants White Rocks to go bankrupt so that he can pick up the land at a low price. But the course here is tiny.'

'Not if you get rid of all the chalets. And this reception building will make the perfect clubhouse. He's promised me my own high-class restaurant, to serve members, plus I'll buy stakes in the place.'

I put down my drink. 'So, getting to know me was useful. You asking me for any extra details regarding the Maddocks' latest ideas was keeping you ahead of the game so that you could destroy all their hard work.'

'Sorry, Kate.' He took my hand. 'I . . . I really liked you as time went on.'

'Yes, enough to tamper with my mike and CD, plus ruin the ABBA evening.' I shook my head. 'As for the fireworks, that was just plain dangerous.'

'I never knew they were in there. I just lit a candle and hoped the smoke alarm would set off so that everyone would have to evacuate the building and the evening would be ruined.'

'And the fishing trip?'

He shrugged.

'Lucas!'

'All right! Yeah. Ten out of ten — you got it right. I knew that protest would disturb the day. And my fishing mate owed me a favour. I asked him not to turn up.' He sipped his wine. 'Of course, I'll deny everything — as will the Peppards. And you know Mr Peppard — he'd probably sue the Maddocks for defamation of character.' He put down his glass, turned to me and took my hands. 'Oh, Kate, why not jump on board? You're a great waitress. I'll put in a good word for you. No doubt the golf club could do with a singer for all their social events. It could be just the regular gig they are looking for . . . '

'At the expense of the Maddocks? No thanks.'

He squeezed my hands and let go. 'You like him, don't you?'

We both knew he was talking about Tremain.

'It's OK.' He shrugged. 'You're a great girl but not my regular type.'

'And I only hooked up with you, initially, to get a plus-one for this wedding, to impress my friend,' I spluttered. Oops. There had been no need to let that slip.

'What?'

Ears hot, I explained the sorry tale — my school experiences with Saffron . . . our mutual love of Poldark.

Eventually, he chuckled. 'Guess I should be flattered. So, you're no better than me. We used each other — me to pump you for information, you to use my eighteenth-century looks to stick two fingers up at the nemesis from your youth.'

'Yes, but I'm not ruining anyone's living in the process.'

Lucas snorted. 'Oh come on, this place hasn't got a hope, with or without my intervention. I'm just hurrying up the process.'

'You don't know that. It's early days. Without your tampering this week could have been great.' I folded my arms. 'Look. I get it Lucas. Why it's so important to you to succeed. But you can't go trampling over other people's dreams to achieve that.' I straightened. 'I may not have proof of your involvement in things going wrong last week, but I have got proof of your affair.'

His brow furrowed.

'The police will still have that leopard-print bra. It will only take a word from me to raise Mr Peppard's suspicion. Unless you call off this plot with the Peppards and get them to leave, I'll tell him about you and his wife.'

'Whoa. Now wait a minute. You can't.'

'I can and I will. You must leave too. Immediately.'

He gasped. 'Wait a minute, Kate, don't be

280

so hasty.' He ran his hand up my arm. 'Mrs Peppard is no competition for you. Let me take you out tonight. Make it up to you.'

'Lucas.' I pulled away my arm. 'That charmer crap doesn't work on me any more. And in any case, I'm not interested.'

His jaw tightened. 'Fine. Suit yourself. Go break up a marriage.'

'You think I won't? It's not as if they look happy together.' I made for the door, but he grabbed my arm.

'All right. All right. Don't.' He looked away. 'She . . . Angie . . . doesn't deserve that.'

I raised my eyebrows.

'He's not the easiest person to live with.' Lucas gave a wry smile. 'It's kind of sad, how grateful she is for the smallest attention I pay her.'

'But you like her. Why not ask her to leave him?'

'Nah. She's too used to the lifestyle. This set-up suits us both.'

I stared at him. He really was like Poldark, who had feelings for a woman married to another.

'I mean it,' I said. 'Get them to leave or I will make the affair public. I saw the knickers matching that bra in the swimming-pool changing room, when she was taking a dip. Mr Peppard would no doubt recognise them too, if shown the other half of the lingerie set.'

'OK! OK. Just give me some time.'

'Today, Lucas — before you do any more harm. Or I'll tell Tremain everything,' I said, as the swing doors opened slightly.

Lucas snorted. 'How? Done a runner, hasn't he?'

The doors opened wide. 'No. I'm back.' Tremain glared at us both. 'What's going on?'

# 18

'You're back!' A warm sensation burst from my heart and flooded my chest. With difficulty I fought the urge to throw my arms around his neck.

'What were you going to tell me?' he said and turned to Lucas. 'Or perhaps it's better coming from you?'

Lucas sneered. 'Nothing less than you deserve. You've always had it in for me.'

'No. I just prefer team players.'

I looked pointedly at Lucas. 'Shall you tell him or will I?'

He shifted from foot to foot. 'What does it matter? Fine. You get your own way. Me and the Peppards will leave tonight.' He cleared his throat and gazed at Tremain. 'It was never meant personally,' he muttered. 'And good luck with this dump, although you'll need a miracle to turn it around. Say goodbye to Kensa. She's always been decent enough.' He took my hand and lifted it to his lips. After a gentle kiss he let go. 'Take care, Kate. Hope you find a better plus-one for your wedding.'

I swallowed. He wasn't all bad. A bit dangerous like my fantasy Poldark — just lacking the integrity.

He left through the swing doors. As they whooshed closed again, Tremain took a step towards me.

'How are you?' I mumbled. 'We've all been worried. Kensa — '

'It's OK. I've seen her. Apologised. I'm an idiot.'

I stepped nearer. Wrapped my arms around his neck. 'As long as you're OK.'

'I am now,' he mumbled. His strong arms circled my waist and he lifted me up into the air. My legs entwined around his hips and I closed my eyes as our mouths connected. Tenderly, his lips kissed mine and then deeper, with more urgency. Jets of warmth shot through my body, as if I were made of volcanic liquid. Finally, he set me down. 'Come with me. To a beach I know. We need to talk. You need to know everything.'

'Only if you're ready.'

He stared for the longest moment, those leaf-green eyes searching mine. Then he nodded and, by my hand, led me to his van.

On the journey towards Port Penny, I told him about Lucas and Mr Peppard's plan. Face flushed, his fingers tightened around the steering wheel until, in a small voice, I got to the part about me needing a Poldark lookalike.

Tremain burst out laughing, as we drove

through the small town, past tiny cottages and bumpy cobbled roads. 'Guess I should be proper insulted. I mean, you've seen me at Guvnah's, cutting grass, with a naked torso. Obviously you weren't impressed.'

'How do you know about that scene from the TV series? Don't tell me you're a *Poldark* fan?'

'Nope, but Mum loves it. I get a full recap of each episode, when the series is on,' he said and pulled a face. 'It's the one pleasure she allows herself, amidst the stresses and strains of running this place.'

To my surprise, we drove past the pottery — I thought Tremain was going to park there. Instead, we carried on, through the busy centre, and out the other side, going up a hill.

'So, from what you have heard, who do you prefer?' I teased. 'Streetwise urchin Demelza or refined Elizabeth?' As I said those words, I chuckled inside, comparing economically challenged me to posh Mrs Peppard, and Poldark-lookalike Lucas being caught in between. Talk about real life mimicking fiction.

'Oh, definitely Demelza. Airs and graces don't do anything for me.'

I shrugged. 'Funny, isn't it? I think Lucas really cares for Mrs Peppard — it's not just the money.'

Tremain snorted. 'That's a first then. For years he's used his looks to flirt and get favours from wealthy women customers. I sensed there was something between them last year. Mrs Peppard looked devastated when it was time for her to leave.'

'He's . . . He's not always had it easy. His dad asks a lot of him, I reckon, in terms of success and his position in the workplace.'

Tremain didn't answer for a while and then his shoulders relaxed. 'Yep. Expectations are hard, whether they come from someone else or within.' The hill evened out and I enjoyed an amazing sea view, watching trawlers chug along the horizon and seabirds swoop at the back of fishing boats.

'So, where is this beach?'

'Almost there now.'

I glanced sideways and he turned briefly, the look in his eyes melting me. The hill veered down and we followed it, finally turning into a narrow avenue. The occasional cottage lined the way and eventually the road just came to a dead-end at a mass of sand dunes. We parked to one side.

'Not many people know about this cove,' he said, as we got out. He locked the car and I fanned my face. The early afternoon sun made me squint. Tremain held out his hand. My fingers slipped in between his. What was this all about? He seemed so much more sure of himself and calmer. Where had he spent the night?

I soon had my answer as we reached the snuggest part of the cove — a patch of sand, right in front of a small cave. Remnants of burned sticks lay on the ground.

'Here? This is where you slept yesterday?'

He nodded.

'Oh, Tremain . . . ' We sat down on the sand and I held his hand in both mine and squeezed. 'So, you want to talk?'

With the other hand he circled in the sand. 'I do. Finally, I do. That's why this morning, I did what I've been refusing to do the last couple of years.'

I raised my eyebrows.

Still staring ahead, he took a deep breath. 'I . . . went to see the doctor. He's referring me for counselling.'

I squeezed his hand again. 'Losing someone — it's hard,' I said. 'You've done the right thing. Was . . . the red roses . . . two years ago . . . Did you lose someone special?'

Tremain pulled his fingers out of my grip and held his head in his hands. 'Yep.' He said, in a muffled voice. 'And it was all my fault.'

'I'm sure it wasn't,' I said gently. 'Talk to me. What was her name?'

'His.'

'Oh.' I straightened up. Wasn't expecting that. 'OK, so . . .'

He took his hands away and glanced at me, the smallest of smiles on his face. 'No. It wasn't like that. We were just proper good mates.'

'But the roses . . .'

'It had become a joke, you see . . .' Tremain brought up his knees and hugged them tight. We sat in the shade of a rock and had the beach to ourselves, apart from the noise of breaking waves and an inquisitive gull that stood about two metres away and cocked its head, before flying off.

Tremain stared ahead. 'He was called Ben. We joined up together and ended up in the same battalion — deployed in Afghanistan. A couple of years ago we were there, at the tail end of the action before the war came to an end.'

I nodded, not quite sure what to say.

'One day we were out in the field. Bullets everywhere. Adrenaline high. Ben got shot in the leg. I wanted to stay with him, but spotted a group of colleagues ahead who needed cover. It was simply a matter of numbers. There were three of them. Only one of him. I acted on automatic. Training kicked in. I was only gone for a few minutes. Ten tops. When I got back Ben had been hit by the blast of a hand grenade. I . . . ' His voice wavered.

'Carry on,' I said softly.

'It's not pretty,' he said and gulped.

'Go on. Tell me what you found.'

'The bottom half of his body was missing. I'll never forget the smell of his burning flesh.'

I shuffled up and put my arm around his shoulders, throat feeling thick. 'You were doing your job, Tremain. Ben would have done the same.'

He turned to face me, eyes wet. 'Would he? Perhaps he'd have put me first and taken me with him. We were mates.'

I swallowed and recalled him talking about firing Lucas. 'There is no room for sentimentality in some jobs,' he'd said. 'How old were you when you joined up?' I asked.

'Sixteen. So was Ben. He heard me talking about travelling the world and wanted the same.' He bit his lip. 'Juliette — his childhood sweetheart — wasn't happy.

Ah. Ben must have been the friend he was talking about when he mentioned the mate with a Parisian girlfriend.

He half smiled. 'A ballsy woman, she is. One Valentine's Day, Juliette was determined not to behave as a stereotype so *she* sent a dozen red roses to Ben. He never lived it down, and every Valentine's Day after, me and the lads would club together to buy him a bunch.'

'You didn't force Ben to sign up, Tremain. He would have known the risks, the dangers, when he followed you into that career.'

Tremain wrung his hands. 'I went to see Juliette, after his death — after the funeral. She wouldn't talk to me at the service. I knocked on her front door that evening. She opened it and slapped me around the face. Said I'd promised to look after him. Told me it was my fault he ever became a soldier; my fault that he died. That I was a joke of a best friend.'

'But that would have been her grief talking. Have you seen her since?'

He shook his head. 'I couldn't face the resentment.'

I remembered, when we first met, on the golf course, he muttered something about please not resenting him.

'I'm sure she won't now — time gives people perspective,' I said gently. 'You must have mutual friends you can talk to about this.'

'I don't open up. Don't want to get close. Don't want to get hurt again. But then . . . ' His voice cracked. 'I met you. Mad, isn't it? We've not known each other long but from the first minute I saw you, talking about swallows, caring about that injured rabbit and trying to sneak back onto the golf course, the banter, I don't know . . . it sparked something in me. It felt easy. And it made me mad to see you with Lucas. Then the fire . . . '

'Sorry about that,' I whispered. 'It must have been hard to come in and get me — amongst the smoke . . . all the memories.'

'But it made me realise I cared. Apart from my parents, I haven't cared about anyone in the slightest, for a long, long time.'

'And the fireworks?'

'Mum knows I don't like them. The noise. Takes me back. The rotting smell. Ears hurting. Men's screams.' He glanced at me. 'Kate. Walk away now, if you want. Honest. I've . . . I think the phrase is — got baggage . . . on a diva-like scale. Walk away if it's too much. I've taken that first step for help. I'll be OK.'

'I'm not going anywhere — I've coped with you so far, haven't I? Is this . . . post-traumatic stress disorder?'

Tremain wiped his face and straightened up. 'No. Not full-blown. To me that's like people saying they've got OCD just because they like to, I don't know, arrange their groceries in a certain way. I've got a mate with PTSD. He's lost it a couple of times in the last year. Ended up with a conviction.'

I flushed, remembering how Izzy and I wondered if Tremain might have been in prison.

'Once, after a drunken rampage, his family couldn't find him,' he continued. 'The poor sod had taken refuge in a wheelie bin. So . . . ' He cleared his throat and moved to sit opposite me. 'That's not me but I . . . I just need to talk it out, I guess. The guilt I feel about Ben's death. The graphic memories that mean I don't sleep well.'

I took a deep breath. Perhaps now was the time to tell him about Johnny. But then no. This was Tremain's moment; time to concentrate on him.

'What?'

'Nothing,' I said. 'It can wait.'

'Kate. No more secrets between us. Let's start with a clean slate. Please.'

My heart raced and said open up to him. Follow your heart, Kate Golightly. 'I can sort of relate to the guilt. Ten months ago . . . my boyfriend, Johnny . . . '

'He left, right? I remember you saying. What happened? Did it end badly? You think you were to blame?'

'I'd been on at him all evening — said I had cravings for a takeaway curry. I'd had a glass of wine and didn't want to drive. I could tell he didn't feel like going out but I

292

persuaded him. Johnny was so good-natured.'

'And he never came back?'

My vision went blurry. 'No. It was October — when we'd had all that torrential rain and flooding. He had an accident. Straight into a lamppost. Killed instantly.'

'Oh, Kate.'

'I felt so guilty — my stupid cravings sent him out. But I hated him for a while too — for months — because he'd lost control after trying to avoid a cat in the road, according to a witness. He skidded on the saturated road.' I threw my arms in the air; 'He died for a cat. Appropriate really — him working for the RSPCA.'

Tremain studied my face. 'You do what you have to do in that split second. Me charging forward to cover colleagues. You rushing into the burning chalet.'

'Yes, but I thought there was a person in there.'

'What if you'd heard a dog yelp?'

I swallowed. 'I know,' I said eventually. 'Over recent weeks I've finally become less angry — and had talked it out with him.'

Tremain's brow furrowed. 'How?'

My eyes filled again. 'His family memorialised his Facebook page. Plus, they were keen for me to stay in touch with them as I was a link to their . . . their dead son.' I swallowed.

'But it meant I could still message, even though all my words remained unread. Just as well, really — I was furious at first. Swore at him. Asked how he could risk our future like that. Then, over time, I just messaged when I felt low. Or needed advice. Or just to tell him the things I'd never tell anyone else.' I smiled. 'Must make me sound bonkers.'

Tremain shook his head. 'No. Sometimes I still talk to Ben.'

'Right at the beginning — ' my voice wobbled ' — I so wanted him to reply. For the first weeks I almost managed to convince myself that we'd only broken up and that he was reading my messages and then just marking them unread.'

'Weirdly, that must have been a comfort,' said Tremain. 'A coping mechanism. Better than drinks or drugs.'

'How did you manage, in the early days?' I said.

'I haven't told Mum this, but I slept rough for a while. Got beaten up a few times. Didn't bother me — I felt numb, like I deserved it.'

'And what made you leave the streets?'

'Say what you want about Dad, but we'd kept in touch — I didn't want to upset Mum who is on her own. He had his new girlfriend for support. I still didn't tell him everything but he worked out I hadn't got a place to live.

He tried to persuade me to move in with him but … I needed the time on my own. Anyway, eventually, Dad let slip that he'd heard on the grapevine Mum was struggling. Unless he said that on purpose because he knew it would shake me up.'

'But he left her!'

'I know. Doesn't mean he didn't — that he doesn't — care.'

Guess I'd only heard Kensa's side of the story.

'So, you headed home.'

He nodded. 'Exercise helps me release the anguish, now.'

'Like when you were running around screaming on the golf course?'

'Yep.'

'Singing does it for me,' I said. 'Helps me empty my mind.'

We looked at each other. No words necessary. We kind of had common ground.

He stood up and pulled me to my feet. 'Fancy a paddle?'

I smiled. 'No. Not quite yet. There's something else I need first.'

'Me too.' He stepped forward and held my shoulders. Lips on mine. Volcanic heat erupting.

'Oh, Tremain,' I whispered, as I pulled away for breath, my hand running over his short hair, his fingers trailing a line down my back. We fell to the ground and I pressed up close, heat emanating from him. As we kissed, I experienced a sense of release — the shedding of past romance. Now nothing mattered but Tremain. Making him better. Feeling that hot mouth on my skin. Listening to his reliable heartbeat.

'What about the scar?' I said as, hand in hand, we eventually ambled towards the beach. 'I saw it when you were gardening at Guvnah's. Did you get it in Afghanistan?'

'You'd think so, wouldn't you? Nah, someone mugged me when I was fifteen. That's one reason I wanted to go into the army — to learn how to protect myself. You say Ben knew the dangers of signing up, but we were just kids. I, for one, didn't think about the consequences of everything I was going to have to see and do.'

We reached the waves. Slipped off our shoes and socks. Cool water trickled over our toes. He kicked some up at me.

'Don't push me too far,' I said, in a teasing voice. 'You may be army material but never challenge the deviousness of a woman and — Ow!' I pulled a face and hopped up and down. 'I think something just bit my foot, can you take a look?'

Concern crossed his face and he bent

down. I giggled and pushed him over.

'That was a mistake,' he said, finding his balance, trousers and top dripping. Solemnly, he shook a finger. I started to run.

★  ★  ★

'Of course he caught me,' I whispered to Johnny as, that night, I sat in my bedroom, looking at the red wind spinner. I'd pulled my suitcase out from under my bed. I held the scarlet metal and ran a finger over the curves. 'It was good to see him laugh. You'd like him, Johnny.' Tears filled my eyes. 'I loved you so much. You were the best. And . . . I just wanted to check you knew that I'm no longer angry. I had no right to be. If you hadn't cared and just run over that cat, you wouldn't be the Johnny I knew. Plus . . . I'm sorry I sent you out for that curry.' I sniffed. 'But you know me after a glass of Pinot Grigio.' I gazed at the heart-shaped strips of metal. 'You'll probably be relieved to hear that I won't bother you with my crazy messages any more. All these last months, I had so much to say — advice to seek, problems, stories and jokes to share — but you see really . . . ' My chest squeezed. 'I guess it was what you'd call a long goodbye.' My throat ached. ''Cos we never got the chance to do that, did we? Say our farewells? So that's what this is. I wanted to do it properly.'

I took a deep breath. 'Thanks, Johnny. For everything. You taught me so much about loving. Sharing. Supporting. And laughing — we did a lot of that. Remember that time we almost got thrown out of the cinema when, hamster-like, you puffed your cheeks up full with popcorn?' My eyes tingled. 'You made me happy. Gave me confidence. And . . . I remember once you saying you felt the same. That me following my singing vocation made you surer than ever that you'd chosen the right career; that memories of fulfilling dreams would keep us content in our final years, not a pile of money.' My voice broke. 'I'm glad you followed your heart and started to achieve your goals before . . . before your time here was over.'

I stifled a sob. Sat up straighter. Cleared my throat. Very slightly, my lips upturned. 'So, sleep tight, sweetheart. Rest peacefully. It's goodbye now.' I kissed the wind spinner for the longest moment, then put it back in the suitcase, which I zipped up and slid back under the bed.

# 19

What a difference two weeks can make. I looked sideways at Tremain and longed to tear off the blue suit and smart tie he wore. The fine cut showed off his broad shoulders and solid neck. Hair newly shaved — hmm, you've got it, I couldn't wait to kiss him later and run my hand over that bristly head; to see the brow lines disappear as that veiled look of vulnerability gained confidence.

'Lovely service, wasn't it?' I said to Chelsea, who sat to my left. Yes. I'd brought Tremain to Saffron's wedding. With his fine torso and brooding, moody way, I should have known from the start that he was really my Poldark. I smiled brightly, trying not to remember how Chelsea had laughed at me, along with Saffron's cronies, at school. She had two toddlers now and was more laid-back about her appearance than I remembered, with lipstick that didn't exactly match the shade on her nails.

'Didn't Saffy look beautiful? The laced cleavage on that dress is exquisite.' She cleared her throat. 'Love your outfit, Katie, by the way. The fifties style really suits your figure. Makes me wish I'd got bigger boobs.' She pulled a face. 'Mum promised me I'd go up a size after having kids, but I'm still waiting for that to happen.'

We laughed. I know. Weird. Everyone on our table was so polite. It was as if the school years had never taken place. I gazed opposite. Take Ryan, who always called me Tracy after the lead dumpy teenage character in *Hairspray* — his life goal had been to impress Saffron. Yet now he couldn't have been more polite when I arrived and insisted on fetching me and Tremain each a glass of Bucks Fizz.

I gazed around the hotel conference room, at the round tables decorated with pink roses and white lilies. As well as her dress, Saffron's wedding breakfast had been exquisite too, with a goat's cheese tart to start, followed by leg of lamb and vanilla panna cotta for dessert. Cream curtains framed the huge windows and silver confetti hugged the ceiling in a net, all set up to be released onto the dance floor.

Under the table, a hand grabbed mine and squeezed my fingers. Tremain's eyes twinkled.

'So. Straight from here we go to your pad and pack your stuff, right? Then we can get off first thing in the morning. It's a proper long drive back to Cornwall.'

I nodded. 'The speeches are done. Our cue to disappear.'

The laughter left his eyes for a second. 'You're still sure? About coming back to Port Penny with me?'

I squeezed his fingers back. 'Crazy, isn't it? Me moving down South to help you and Kensa. Me, running Izzy's mini Donuts & Daiquiris and singing for guests . . . It's all happened so quickly.' I shook my head. 'Am I certifiably crazy, what with Greg moving here to take my position at Izzy's main branch? He and I are effectively swapping lives.'

It looked like Izzy got her Disney prince after all and we had celebrated by having one of our holding-hands, jumping-up-and-down moments. Swiftly followed by a few tears. We'd miss each other but vowed to visit. And Skype. Plus, chat on WhatsApp.

'Yep, you are mad.' Tremain grinned. 'Perhaps you should see a counsellor too.'

I leant forward and kissed him firmly. 'Nah. No need. I'm lodging with Guvnah now, until I find my own place. She's sharper than any psychiatrist.' Tremain's first hospital appointment had come through for two weeks' time. 'I can't believe I'm going to be living near my gran again.'

Tremain had wanted me to move in with him but, ever independent, I felt it was early days. Even though my heart said he was the man I'd get old with, I needed to take my

301

time if I were to start relying on someone again.

'And it was a brainwave of yours, so it was, to suggest we offered Lucas's job to Shirl Jones and make Earl caretaker. That will free me up to do many other jobs.'

'I'm not just a pretty face, you know,' I said airily.

'I know,' he whispered in my ear. 'You've also got pretty legs, pretty thighs and pretty — '

'Really?' I murmured, cheeks hot.

He nodded. 'Not that any of that matters,' he murmured. 'I've always thought the important thing is to love with your soul, not your sight. I'm yours for keeps, if you want, Kate. Heart, soul, body . . . they all belong to you.'

I replied with the longest of kisses.

'Katie! Thank you so much for coming.'

I pulled away from Tremain, ears hot, and looked up.

'Saffron. Oh, um, hi. It's been a lovely do. Thank you for inviting me . . . us.'

She smiled. What lovely white teeth. Porcelain skin. Lush blonde hair. Some things never changed.

'Is this Ross?' she said and turned to Tremain. A quizzical look crossed her face. Tremain looked nothing like wavy-haired,

New Romantic Poldark.

'No, this is Tremain.'

'Proper pleased to meet you,' he said.

Saffron gasped. 'Oh, I do love a Cornish accent. I wanted to have a *Poldark* theme for the wedding but Mum and Dad were horrified; said that getting married was serious stuff.' She laughed. 'Perhaps I'll do a themed party for our first anniversary. Katie, I could book you to sing.'

I gave a stiff smile.

Her cheeks flushed and she cleared her throat. 'Would you do me a huge favour, Katie — I absolutely must go to the Ladies' room, but need help with my skirts.'

'Oh. Perhaps Chelsea . . . ' I turned to my left but she'd gone.

'Please,' said Saffron, in a bright voice. 'I'd be terribly grateful.'

'Won't be a minute,' I muttered to Tremain and stood up. My stomach churned. Was there some ulterior motive? Perhaps she wanted to corner me in private so that she could reel off a list of her amazing achievements. I took a deep breath. Don't be ridiculous. With all those metres of silk, she probably did need a hand.

'He looks nice,' she said to me, as we left the conference room and headed left, along a corridor, to the toilets.

'He works at a holiday resort. I'm moving there next week,' I said.

'Really? That's amazing. Living in the South-west, eh? Lucky you. Just think of all those sunny days, the ice creams and beach barbecues . . . I'm envious.'

I pushed open the door to the ladies' and we both headed in, stopping in front of the mirror to check our make-up.

'Envious? You've got a career teaching. Now you're married.' I shrugged and met her face in the mirror. 'I never thought I'd hear you admit to wanting something I'd got.'

She fiddled with the sleeve of her dress. Now was the moment to ask why I was really here. Funny. Since deciding to bring Tremain, I'd lost all impulse to impress her. Tremain was my man. She could like him or not. In fact, I'd suggested to Tremain that we back out of coming at the last minute but he said no — he'd already got my sense of curiosity sussed. He knew I'd always be asking myself what her true motive for inviting me had been.

Saffron looked around. The toilets were empty. She turned away from the mirror and leant against the basin unit. I did the same.

'Katie . . . '

'It's Kate, now, actually,' I said.

'Kate . . . I invited you here because . . . I

wanted to say sorry,' she blurted out. 'For the way I was when we moved up to high school.'

Wow. I stared at her, looking for a sarcastic twitch of the mouth. Nothing. Just wide blue eyes staring back.

'Why? After all these years?'

She fiddled with a pearl teardrop, sewn on to her bodice. 'I always felt bad — may not have shown it, but you and me, we were best friends at juniors.' She smiled. 'How we'd always go to each other's house for lunch on a Saturday. I'd scrunch up my crisps and drink them from the bag, whereas you would put yours in between bread. Happy days.'

'So what happened? Why did you ditch me?'

'I never intended to. It's just . . . Remember how I got bullied in top juniors — when Dad lost his job? My parents couldn't afford a birthday party. Nor the fashionable clothes everyone else wore to non-uniform days. They called me Second-hand Saffy.'

I shrugged. 'Guess I never saw it as bullying — I was always used to feeling like the odd one out and just accepted the pecking order. With all my siblings I never got new clothes so had never even appeared on the radar of being cool or fashionable. Whereas you were and then you lost it all.'

She nodded. 'And then my family came

into an inheritance, just as we started high school. Dad started his own business. Things took off big time and it was great making new friends without the baggage of the old me who couldn't even afford to go to the cinema.'

'You had designer clothes. Threw the best parties — not that I was ever invited.' I gazed at her chin which wobbled slightly. Those blue eyes glistened. Age and hindsight were great gifts. 'It's OK, Saffron. I didn't fit your new image. We were kids.'

'But we used to be best mates, Katie — Kate. I've . . . never forgiven myself. Looking back, I can see I bought most of those friends, giving them designer handbags I didn't appreciate because I already had so many, inviting them around and providing the most amazing snacks and drinks.' She gave a wry smile. 'You never cared about any of that stuff. That last year in juniors, when my family was skint, I didn't have any money to buy you a birthday present . . . '

'So you made me a gift voucher — worth one hour of you doing my maths homework.' I grinned. 'That was one of the best presents I ever got. I never did get algebra or geometry.' I shrugged. 'So why now, Saffron? Why friend me on Facebook and dig up the past?'

A guest came in and headed into a cubicle.

Saffron turned around to the mirror again and I followed. We looked at each other in the glass.

'I . . . I've been nervous about inviting you. That's the real reason I left it quite late. None of my family had really dropped out because they're ill. That was just an excuse. You see, since becoming a teacher, I've seen how cruel children can be,' she said, in a lower voice. 'Excluding pupils for no good reason. Name-calling. Insults. It's all about the cliques.' She squeezed my arm. 'To be honest, I'm amazed at how you withstood it. Not sure I could. Like a couple of kids in my form . . . it's often the most hard-working who get sidelined, but it doesn't stop them — they just keep their heads down and get on, and achieve brilliant grades.'

'I must have been the exception then! You were always the clever one. But I was lucky. Guvnah was there to turn to. She offered great advice as someone who never followed the crowd.'

Saffron's face lit up. 'How is she? Still painting?'

'Yes. Granddad died. She's remarried. Lives in Cornwall. We'll be close to each other again.' And, as the guest left the cubicle and washed her hands, I told Saffron all about my recent weeks in White Rocks.

'Wow,' said Saffron when we were alone again. 'Good thing you took Izzy up on her offer of a holiday, then, otherwise you'd never have landed a job with regular singing work.'

I blushed, tension leaving my body as I saw occasional glimpses of the old Saffy — the one I knew as a little girl before we started worrying about boyfriends and body image. 'Well, there was a good incentive to go down there . . . ' I preceded to tell her all about my plan to find a sexy Poldark lookalike for the wedding.

Saffron giggled. 'Oh, Kate. That erotic writer sounds hilarious. And I wish you'd got a photo of Lucas.'

I grinned. 'So, I'm really glad you invited me today, Saffron, because otherwise I might never have gone to White Rocks and met Tremain. And — ' I nodded my head slightly ' — it's been good to catch up. Thanks for . . . sharing.'

Saffron leant forward and hugged me. 'Thanks for being gracious about it. Right.' She started to lift her skirts. 'You were going to help me into a cubicle . . . '

★ ★ ★

As it was, Tremain and I stayed until the end of the wedding. Packing could wait until tomorrow. And I had more school friends to meet. None were as open as Saffron but all were interested in my life — and my boyfriend.

'Funny, isn't it?' I said as we smooched to a slow dance, lights dim, fairy lights hanging from the ceiling. 'I hated some of these people at school and the cutting words that tumbled out of their mouths. Yet now . . . they seem OK.' I leant forward closer, heart pulsing as we rocked side to side. 'It's like you and Ben both joining up when you were sixteen. You can't blame yourself — or should Juliette — for decisions made by the person, or rather the child you were back then.'

He stood back. Tucked my hair behind my ear, then his hand moved to the back of my head and tenderly he pulled me forward. Feeling slightly dizzy — from too much champagne or Tremain, I knew not — I kissed him back.

'Wish I'd known you back then,' he whispered eventually. 'I'd have enjoyed making some very wrong but enjoyable decisions.' He winked

'Do you think I'm making the right decision? To move to Port Penny? What if you and I don't work out?' I gave a shy smile.

'You'll always have a job there, Kate. My life wouldn't be worth living if Earl ever found out that I'd given you the chop!'

I smiled. 'He's a lovely bloke. And little Pearl has offered to be chief taster of any new doughnut flavours. As for Shirl . . . '

He nodded. 'Her cooking is spot on for our new market. Last week's guests loved her sharing platter with onion rings, garlic mushrooms, ciabatta and all those dips. And your singing evenings also went down pretty well — especially the Take That and Spice Girls one. As for the talent show . . . '

'That family dressed up as the Kardashians . . . '

We both grinned.

'Plus, how many toy Rocky Rabbits have you sold?' I said.

'Sixty-four last count.'

'Good, but not nearly as many as the hot dogs Geoff handed out last week.

'I'll be interested to see how Guvnah's painting classes go. If the holidaymakers like them, it got me and Kensa thinking — we could offer more specialised weeks during the quieter winter months, where people could learn an activity.'

The song ended and we sat down to finish our drinks. 'And what if Lucas was right?' I asked. 'Him saying that only a miracle will save White Rocks and next year you still go bankrupt?'

Tremain looked at me. 'As long as I've got you, Kate, nothing else matters. I can work as a handyman or gardener.'

'With your top off. Using a scythe.'

'That's sexist!' he said, using the words I'd once used against him.

'But incredibly sexy,' I said and closed my eyes as our mouths met . . .

# Epilogue

And that was it. The tale of my quest to find a Poldark plus-one. Well almost. I'm thinking it would be rude not to fill you in on the latest gossip. You see now —   six months later —  the new changes have become more concrete. My best mate and Greg are getting on great. Turns out that, like Izzy, he's got the cleverest business brain. The two of them are already pitching a second mini Donuts & Daiquiris to another holiday resort. Just after Christmas, they moved in together and every month or so we've met up. In fact, we stayed at their new pad a couple of weekends ago. They wore matching tie-dye T-shirts and have bought the cutest pug dog. She's called Manhattan, after the cocktail —   Hattie for short.

Earl, Shirl and Pearl have all settled in well at White Rocks and lifted a lot of the stress from Kensa. Earl can work wonders with his toolbox and Shirl has the knack of making lush meals out of the simplest ingredients. Pearl and I sing together as often as we can. She is also the prime doughnut taster. In fact, she is one talented little girl and often visits

Guvnah, who says her new young friend is something of a painter.

Talking of Kensa — remember the bank manager I mentioned, who went above and beyond duty to give her help? Seems his interest wasn't one hundred per cent professional. Last November, they started dating and his expert, now hands-on advice — alongside all the rebranding changes — seems to be helping the resort recover. Plus, Tremain's estranged parents get on much better. Kensa found out that her ex had alerted their son to the fact she was struggling to run White Rocks alone. While she didn't accept his invitation to the christening of Tremain's new baby half-brother, Kensa did send a gift and card.

So, I guess that just leaves me to give you an update regarding me and my man. He's still the most swoon-worthy kisser, with mesmeric leaf-green eyes and an air of capability that fulfils all my politically incorrect beta female needs. Plus, he doesn't run around shouting so much. Counselling is helping. Tremain has even become more sociable and joined a local football club. I've moved in with him, too. We have our own chalet at White Rocks. He snores and I hog the duvet. I'd almost forgotten how special those mundane things were.

And then there are the not so mundane

things. Like the way he listens to all the new songs I've been writing and gives me his honest opinion. Or how, a couple of months ago, I finally convinced him to visit Ben's widow, Juliette. I sat in the car outside. He hasn't spoken about the meeting to me yet, but ever since the visit he doesn't seem to mind talking about Ben so much.

Funny, isn't it? What has resulted from my quest to find a smouldering, charcoal-eyed, ruffle-haired Poldark plus-one? My plan didn't go as intended. I guess Tremain is right. In the end, all that matters is to love with your soul, not your sight . . .

We do hope that you have enjoyed reading this large print book.

Did you know that all of our titles are available for purchase?

We publish a wide range of high quality large print books including:
**Romances, Mysteries, Classics**
**General Fiction**
**Non Fiction and Westerns**

Special interest titles available in large print are:
**The Little Oxford Dictionary**
**Music Book**
**Song Book**
**Hymn Book**
**Service Book**

Also available from us courtesy of Oxford University Press:
**Young Readers' Dictionary**
**(large print edition)**
**Young Readers' Thesaurus**
**(large print edition)**

For further information or a free brochure, please contact us at:
**Ulverscroft Large Print Books Ltd.,**
**The Green, Bradgate Road, Anstey,**
**Leicester, LE7 7FU, England.**
**Tel:** (00 44) 0116 236 4325
**Fax:** (00 44) 0116 234 0205

*Other titles published by Ulverscroft:*

## STELLA'S CHRISTMAS WISH

### Kate Blackadder

It's six days before Christmas, and a phone call to her London office is about to impact Stella's life in ways she could never have imagined. Her grandmother Alice, far away in the Scottish Borders, has been hurt in a fall. There's only one thing for it: Stella must journey north to help Alice while she convalesces. But when she returns to her little Scottish hometown, her grandmother's health is not her only concern. Relationships which have lain dormant for years are rekindled, and fresh opportunities present themselves — if only Stella will dare to take them . . .